M000215013

DIG TWO GRAVES

DIG TWO GRAVES

A Thriller

SARAH ENGELL

Translated from Danish by Sinéad Quirke Køngerskov

Podium

SAGA
EGMONT

All rights reserved. No part of this publication may be reproduced, stored in a retrieval system, or transmitted in any form or by any means electronic, mechanical, photocopying, recording, or otherwise without prior written permission from Podium Publishing.

This is a work of fiction. Names, characters, places, and incidents are either products of the author's imagination or used fictitiously. Any resemblance to actual events, locales, or persons, living, dead, or undead, is entirely coincidental.

Copyright © 2021 by Sarah Engell

English translation copyright © 2021 by Saga Egmont

Cover design by Podium Publishing

ISBN: 978-1-0394-2138-7

Published in 2023 by Podium Publishing, ULC
www.podiumaudio.com

DIG TWO GRAVES

CHAPTER 1

It was forbidden to cry anymore. The cherry tree blossomed, dropping pink snow over us as we sat on the grass.

It was best if someone volunteered. Otherwise, Father would have to choose.

We had been left in the garden to think about it. Not allowed to come in before he said.

That was a long time ago now. The shade of the tree had moved far over the lawn. Every time I looked at the house, I got a stomachache.

"I have to pee," I whispered.

"Me too."

Several petals fell through the air. In the distance, a cow bellowed. A long wailing sound that hung long over the flat fields with yellow winter rapeseed and newly sprouted peas.

I closed my eyes. I wished I could fall asleep, but my eyes kept opening. Like my little sister's doll when you sat it up.

"Maybe he forgot about us," I whispered.

"Maybe."

I looked at the house again. The dark windows. The closed door.

With every gust of wind, it looked as if the house was bristling. There were vines all over the red bricks. Large, deep-green leaves with white streaks that resembled veins. The house had almost completely disappeared. It made me think of when we were smaller and we would bury each other in the sandbox. The feeling of not being able to breathe.

The leaves lifted again. I couldn't stop looking at the house and the closed door. The stomachache got worse, and my feet walked over there of their own accord.

The blood rushed as I took the handle. There was no lock, and even though I was terrified, I stepped inside.

The incense sticks had been burning since yesterday morning. Still, there was a pungent smell in the house. My fingertips stroked the raw brick wall in the hallway. I didn't dare turn on the light. I walked on tiptoes, striving to step on the right floorboards, past closed umbrellas and velour shoes with thin straps. It was dim here. All the curtains were drawn.

A creak. I froze. Saw that my foot had stepped on the wrong spot. There was a faint hiss. Like someone breathing, and I thought of sleeping dragons. Spirits and monkeys and scaly snakes with the heads of lions.

Don't let your imagination run wild. That's what the adults would say if they were here.

The incense sticks were patchouli. Little sister's favourite.

My feet started walking again without my giving them permission.

The house was really cold. How had they made it so cold? Outside it was May and the whole garden was in bloom.

The kitchen door was ajar. On the stove, blue gas flames whistled under a pot of vegetables. That was the sound I had heard. It smelled burnt. I wanted to turn it off, but I didn't dare.

On the living room door hung a drawing of a tiger. It was stuck up with tape. The tiger's teeth were very long. The longer they were, the more forbidden it was to enter.

I pressed down the handle as gently as I could. The living room was gone. The only thing I could see were white sheets hanging from ceiling to floor. I squatted and lifted up the edge of the sheet. My stomach sank when I spotted her. I hadn't heard the slightest sound of anyone in here. She sat as quiet as a mouse on the sofa. Only her hands moved. She was folding paper flowers. White, pink, and red. She did it quickly and without looking up. My heart was pounding as I sat under the edge of the sheet. I couldn't stop looking.

Her hair. It was so long. I had never seen it hang loose. It was black and shiny and just as beautiful as the collages in our fairy-tale book. I had never seen Mother look like this before.

She lifted her head and spotted me.

Electrified seconds passed as we stared at each other.

She laid down a half-finished flower and came over with quick steps. "Haven't I told you that you're not allowed in here?" She pushed me back through the hall. Her nightgown was crumpled and she was barefoot on the cold floor.

"Your food is burning," I said.

She pushed me out into the garden without answering.

There was a click as the lock was turned.

I ran around the house to the kitchen window. Mother's hand came into view as she set it on the latch. I could smell the burnt vegetables. The curtains moved slightly in the wind, and I tiptoed over to the open window to look inside.

Mother was poking around the pot with a bamboo spoon. She picked up something that looked charred. Stood for a while looking at it. Then she put down the spoon and pressed her hands against her eyes.

It felt like she was pressing my eyes, too, and I had to look at something else. At the packages of dried mushrooms and the steam cooker. Soy, vinegar, fish sauce. The sharp knives that hung on the wall.

Only now did I see them. All the dishes displayed on the dining table. I'd never seen so much food before. Not even for the Moon Festival.

I tried to feel hungry. But I only felt nauseated.

I gave a start when the window was closed. I just managed to see Mother's wet eyes before the kitchen disappeared.

I put my hands in my pockets. Kicked a yellow dandelion. On the other side of the pea fields, the windmills stood still. The sun made the clouds glow orange.

With my hands in my pockets, I walked back into the back garden. My brother stood up under the cherry tree.

"Did you see anything?" he asked.

"Not really. But there's mounds of food in the kitchen."

"Century eggs?"

I nodded.

5

He hit a branch so it snowed even more. Pink petals fell onto the grass around us.

"You are the eldest," he said. "Of course Father will choose you."

"But you are their favourite son. He will definitely choose you."

We scowled at each other. A quivering atmosphere filled the air. I thought of necromancers and gold dragons and noisy processions marching through cobbled streets with drums and brightly coloured silk garments.

It was quiet here. Flat fields, thatched houses, and red-and-white flags that had to be taken down when it got dark. Far away, the neighbour's cow bellowed again.

"Father will choose you," he repeated. "I can feel it."

"I can feel you are lying," I said. Suddenly, the door was opened and Father appeared.

The quivering atmosphere intensified, as if he were compressing the air as he walked through the garden towards us. His black hair was covered with water. The side parting was drawn as though with a ruler. He looked tired.

"Wu-Chao. Wu-Kang." He smiled at us. Raised his hands to call us closer.

We walked forward slowly and stood in front of him.

"My sons." Father laid one hand on my brother's shoulder and one on mine. His body looked like ours despite the fact that we were only eight years old: slender and not very tall.

"Family is the most important thing," he said. "Always."

We nodded.

"Do you understand?" he said.

We nodded again.

His eyes narrowed, so they became even smaller than usual.

"Today is a day of celebration. I would like you to respect that. No more tears. No more discussions. Today we are happy. All of us. Okay, boys?"

My brother looked down at the grass. My stomach whirled round and round, like the washing machine on a spin cycle.

"Being able to do something for one's family is the greatest joy a person can experience. We live in a country where that is not always understood. A country where one is closest to oneself. But we are lucky. A strong culture bears us. A culture that makes us invincible. Not least on a day like today."

This time, it was just me who nodded. My brother stood with his head bent down. Probably trying to make himself smaller than he was.

"Remember your grandfather worked for the emperor himself. You were born into a powerful lineage."

He always said that when he wanted us to do something we were afraid of. We knew very well that Grandfather had only worked in the administration. He hadn't even met the emperor.

"What do you say?" asked Father. "Will one of you step forward?"

His eyes were like flint. Black and hard. My stomach whirled faster and faster as I looked into them.

"Well," he said. "Then I must choose."

He looked at us alternately. His two eight-year-old sons.

"Smile, boys," he said. "Remember, it is a celebration. It will not do to have a sad bridegroom."

CHAPTER 2

Small threads of blood swirl around the toilet bowl, and I flush for the second time. I stand for a moment with my knickers around my knees, not wanting to change the sanitary pad. I think I can wait until the next time I have to pee.

As I pull up my knickers, it occurs to me that I had the exact same thought the last time I peed.

I tighten the belt of my dressing gown and go over to the sink. Get lost in a trance over the turquoise glass mosaics on the wall.

The tap sputters on and I wash my hands. Doubt whether I have already done it. The soap foam smells synthetic. It's the cheap one from the supermarket that I don't like.

The sound of car tyres on gravel makes me look up. Through the blinds, I can see a police car stopping in front of the house. The windshield wipers are on at full speed, though only a mist is falling. Cawing, a few crows alight from the gravel road and disappear over the stubbly black fields, where the rapeseed no longer blooms. My pulse rises as I watch the lights of the police car go out. The front doors open and two officers step out. Torben slides his hand over his big, full, red beard before putting the police hat on his head. The other officer is a woman I haven't seen before.

They stand for a while looking at the boxes in the front garden. The drizzle has turned the cardboard dark brown. Torben says something and the woman nods. They turn to face the house and start walking towards the front door.

I stumble over the pack of nappies as I back away from the bathroom window. I squat beside the toilet. Hold my breath.

They spotted it. Of course, they spotted it.

The doorbell rings.

Close to my ear, the toilet makes a faint, trickling sound, and I close my eyes.

I should have been prepared.

The doorbell rings again.

"Eva! Steen!" I jump when Torben calls from out there.

The sound of our names pulls me back to reality. I lean on the toilet and get up. What am I doing? Sitting beside a toilet, hiding from the police?

I rummage in the pocket of the dressing gown, find the box of Ga-Jol liquorice, and put some in my mouth.

In the mirror, I am strangely blurry, like a photo taken with a shaky hand. My eyes look panicked and I straighten my bun, trying to tame a few grey hairs. I look at my reflection as one would look at something broken. Then I go out to open the door.

The September air is fresh and moist, from drizzle and long grass. Behind the burst clouds, a pale sun has already reached high in the sky, causing me to squint.

"Well?" Torben gives me a pat on the shoulder. "Did we wake you?"

"A little."

"Sorry about that. How are things going at home?"

"So-so."

He rubs his beard. Looks towards the cardboard boxes on the grass.

"I'm really sorry about this," he says. "To have to come for official purposes, given the way things are right now."

I look at the gun in his belt. The handcuffs.

"But I thought it was better that it was me who came."

I nod slowly.

"Hi there." The woman extends her hand. "Dagmar. I'm Torben's new partner."

"Hello."

Her warm handshake makes me aware of how cold my own hand is.

"Is your husband at home?" asks Dagmar.

"What?"

"Yes, I apologise for coming unannounced," says Torben. "I know you …" He gestures with his hand.

I tighten the dressing gown's belt, even though it's already tight.

"Is Steen in there?" Torben nods past me. "We would just like to talk to him."

I put my hand against the doorframe, blocking the path. "Unfortunately, it's not a good time. He's … sleeping."

Dagmar pulls up her sleeve and looks at her watch.

"Could he ring you back?" I ask. "When he wakes up."

"We would very much like to talk to him in person," says Torben. "It won't take that long."

"You can just tell me and I'll give him the message."

"As I said, we would very much like to talk to him in person. It's about his father."

This makes me so confused that my arm falls down by my side again.

"Steen's father?"

"Okay," I say. "Come inside."

With my foot, I push aside the parents-to-be gift basket that I still haven't removed from the doorstep and taken into the house. The rain-soaked cellophane sticks to a heart-shaped box of chocolates and a bag of coffee beans. The card is completely rained to bits.

Torben and Dagmar step into the hall. Her eyes glide around the half-dark, cluttered room.

"I've always wanted one of these." She slaps the naked brick wall. "We live in a redbrick house, too."

"Removing the plaster makes such a mess," says Torben, when I don't answer.

I remove the pile of sweaty sheets lying in the way. I push the unopened letters from the council under some advertisements and drop a packet of wet wipes on the floor. All the muscles in my body tense. Is it illegal that I didn't call anyone? That I just let him lie there?

"Sorry about the mess," I say. "There's been a lot going on and I ..."

"Don't worry about it," says Torben. "Will you wake Steen and tell him we're here?"

"Of course. Yes. One moment."

We go into the living room together, and they stand by the fireplace while I hesitantly approach the closed door to the bedroom.

I push down the handle and tiptoe in, even though I know he's already awake. He's guaranteed to have heard everything that's been going on since the doorbell rang.

I look at the yellow backs of Steen's hands and the bare soles of his feet. He's lying there like he usually does, with his arms down along his sides and his feet outside of the duvet, so he doesn't get too hot. The clock on the wall is ticking. I remain standing. Trying to calculate how much time it would take to wake a sleeping man.

"Sorry," I whisper before returning to the officers. They are still standing by the fireplace. An old, built-in one with neat carvings that we haven't dared use since we lit it the first time and the whole living room filled with smoke.

"Okay," I say. "He's in there."

The officers edge around the full clotheshorse, the bucket of cold, brown soapy water, and the rubbish bags that I haven't carried out yet.

"Wait!"

My outburst stops them.

Torben looks at me questioningly.

"It's just that ..." I straighten my hair again. Try to breathe normally. "Don't be alarmed. But he can't move."

"What?"

"It's because ... He's been paralysed."

I whisper the word, but as soon as it passes my lips, it swells up and fills the living room like an oversize piece of furniture.

"But ..." Torben looks at the bedroom door. "The last time I saw him, he was ..."

"It happened very recently," I say. "Twelve days."

"What happened to him?"

11

"We don't really know."

"Did he fall off something?"

"Not as far as I know."

"But a doctor has seen him?"

I nod. "Doctor Møller says that it's a completely normal reaction given what we've been through. He says it should go away in a few days."

"But did you not say he's been lying here for twelve days?"

"Steen has always been very sensitive. Doctor Møller knows that well. We have to give him time."

They exchange a glance and I start sweating under my arms.

"Shouldn't he be in hospital?" asks Dagmar.

"Doctor Møller thinks it's best that he's in a safe environment."

The more I distort the truth, the more I sweat. In reality, Dr. Møller had said exactly the same thing as Dagmar. Even took out his phone to ring the hospital. But I talked him out of it. Begged him to keep it between us.

They can't take him from me. Steen is the only one I have left.

And I can't be on my own in the house. Not anymore.

"That's awful," says Dagmar. "And now his father on top of everything else."

"I think you're mistaken," I say. "Steen's father died four years ago."

"Yes," says Torben. "That's the point."

I look at him confused.

"I'm sorry," he says. "Misfortunes rarely come alone."

"Misfortunes?"

He nods towards the bedroom door. "Let us talk to Steen."

The bedroom is dark behind the rolled-down blinds. It stinks of full nappies, and Torben slowly enters. So slow that he stops.

Steen's hair is styled in the front. The back is flat and matted. There is a clear line of where I haven't been able to reach with the brush. On his bedside table is a pink feeding cup with flowers.

On my side, the sheet is crumpled and the duvet is on its way over the edge. My phone is charging on the pillow. On my bedside table is a jar of sleeping tablets and a packet of Natracare New Mother postpartum pads.

"Should I change him before we talk?" I say.

Torben pulls the hat back and forth on his head.

"It won't take that long," I say. "You can wait in the living room meanwhile."

"It's okay," says Dagmar. "This is fine."

She edges around Torben to the double bed. Kneels a bit to come down to eye level.

"Hello, Steen. Sorry for the intrusion. My name is Dagmar. I'm Torben's new partner."

Steen's eyes flicker between the officers and me. As if it's only now dawning on him that we're here.

"What's going on?" he asks.

"Unfortunately, there's something we have to tell you," says Dagmar.

"What?" Steen looks at Torben.

"Should I lift you up a little?" I ask. "Would you like another pillow behind your back?"

He blinks twice.

"Okay." I turn to the officers. "Would you like some coffee?"

Torben holds up a hand.

"Something to eat, then? I don't really know what's in the fridge, but sometimes there's a cake."

I can hear how nervous I sound.

"No, thank you." Torben walks closer to the bed. There is something awkward and reluctant about this otherwise robust man. His arms hang limply and I think about how they used to greet each other. Torben's shouts and Steen's outstretched arms. Two men who hugged and slapped each other on the back, hard, several times, like when you want to knock the last bit out of a bottle of ketchup.

"Steen, old boy. What's the matter with you?"

"Yeah, it's not good."

"Eva says you're paralysed?"

"From the neck down."

Torben takes the hat off and holds it in front of his chest.

"If I'd known, I'd have made sure to drop by."

Steen blinks three times to signal that's okay. He's probably so confused right now that he forgot that it's only the two of us who understand blink language.

"What the hell are we going to do with the old boys' team now?" says Torben. "You have to get back on your feet again so we don't get thrown out completely."

"I'll do what I can."

"But I still don't understand … what happened to you? A healthy man in his prime. How did you end up like this?"

"I don't know."

"It happened all of a sudden," I say. "From one moment to the next."

Torben shakes his head. Says it sounds completely incomprehensible.

"It's not even three weeks since your winning penalty kick. The boys are still talking about it. And now you're lying here."

"Yeah."

"Is there anything I can do? Just say, if there is. I can do a shop for you or come by with some dinner? I make a pretty good lasagne, if I do say so myself."

"We can handle it," I say. "But thank you."

Torben nods. He shifts his weight from one foot to the other, as if he can't decide whether to embrace Steen or to hurry up and get the conversation over with and get away from here.

A bluebottle flies around the room and lands on one of Steen's big toes. I wave it away. All three of us watch it as it flies around the bedroom and lands on his big toe again. It crawls over the sole of his foot. Small, black legs.

I wave again. Keep waving until the fly gives up and settles on the wall instead.

Dagmar looks at her wristwatch.

"I'm sorry, but we have to move on, Torben. Patrol."

Torben turns his hat in his hands.

"It's almost unbearable. To come with such news when you're already …" He gestures with his hand.

"Unfortunately, we bring you some unpleasant news," says Dagmar. "Would you like to sit? Or … would you like to sit, Eva?"

I look around the bedroom, but there's only the double bed.

"It's fine," I say. "What about you? Should I get some chairs?"

"Don't worry about that. We'll be heading off again soon." She looks at Torben, who nods and puts the hat on his head.

"The thing is," he says, "we got a call from the church this morning. Something happened last night. Vandalism. In the graveyard."

"The graveyard?" I whisper.

"It's your father, Steen. His grave ..." Torben changes position. "We're very sorry to have to bring you this news. It was the verger who contacted us. He discovered that something had been written on the headstone."

"You mean graffiti?" I ask.

Torben shakes his head.

"It turned out to be a kind of paint. It was done very neatly. With a thin brush. The person concerned went to some effort. Still, it was hard to decipher. The rain destroyed much of it. And then we had the extra challenge that it wasn't letters, but Chinese characters."

There's a moment's silence where only the ticking of the clock can be heard.

"Naturally, we are getting it translated," says Dagmar. "But it's hard when some of the paint has run off."

"Initially, the verger thought it was just a prank," says Torben. "But when he looked closer, he saw that someone had dug up the ground."

"It had been raked and everything," says Dagmar. "And the gravel and everything had been put back."

"The person in question really tried to leave everything as it was," says Torben. "But we got forensics in and they confirmed our suspicions."

He pauses for a moment. Then he says:

"The grave was opened."

CHAPTER 3

The dragon in front of our house was made of iron and old car parts. Half reptile, half bird with four legs and large nostrils.

Usually, dragons lived in caves, like unicorns, and only appeared to humans when something important was about to happen. Our dragon stood here every single day, but there was something new about it now. Something in the green glass eyes. A warning?

"Come," said Father for the second time. He held my shoulder. When he'd said it the first time, I had run. Father caught up with me in the front garden.

"She is waiting for you," he said. "Inside the house."

"I have to pee."

"I need you to be strong. Your wedding day should be a happy day."

"I'm eight years old," I whispered.

My voice was so low that I didn't know if Father heard it. Maybe he just pretended he didn't.

"Go in to her," he said.

My body couldn't do it.

"Family is the most important thing," said Father. "Remember that."

I nodded. Either you were a part of it or you were on your own.

Being on my own was the scariest thing I knew.

Father laid a hand on my back. Forced my legs forward.

On the way up to the house, I turned around. The dragon's green eyes were watching me.

Water splashed in the cistern and I looked at the wall. I stood for a long time by the toilet after it had stopped dripping. If I looked long enough, faces appeared in the turquoise glass mosaics. People with long beards and hats. With open mouths and eyes that stared back at me.

There was a knock on the door. There was no lock. Otherwise, I might never have opened it again.

Inside the house, the smell of incense had intensified. It smelled of deep fat frying and Mother's perfume, too. She had put on her fine silk dress, the one with red birds. Her long black hair was curled up and fastened with two chopsticks.

"First you have to find her shoes," said Father.

"Are they missing?"

"A bride is not complete until her husband finds her shoes and puts them on."

I looked at the hall bench. On the top shelf were three pairs of ladies' shoes in velour fabric with flat heels and thin straps. But they were Mother's.

Father nudged me. My legs felt weird. Even though he didn't push hard, I nearly fell.

"Meanwhile, the groom searches, and all the wedding guests push and pull, making it harder." Father pulled my arm. It didn't hurt. Still, it burned behind my eyes.

But it's just us, I wanted to say. Instead, I stood completely stiff, rubbing myself in the spot he'd grabbed.

"Maybe we could help a little?" said Mother.

Father ran his hand through his hair. Ended up ruining the side parting.

His silence filled the room. It leaked out of him like smoke from a dragon's nostril. Maybe he thought he should have chosen my brother instead.

"Bird, fish, or in between?" I asked him.

He blinked. Looked at me.

"Bird," he said.

I looked up. The ceiling was decorated with yellow lanterns of thin rice paper, and I walked around the hall. I lifted jackets and pulled out drawers. The tiger was still hanging on the living room door with his big teeth. A tiger drawing had been put on the kitchen door, too. It was as though the house was shrinking.

I walked back and forth. It was hard to concentrate. "You have to say hotter or colder."

"Colder," said Father. "Very cold."

I went the other way, back towards the living room door.

"Warmer," said Father. "Warm on your hair."

I looked up.

There they were. On the shelf with father's hats. Two small white bridal shoes.

Father helped me get them down. I waved with them, but Mother didn't smile.

"I'll get the soup," she said.

It was hard to eat without breathing. The taste made my nausea worse. Soy, vinegar, mustard sauce, pepper, salt, and sugar. All five flavours should be there. Sour, sweet, salty, bitter, and umami.

"It is important you eat it all," said Father.

I didn't dare ask why. He had the same expression as when he picked up the box of dead butterflies. The ones he used in his fairy tales. His stories were always creepy. They were about curses and evil warnings, dog howls and crow screeches. About ghosts, flames, and hungry spirits flying around the streets like bats.

Mother watched me as I ate. She had put earrings on and had blackened her eyes, which she eventually had to remove because it was constantly smearing.

Maybe she hadn't heard Father's rule that crying was forbidden from now on.

When I had eaten the soup, I had to change. Father led me into the playroom. It was very cold. The windows were covered with paper. It looked like a birthday tablecloth, only without the Danish flags.

The beds were made. I had never before seen the duvets so neat. They were completely smooth, and only when Father laid a hand on my shoulder did it dawn on me that he had said my name.

Slowly I took off my clothes. I had goose bumps.

On a hanger next to the mirror hung my new clothes. They looked like a small, flat person. Black suit. Red tie.

When I sniffed, I could still sense it. Below the incense and deep fat fryer and Mother's perfume. The sharp smell that had come into the house.

Father tied my tie. Took it off and tied it again. It was still too long, but he gave up on making it better. Pointed at the patent-leather shoes. I put them on. He straightened me up and looked at me in the mirror. My heart felt like a tiny metal drum playing too fast.

Father squatted down and tied my shoelaces. The patent-leather shoes were black, just like the suit. The socks were black, too, and my hands were shaking.

"She is so beautiful," said Mother, who had come in to us. "Don't be nervous."

Father laid a hand on my back and pushed me back towards the hall.

All three of us stood in front of the living room door. Stood without saying anything.

The tiger looked at me, like the metal dragon out in the garden had done. As if it wanted to say something.

Father patted me on the shoulder before entering the living room and closing the door behind him.

Shortly afterwards, the bells began to chime. I thought of my brother who was still outside.

Mother patted me on the cheek and peeled the tiger down from the door.

"So, it is now," she said. "She's waiting for you in there."

I clutched the white silk shoes in my hand.

On the bottom of them was written "Size: age 6."

CHAPTER 4

"Has the grave been opened?" I shake my head. "Opened *how*?"

"Like I said, the verger discovered that something was wrong," says Torben. "And, unfortunately, it was worse than we feared."

He clears his throat. Shifts his weight from foot to foot.

"I'm really sorry to have to tell you this, Steen. But your father ... he's no longer there."

No one says anything for a long time. Only the buzz of the bluebottle breaks the silence as it takes off from the wall and flies around the bedroom.

"Do you mean ..." Steen looks from one to the other. "Someone stole the body?"

Torben nods. "Or ... what was left of it."

The thought makes me feel sick. A four-year-old corpse.

"But," I say, "who would do such a thing?"

"Apologies for not being able to tell you more at the moment," says Dagmar. "Forensics are investigating the coffin, and hopefully we'll find out what the Chinese characters mean soon."

The double bed creaks as I plonk down next to Steen. Talking about the graveyard makes me dizzy.

"I'm really sorry." Torben looks as uncomfortable as I feel. "Can we do anything for you?"

"I don't know," I say. "It's a bit of a shock."

"Forensics left everything as nicely as possible, of course" says Dagmar.

"Thank you," says Steen.

"The verger couldn't tell whether anything else had been stolen from the grave," says Torben. "Candlesticks and vases and what have you. He suggested that you go down yourself to inspect whether anything is missing. But that's …" He looks at the duvet covering Steen's body.

"Never mind," says Steen. "There was nothing special on the grave. You don't need to do any more there."

"I can go down," I say. "I can take some pictures of the grave so you can see if everything is all right."

"I can hardly remember what it looks like." His face winces.

"I'll lay a flower tomorrow, too," I say. "From both of us. What kind of flowers did your father like?"

"I don't know."

Torben extends his hand towards Steen. Pats him on the shoulder several times.

"He can't feel it," I say.

"What?"

"When you pat him on the shoulder. He can't feel anything."

"Oh … no. Of course." Torben removes his hand.

"Are you okay?" he says to Steen.

"I don't really know."

"It's a bloody mess. If I knew which sicko—" Torben interrupts himself. Glances at Dagmar and straightens his hat.

"We'll contact you as soon as we know more," he says. "The coffin has been sent for examination, and we are doing everything within our power. And just you ring if there's anything I can help with."

"Thank you," says Steen.

"Would you like to inform the other next of kin yourself?" asks Torben.

"No," says Steen.

"Well, you're the sole owner of the grave, so it's up to you. But we are happy to contact the other family members. Your adoptive mother is still alive, isn't she? Should we inform her?"

"Do what you want. Just don't involve me."

The sound of the doorbell interrupts us.

"I'll get that." Dagmar goes out.

Steen closes his eyes, as if it's too exhausting to keep them open any longer. The smell of his full nappy hangs heavily in the air, and Torben's eyes zoom around the room like the bluebottle that is constantly taking off and landing again. Them being here feels wrong. Like sitting on a public toilet with an open door. But beneath the shame is something else. A budding idea.

"Well," I say. "If there's nothing else, I think Steen needs some rest now."

"Of course. I'll contact you when we know more. Get well soon."

"Thank you," mumbles Steen.

"And if you change your mind about that lasagne, just call."

"We will."

We walk out of the bedroom and I close the door behind us. Pull the handle an extra time to make sure it won't open again.

Torben looks at the clotheshorse, where Steen's pyjama shirts are hanging with limp arms. He pulls out his collar. "We've been talking about how we haven't seen you much lately. But we didn't want to force ourselves on you. We had no idea …"

"Don't worry about it," I say. "But I'd be grateful if you kept a slightly low profile. People are looking at me a lot already."

He makes a movement as if he is zipping his mouth.

"Will you say it to Dagmar, too?"

"Of course."

"Thanks. Would you come out into the kitchen with me, please?"

He glances to the door behind us. Nods.

The kitchen stinks of overripe bananas. The sink is full of half-empty coffee cups. On the cooker is the pan with the fried eggs and bacon from this morning. I thought I'd put it in the fridge.

"Sorry we're not so chatty at the moment," I say. "Everything is a bit chaotic. But I'll contact Steen's mother. You needn't spend time on that."

"But Steen …"

"Steen is not himself at the moment. Understandably. But, of course, I will do it. There's just one thing."

"Yes?"

"I don't know who his mother is."

He raises his eyebrows.

"We lost touch. Or rather, I've never actually met her. But I think now is a good time. If you have her address."

"You've never met Steen's mother? How long have you been together?"

"Eight years." I shrug. "You know Steen. Once he decides something, he's stubborn about it."

Torben smiles. Says I've got that right.

"Excuse me?" Dagmar comes out into the kitchen to us. "It's the postman. He needs a signature. I tried to say it wasn't a good time, but he insisted."

I follow her out to the front door, where a postman is standing with a large cardboard box by his feet.

"Hello, hello," he says. "Eva Hegner?"

"That's me."

"There's post from the great abroad." He shows me the delivery note.

My stomach turns when I see what it is. The car seat. The one we ordered from a German website after reading hundreds of reviews to get the safest model.

"Just put it there." I point to the rain-soaked cardboard boxes in the front garden.

The postman follows my gaze.

"Are you sure?"

I nod.

Torben comes to me. Looks at the delivery note.

I ignore his eyes.

"Can't you send it back?" he asks the postman. "Isn't there something about a person being able to refuse to accept a package?"

"It's okay," I say.

He looks at me questioningly, but I can't explain it. I can't bear the thought of sending it back.

"All righty. I just need an autograph here, so." The postman holds out a touch screen, and my handwriting almost looks like itself.

"Have a nice day." He tips his sunhat and walks back down the driveway.

I stick my hands in the pockets of the dressing gown and stand looking at the cardboard boxes.

There are five now.

"Are you okay?" asks Torben.

I shrug.

We go back inside and I close the door behind us. Realise that I'm counting my breaths.

Torben pats me on the arm and signals that I should remain standing. He gets out his phone and puts it to his ear.

"Torben," he says. "We're still out with the next of kin. Can you find the address for Steen's mother? I don't know her name."

He pats his pockets and fishes out a small, crumpled notebook. He clicks out the tip of a ballpoint pen and stops.

"What?" he says.

The wrinkles in his forehead deepen as the voice at the other end speaks.

"Are you sure that's the correct name?" he asks.

The voice at the other end is a faint murmur. I can't hear what's being said.

"Okay," says Torben. "Thanks for that anyway."

He ends the call and writes something in the notebook. Tears off the top page and folds it in half.

"Here," he says, handing it to me. "Steen's mother's address."

I snatch the paper, clutching it in my hand before I put it in one of the dressing gown's pockets.

He gives me another pat on the arm.

"And maybe we should send someone from the social services? So you can get some more help."

"We're getting all the help we need. Thanks, though."

He looks around the room.

"My sister comes all the time," I say. "She's a doctor."

His phone starts ringing.

"Excuse me." He puts it to his ear and signals "two minutes" before going to a corner of the living room and saying "Hello?"

I touch the paper in my pocket.

"Do you read many books?" Dagmar peruses our bookshelves.

"I did once."

She pulls out a book. Pushes it in again.

Torben has fidgeted a clothes peg off the clotheshorse. Stands there opening and closing it as he talks on the phone. Says "I'll be damned" and "yes, we're here now."

"I don't get to read as much as I'd like to, either," says Dagmar. "It's difficult when you're so busy, isn't it?"

I nod without looking at her. My body feels cold under the dressing gown and I think of Steen in the bedroom. The headstone with paint and *I'm really sorry to have to tell you this, Steen. But your father … he's no longer there.*

No matter how much I rub my hands together, I can't get any heat into them.

"This is really nice, this one." Dagmar has gone to the fireplace. "Did you do the brickwork yourself?"

She slides her fingers over the carvings. Looks at me when I don't answer.

"It came with the house," I say finally.

Torben hangs up and comes over to us.

"That was forensics," he says. "About the coffin."

"Yes?" Dagmar turns away from the fireplace.

"There was paint on the inside of the lid, too. The red colour was hard to see on the wood, which has started to rot. That's why they missed it initially."

"I didn't think there would be any coffin left after four years," I say.

"He was buried in a solid oak coffin, which has a long shelf life."

"Solid oak," I say. "That sounds expensive."

"Yeah. Why?"

"I just never got the impression that Steen's parents had a lot of money."

"They obviously prioritised a good coffin." Torben shrugs.

"But what did it say?" says Dagmar. "On the coffin lid?"

"The same Chinese characters as on the headstone. Only difference was they were easier to decipher. We should get an answer to what they mean shortly."

CHAPTER 5

She was in there already. I clutched the white bridal shoes in my hand. Father held two shiny silver bells, which he rang as I stepped through the door, and I didn't dare look at her face.

The number of gifts surprised me. A house, a horse, a refrigerator. A crock of silver and a gilded birdcage with a blue-breasted quail.

Mother pushed me forward.

My shoes were noisy against the floor as I walked through the room and stood next to my bride.

The word felt strange. *Bride.* She looked really small.

I glanced at her out of the corner of my eye.

Mother was right. She was very beautiful. Still, I didn't really know her. She was wearing a white silk dress. Her hair was brushed and shiny. A fine mother-of-pearl colour was applied to her eyelids. In her hands, she held a white lily. Only after some time did I see that it was made of paper.

"Are you ready?" said Father.

"Yes," I said.

Father put down the two silver bells and came over to us. His tie was red, just like mine. On one breast pocket was a gold pin. That was what I looked at when he started talking.

"We are gathered today to unite a young man and a young woman in sacred marriage."

He spoke loudly, despite it being just us. The words echoed in the quiet room. Mother stood next to him, looking down at the floor. Father told me about the beginning of the universe, about how everything was connected, and all the while I thought about butterflies and spirits and about being buried in the sandbox. I thought of my brother who was still outside.

Father patted me on the shoulder. "Are you there, Yin-Yin?"

"What?"

"It is you now."

I blinked hard and it was all there again. The silver bells and the wedding gifts. A house, a horse, a refrigerator. And right next to me: her tiny bare feet.

Yin-Yin. Father always called me that when he wanted me to do something I didn't want to do.

I kneeled down. Took one of her ankles. It was hard to get the bridal shoes on. Her feet were so small, and even though she didn't say anything, I was afraid it was going to hurt her. I closed the little silver buckles and got up again. Father patted me on the shoulder.

He took a jewellery box out of his jacket pocket.

"Do you, Yin-Yin, take Wu-Lin to be your wife?"

"I do," I said.

"And do you, Wu-Lin, take Yin-Yin to be your husband?"

"I do," said Mother when Wu-Lin didn't answer.

The rings were thin and shiny. Looked like real gold.

Wu-Lin's skin resisted as I pushed a ring down over her knuckle.

I put the other ring on myself. Bent and stretched my fingers.

Mother wiped her eyes again, and Father held his palms over us.

"I hereby declare you man and wife. You may kiss the bride."

I looked at Wu-Lin. Looked away again.

My metal heart drummed and drummed. The rest of my body stiffened.

"You are a big boy," said Father.

I nodded. I was wearing a tie, just like Father. I could do this.

There was a rushing in my head as I held my breath and leaned forwards. Then I kissed Wu-Lin on the mouth.

CHAPTER 6

Steen's mother's address is on the coffee table. I look at it every time I walk by. I chew hard on the handful of Ga-Jol liquorice I threw into my mouth as soon as the police were gone, but I still have a strange taste in my mouth.

I get the nappy-changing things ready in the bedroom and start undressing Steen. His skin is moist with sweat and has a pallid-yellowish colour that makes me think of plasticine and margarine, and of German children who were imprisoned for so long that they were in danger of dying of vitamin D deficiency.

As I struggle with the buttons of Steen's pyjama shirt, I feel like googling them again. Just google someone. Someone who might understand.

Steen and I should talk about his father, but I can't bring myself to mention the graveyard. Can't stand thinking about that place.

The buttons keep slipping between my fingers. It is the restlessness in my body. The address on the coffee table.

Steen's breathing is fast. As though he's breathless from my fumbling.

I smile at him, but he doesn't smile back. His body is warm from the bed, and the little curly hairs on his chest are flat and stuck to his skin. His arms are heavy and limp, and I have to constantly support him with my head. Even though I've done it a million times, it still feels awkward. Like a little girl with an oversize doll.

In the living room, the television is on. The volume is turned up high. It's getting harder and harder to drown out the silence. It's mounting up, like the cardboard boxes in the front garden, and I miss him. Even now, as I am pulling off his underpants, I miss him.

I wring out a cloth in some water and start washing him. At first, I used to put the nappy on wrong so his faeces pushed their way up his back. I tried to smile as I dried him. I cried only when I was on my own.

I don't cry anymore now. Just freeze.

"Are you ready?" I say.

He blinks once. Yes.

I put his legs up on my shoulders and take a deep breath. Balance my feet and remember to mind my back as I lift him up and get the new nappy in place. My arms shake and my pulse pounds with the exertion and the fear of dropping him.

There's guaranteed to be an easier way. Some equipment of some kind. But I dare not call the authorities.

"How does that feel?" I ask.

"I've no idea."

I check that the nappy isn't too tight with a finger.

He avoids my eyes. Looks up at the ceiling, as if waiting to get it over with.

I take the baby brush and comb his beautiful black hair. It keeps sticking out on one side.

"You don't have to do so much," he says.

"Of course I do."

I smear Vaseline on his lips and try to make eye contact again, but his expression is distant, as if he isn't really there.

"Should we wait to deal with your work?" I say.

"It's fine. I'm ready."

"Can I read something for you instead?"

"Let's just get it over with."

I get up and pick up my computer. I sit on the edge of the bed and log in to his Gmail.

Hi, Steen. We need a CMS employee from November and three months on. Do you have time?

Steen clears his throat. "Thank you for your inquiry. As I have explained on my website, I am not taking on any new assignments for the moment. I hope …"

"One second," I say, typing the last words.

"I hope you can find someone else. Best regards, Steen."

The football club has sent something about a competition. I delete it. An email has also come in from the municipality.

Remember to enrol your child in day care …

I delete before I have time to read more.

Hi, Steen. Did you get the invitation to the student reunion? It's just so we know how much food and drink to buy. Best, Claus.

Steen's eyes meet mine. There's something claustrophobic about it, like he's trapped in there, in the black eyes.

"Hi, Claus. Thanks for the invitation, and sorry I'm only getting back to you now. Unfortunately, I can't come that day. Hope you have a fun evening."

I press send and scroll on. I can feel his eyes in the meantime.

Time to make a dentist appointment. Delete.

Special offer on a spa weekend. Delete.

Hi, Steen. You didn't show up for your appointment with psychologist Rikke Villemose, and we …

I freeze.

"And we what?" he asks.

"Sorry, can we do the rest later?"

One blink.

I shut the computer and put it away. Breathe into my palms and rub them against each other.

When I look at Steen, he's looking up at the ceiling again. His face is glistening.

"Are you sweating?" I ask.

One blink.

I pull the duvet off him.

"I think it's freezing in here," I say.

He quiets a little.

"Are you going back tomorrow?" he asks. "To work?"

"I'm not leaving you. Never."

I put my hands around his face and hold it.

"No one is allowed to take you from me. I promised. I'm keeping it."

He lifts the corners of his mouth. It's almost a smile and I hold on even harder.

"It's the two of us against the world," I say. "Nothing can change that."

"It hurts a little."

"What?"

"Your hands."

I let him go again abruptly. Straighten myself up.

His chest moves up and down every time he breathes.

"Are you still sweating?" I ask.

"I don't think so."

"You can lie for a little while without a duvet. Would you like that?"

"You decide."

I insert a finger under the elastic edge of the nappy and check again that it isn't too tight. The first week he got red marks and I kept thinking: *Would I even have been able to look after a child?*

I run my hand over his leg. Let my hand slide up and down several times.

"Can you still not feel anything?" I ask.

Two blinks. No.

We came up with the blink language during the first few chaotic days, when we had no idea whether the paralysis would get worse. Whether in time it would also take his voice away from him.

I don't know if it's the tiredness making him communicate in blinks, or if he still fears that his voice will disappear.

The bed creaks as I lie beside him. I caress his smooth cheek. There's a little nick under his chin, but otherwise, I'm getting a handle on how to shave him, too.

With my index finger, I follow his fine, flat-bridged nose and his lips that always turn downwards but with a small curl on each side, as if a smile is hiding in there. I miss that smile.

It's as though his eyes have turned blacker than ever. As if something deep inside him is broken, and sometimes I'm afraid it can't be put back together.

I picture how the police came in here again. Their uniforms and flickering glances when they saw him lying in the bed with nappies and matted back hair.

"I'm sorry I let them in," I say. "They kept ringing the bell and I think they saw me in the window."

Three blinks. It's okay.

"Do you think they'll send someone out?" I say. "Social welfare, or whatever it's called?"

"It was Torben."

"But the other one, maybe?"

He doesn't answer. Just stares at the ceiling.

"What do you think they mean?" I say. "Those Chinese characters?"

"I've no idea."

"Maybe it's a coincidence that it was your father. Some people would do anything for some jewellery and a gold tooth."

"Maybe."

"But it is strange that they took the time to paint them with a brush."

He grimaces.

"I'm sorry," I say. "Should we stop talking about it?"

One blink.

In the living room, the television repeats the same monotonous canned laughter.

"Every day I wish we could talk about something ordinary," I say. "I've completely forgotten how to talk about something ordinary. What did we talk about in the past?"

"Could I have some water?"

I lean over him and get the feeding cup. Tip it gently so it doesn't run.

"More?" I ask.

Two blinks.

"We'll get you well again," I whisper.

"Do you think?"

"I promise."

I can hear him swallowing and my stomach clenches. As the days pass, the nagging fear that we'll be having this conversation for the rest of our lives grows.

I think of the note in the living room.

"Maybe we should contact your mother?" I say.

"Why do you say that?"

"I just thought it would be good for you. She probably needs to talk about what happened in the graveyard, too?"

Two blinks.

"Are you afraid she's going to find out what happened to you?"

"We're not talking to my family."

"But maybe we could start? Maybe she knows what's wrong with you. Maybe it's something hereditary? Maybe she can help us?"

He blinks hard twice.

"Sweetheart … I'm trying to help you. Don't you want to get well again?"

"I just need peace and quiet."

"That's what you always say, but so far there hasn't been any improvement."

"Can't we just let it go? I am so tired."

I lean forward and kiss him on the forehead.

"We'll figure it out," I whisper. "As long as we stay together, we'll figure it out."

And the rest I'll have to do on my own.

CHAPTER 7

The flash made me close my eyes.

"Smile," said Father. "No one wants to have sad wedding pictures."

We sat on the couch while the pictures were being taken. Wu-Lin in her white dress, me in a suit and tie. It was hard to smile. My mouth grew more and more sore, just like when I was at the dentist to get a very large hole fixed.

"That's it, yes," said Father. "And then just a few where you can see the gifts."

He moved farther away in the living room. The camera was old and the flash huge. It made me think of lightning and of being pulled under a treetop by my father's hand. Having a "no" sitting in your throat like a sharp boiled sweet.

It was decorated so much that it didn't look like our living room at all. Lanterns. Paper flowers. Dizzying mobiles. In the fireplace, even the old papier-mâché tiger had been given a party hat.

We finally finished taking pictures and Father put the camera away. He took a spring roll from a dish and crushed it between his teeth while looking out into the back garden.

"More food?" asked Mother.

"No, thank you," I said.

Mother covered the dishes with tinfoil. Carried them out into the kitchen.

Wu-Lin's face was turned towards the empty dining table. I gave her hand a squeeze. She didn't squeeze back.

Mother came back. The silk dress with birds rustled every time she took a step through the quiet living room. In her hands, she carried a palace of paper. She placed it on the coffee table in front of us. It was very beautiful. It was purpure coloured with a yellow roof and was the size of Wu-Lin's doll's house.

"There you are, children," she said. "This is where you are going to live."

I looked at the little palace, at the paper-thin walls and the neat carvings that were supposed to represent windows.

"You will be happy there," said Mother, patting both of us on the cheek.

Father poured baijiu into four crystal glasses.

"Cheers." He lifted one.

All the new rules were making my head spin. Were children allowed to drink alcohol today?

I took a tiny sip. It tasted like sniffing a strong marker.

Wu-Lin didn't drink anything.

Father put a record on the gramophone and lowered the pickup arm.

"Weddings should be noisy," he said. "All weddings should be noisy."

The living room glowed red, and Wu-Lin grew heavier and heavier in my arms as I turned around with her.

You will be happy there.

I suppressed a moan. Whispered sorry every time I stepped on her long wedding dress. She was really heavy now, and her arms were completely stiff, as if she didn't want to hold on to me.

Mother came over to us on the dance floor. She pressed her lips together and blew soap bubbles at us. They burst every time they hit something.

I liked it better before. When we wore ordinary clothes and played outside in the garden.

Now Wu-Lin was very cold and quiet, and I didn't know what to say to her. I didn't know how to dance with her.

I'd never danced with my little sister before.

CHAPTER 8

There's a knock at the door. Three fast raps followed by three slow ones. The sister knock.

I pull the duvet up over Steen and go out to open the door.

Outside, the drizzle has stopped. Klara gives me a hug and a bag of chops that are so fresh there's still blood on them. Her cheeks are red and her hair flutters in the wind. Over her shoulder is her brown vet's bag.

"Well," she says. "Anything new on him?"

"Unfortunately not."

She takes off her shoes in the hall, hangs up her outdoor things, and takes the chops out of my hand. Puts them in the fridge.

"You smell like a pigsty," I say. "Did you come straight from Mum and Dad's?"

"There was a sow in difficulty. And someone has to visit them."

I ignore her reproachful eyes and go to the bedroom. "I got some eggs and bacon into him this morning, and almost two hundred millilitres of water this morning. But I think he's getting more and more pale."

Klara goes inside and lays a hand on his forehead.

"Hi, Steen." She clicks up the metal hinges of her bag. "How are you doing today?"

"About as good as I look."

She takes out a magnifying glass and looks at him through it. His eyes, his tongue.

"And you haven't thought of anything since I was last here?" she says. "That you fell off your bike or hit your back somehow?"

"No."

"A car accident? An accident of some kind at work?"

"As an IT consultant?"

"And you're sure there have been no symptoms of a blood clot or anything?"

"Do we have to go through the same questions every time?"

"I just think it's so refreshing to have a patient who can actually answer."

She winks at him and puts her stethoscope in her ears. Listens to his breathing and heart. She lifts and lowers his arms and legs, and I stick two fingers in between the blinds and look out into the back garden.

Less than two weeks ago, he was walking around on the grass. He was wearing sandals and had sunglasses on his forehead and was waving at me through the window. I think of our two cars. Whether I should sell one. When do you make those kinds of decisions?

"Can you feel this?" asks Klara behind me.

"No." There's something apologetic in Steen's tone, and I find the scene harder and harder to look at it. The vet examining my paralysed husband.

I sniff. Feel like opening the window. This strange smell. It's like it's seeping out through the pores of my skin and settling in the brickwork. My urine, my breath, the entire building. As though it's penetrating through the walls and up from the basement.

I think of all the things that Klara has carried down there for us. Stacks of cardboard boxes and toys that have never been played with. Maybe I should get her to carry the new boxes in the front garden down there, too.

Klara pulls off the rubber gloves, presses sanitiser into the palm of her hand, and rubs it between her fingers. Her hands look like Dad's. Strong and broad.

"I have to give it to you," she says. "You're in amazingly good form, Steen. Had you been a dog or a pig, your muscles would already have begun to atrophy."

"Thanks for the compliment." Steen sends her a small, flat smile and she pats him on the cheek. Flaps the duvet and covers him up again.

"Haven't you had a shower yet?" She looks at my dressing gown.

"I just wanted to see to Steen first."

She comes over and takes my arm. Pulls it.

"You've lost weight again."

"Not that much."

She brushes something off one of my shoulders. Looks down at me.

"Do you know why they call it a dressing gown, sis? Because you wear it while you're getting *dressed*, not for the whole day."

"Then it's a good thing you can call it a bathrobe instead."

"That requires you to actually have a bath."

"Okay. We could also just stop talking about my clothes."

She throws out her arms. Makes an encouraging *tut* sound, like when she has to run a stubborn horse back into the pen.

"Come on, let's go out and have some lunch. What do you say, Steen? I have your father-in-law's homemade liver pâté with me. The one with bacon."

"No thanks."

"You're a really cheap date. Well, you have to have just one slice of bread."

She pats me on the back as a sign to go first.

"Does my breath smell strange?" I ask as we close the bedroom door behind us.

She sticks her nose to my mouth. Sniffs a few times.

"It smells of liquorice," she says.

"Does it smell rotten?"

"Stop that now."

"I just want to be sure."

"I told you that's all in your head."

"You're not just saying that?"

"Come out and have some lunch. If I know you, you haven't eaten anything since I was here yesterday. You must be starving."

She follows me out into the kitchen with the used rubber gloves between two fingers. The bin is full, so she ties a knot on the bag and puts in a new one.

"Are you sure I can't pay you something for all your help?" I say. "What are you paid an hour as a vet?"

She places the full rubbish bag by the kitchen door. Turns on the tap and starts washing her hands.

"To be honest," she says, "I'm not sure about this anymore."

"This?"

"I'm not a real doctor."

"I trust you."

She turns off the tap and wipes her fingers on a tea towel. Stands for a moment, looking out into the air.

"I trust you," I say again. "And I would very much like to pay you for your time."

Klara takes the frying pan from the cooker and scrapes off the hardened bacon and eggs into the rubbish bin. Opens the fridge and starts taking out the cold cuts she herself bought and put in there. Curried herring. Egg salad. Gherkins.

"He's been lying like that for twelve days now," she says. "Twelve days. And you haven't been out of the house since."

"I was in the hospital yesterday. And I often visit the graveyard when Steen is taking a nap."

"You know what I mean. All your time is spent changing nappies, washing clothes, and making food. It's not good for you."

I shrug. I was prepared for that. I'd been waiting to take care of that other human being who couldn't do anything for themselves for months.

"I really understand that it's difficult after what you've been through," says Klara. "But I also think I've been patient. More patient than I should have been, perhaps. But now ..." She smells a carton of milk. Pours it down the sink.

"There is no improvement in him at all. It's time for professionals. I think we should get him to the hospital. He needs to be examined."

"I don't trust the system."

"Sis." She takes my hand. "It wasn't the hospital's fault that it went wrong."

I pull my hand back.

"I can easily take care of Steen at home. You said yourself that he is in amazingly good form. I can do this."

"But maybe he needs medical treatment. And what about you? What about your work? Aren't you supposed to start tomorrow?"

"I've extended my sick leave."

She sighs and I look at the sandwich things she's taken out. Pieces of meat wrapped in plastic.

"I just don't think I'm ready," I say. "All those kids."

"It will be fine."

"But what about Steen?"

"That's actually why we have hospitals, sis. For sick people."

"He needs peace and quiet. He won't get that in the hospital."

Klara sighs again.

"Okay. We'll make a deal. You call your boss and say you're coming into work tomorrow, anyway, and I'll come and look in on Steen during the day. I can squeeze him in between a castration and an earmarking."

"And you won't ring the hospital?" I ask as I walk towards the bathroom.

"We'll see how it goes tomorrow, and then we'll talk about it, all right?"

In the bathroom mirror, the grey hairs are sticking up again. They feel like pieces of wire and strange against the palm of my hand, reminding me of the fur on the dead mouse I found in the back garden at Christmas. It looked as if it had deliberately placed itself in the snow. As if it could no longer see a purpose in getting up.

Twelve days, I think, and they flicker strangely slowly past my inner eye. The evenings in the living room, when I apathetically watch the television, trying not to think about why I'm sitting there on my own. I watch cooking shows and commercials and quizzes until I am anaesthetised by meaninglessness. Try not to google, but always end up doing it anyway.

Paralysis. Stillbirth. Suicidal thoughts.

Sometimes my thumb is killing me when I finally tear myself away. Google's algorithm still thinks it can entice me with romper suits and personalised dummies, and I click and click to find ad-free pages. End up on obscure articles that give me a weird sense of solidarity.

Doomsday Danes can live for months without any contact with the outside world.

Every year, 2,000 children die in their mother's womb.

Science confirms that there is life after death.

Only when the clock strikes 22:30 do I allow myself to swallow my two sleeping tablets and lie down beside Steen.

I jerk when a bluebottle lands on my cheek. It slowly climbs up my temple and over my eyebrows. I stand still in front of the mirror, watching how it moves around my face. The wings' network of ribs resembles black veins. The proboscis moves in and out. Then it buzzes off, flies in the direction of the light, and bangs into the windowpane.

I turn away from the mirror before taking off my dressing gown. Turn on the shower and wash myself quickly. Avoid touching my stomach.

Klara puts a piece of rye bread on each of the three plates and pushes one towards me.

"Have some food." She puts cold cuts in front of me. An exhibition of salami, roasted onions, and egg salad.

"Why do you keep looking at my hair?" I say.

"You can tell how an animal is doing by looking at its fur."

"I see."

"You've really gone grey, sis."

"Well, I am forty-three."

"But two weeks ago you didn't have a single grey hair."

"Since when have you been so interested in my hair?"

She reaches across the table and takes my hand.

"I understand. I really do. I'd probably react the same way if it was Alfred lying there like that."

She cuts a slice of cheese and stuffs it in her mouth. Looks at me while she chews.

"I see another box has come," she says, nodding towards the front garden.

"The car seat," I say. "I want it down with the other ones if you don't mind?"

"What about putting it up for sale somewhere? Have you given any more thought to that?"

"I'd rather it was down in the basement."

"But they are brand-new. What good are they doing down there?"

"I don't want to sell anything, that's all."

"But you don't even want to *touch* them. They're just left outside getting destroyed."

"That's why you have to put them down in the basement."

"I don't like it. It's not good for you having all these things around. It is as if you're living on top of a ..." She slows herself down, but the word still hangs between us. *Grave.*

"I said no," I say.

"Then I say no, too."

She sticks the knife into the liver pâté and I can't make out the expression in her eyes. Is she afraid to go down to the basement, too? She hasn't been down there since the funeral. Five days ago.

She spreads the pâté on two slices of bread and puts a gherkin on one. She cuts the other slice into small squares, despite Steen saying he didn't want anything.

We sit in silence while Klara eats, and I look at the bedroom door. The handle. I keep imagining it being pushed down. That Steen comes out with his arms up, that he tears off the nappy and kicks it through the living room like he would kick in a football from the touchline.

Over the cold fireplace, he's still smiling. In front of the town hall with his ring finger raised towards the camera and my smiling face next to his. We had to keep retaking the picture. He kept getting one of his tics as we were standing in the sunshine. An unprompted twisting of the upper body, where the head turns backwards and the shoulder is pulled forward. As if you're trying to look over your shoulder.

He's had those tics for as long as I've known him. But it was worse than usual that day. He seemed happy, but also strangely nervous. When I asked why, he said he was just so infinitely happy to have me. And that the happier you are to have something, the more afraid you become of losing it.

Klara pours buttermilk into two glasses and hands me one. "Have you still not talked to Mum and Dad?"

"No."

"So they have no idea what happened to Steen?"

"They've never shown any interest in him. Why should I tell them anything?"

"They don't mean it like that."

"Well, they didn't come over even once when I was pregnant."

The gherkin crunches every time Klara takes a bite. The exhibition of sandwich things stands like a wall between us and I can't bear to eat any of it. Instead, I lift my glass to seem a little cooperative. Force down a sip of the thick, sour milk.

"Did you remember to buy a washbasin and feeding cup?" I say.

"I thought we agreed that the ones you have are fine?"

"I can't stand it."

"Okay."

"Something white," I say. "Without flowers or anything. Can you bring it with you next time?"

She nods. Pats my hand.

"You have a milk moustache," she says, handing me a piece of kitchen roll.

She eats the last of her food. Says I really should taste the homemade liver pâté. That she doesn't like casting pearls before swine.

"Did they survive?" I ask.

"Who?"

"You said a sow was in difficulty. How did it go?"

"Twelve piglets. Lively."

"Twelve. That's a lot."

"They have what they have, you know."

I nod.

"It was pigs, Eva."

"Why do you say it like that?"

"Because your thoughts are like a dog chasing its own tail. That's why it would be good for you to get back to work. See some other people. Think about something else. Just for a few hours."

"I don't know if I can."

"We got through the funeral. The worst part is over. It's over. Okay?"

"It doesn't feel that way."

"I understand, but nothing else is going to happen now. You don't have to be on alert all the time."

"Did you hear about what happened in the graveyard?"

"No?"

"The police were here this morning. Someone dug up Steen's father."

"Is he gone?"

I nod.

She dumps her food back on the plate. We sit for a moment in silence.

"They asked if we'd inform Steen's adoptive mother," I say. "Of course, Steen said no. But I thought maybe it was my chance to finally meet her."

"And what does Steen say about that?"

"There's no reason to give him more to speculate on."

"So you want to go behind his back?"

I shrug.

"Well," says Klara. "He must have a reason for not wanting to see her. Just like you have a reason for avoiding Mum and Dad."

"Maybe. I just want to talk to someone who knows him. I'm going crazy walking around with all my thoughts."

Klara sits for a while, considering me.

"Okay," she says. "I have to admit that it sounds a bit far-fetched. But it's nice to see you that way again. With hope in your eyes."

"If I promise to go to work tomorrow," I say, "can I leave after we've eaten lunch? Will you stay and watch Steen in the meantime?"

"Now?"

I nod.

"Do you want to drive to Steen's mother now?"

I nod again.

She hands me the same piece of kitchen roll as before.

"Then ring your boss now, too. So I can hear it."

"Thank you, Klara."

I smile and she points to my mouth.

"It suits you," she says.

"The milk moustache?"

"That, too."

We smile at each other and I wipe my mouth with the kitchen roll.

Actually, I'd given up ever getting to know Steen's family. Had even convinced myself it was easier that way.

Now the old questions returned with renewed force. And they were amplified when I unfolded the paper and saw what Torben had written.

Are you sure that's the correct name?

I had stared at Torben's handwriting for a long time. Felt a restlessness spreading through my body.

Yes, that name is really weird.

The address is just as disturbing.

CHAPTER 9

Wu-Lin stayed in the living room while I helped Mother and Father carry the presents outside. The house. The horse. The fridge. There were even two small babies. One with blue clothes and one with red.

We laid them carefully on the grass and Father went into the shed. The fields stretched out, large and empty of people, on both sides of the house. I couldn't see my brother anywhere.

A gust of wind blew through the garden. Mother took my hand and pointed to the blue-breasted quail moving around in the birdcage. The babies smiled with big red mouths. Next to it stood the purple palace. A door the size of a mousehole had been cut.

Mother and Father must have been up all night to get it finished. They must have used almost every single bit of paper, bamboo, and clothing scraps we had.

Father came out of the shed with a petrol can and a box of storm matches.

"What about Wu-Lin?" I asked.

Mother and Father looked at each other. Then Father put away the things and went back into the house.

When he came out again, he had to walk sideways through the door so that Wu-Lin's head didn't hit it. The silk dress fluttered around her legs as he walked across the lawn with her. The strange purple discolouration that had spread over her skin was very evident under the nylon stockings.

Father manoeuvred her down into a white plastic garden chair. Had to exert effort to get the stiff body to sit.

He turned the chair so her face was towards the gifts. There was a gush as he poured petrol over them. The horse. The fridge. The babies. The match was a shiny little shooting star, and white smoke rose up into the sky. Soon the things would rise up there, too. Wait for us.

It was hard to understand.

Father laid his hand on my shoulder and explained it again.

"Fire is a sacred force. When we burn an object, we release its soul. Like when you let a bird out of a cage."

He pointed from the smoke up towards the clouds. "The soul takes the form of smoke, so we can see that it is on the right path. It rises up to the sky. All the way up there."

I put my head back and followed the smoke with my eyes.

"In heaven, everything returns to its proper form," said Father. "Paper houses become real houses. Feathers turn into birds. The dead come alive. Is that not beautiful?"

I tried to picture it.

"So up in the sky, Wu-Lin will come alive again?"

Father nodded. Up in the sky, Wu-Lin will be able to play and laugh and sing and give me a hug.

"But how do we get up there?" I asked. "Me and Wu-Lin?"

Father looked at the fire. The flames were high now. The heat from them burned against my face and I looked towards the white garden chair. Wu-Lin's eyes flared, large and black with the reflection of the fire.

Again, I felt the simmering sensation in my stomach. I was glad that Wu-Lin would be able to play again soon. But the fire. I didn't like looking at it.

"Is that why there's a tiger in our fireplace?" I asked. "Because anything can happen when you burn things?"

"You must not play with fire," said Father.

We stood in silence, watching the fire.

When the flames really took hold of the presents, Father started ringing the silver bells and Mother brought out the wooden fish. It was hollow and shaped like a carp, and she struck it with a stick in time to our father's silver bells.

The two babies looked like they were moving. For a moment, they illuminated the entire garden.

I looked towards the sky. Tried to spot them up there.

Now the purple palace was in flames. The smoke swirled around me. Souls crawled up from the grass and appeared right behind me, hovering around my head and making me dizzy.

I looked at Wu-Lin through the dense smoke. The glow of the flames made the garden chair cast dancing shadows. The paper lily in her hand bobbed, about to come loose from the sticky tape.

The ringing sound stopped, and Father set down the silver bells. Now everything had been sent up to heaven. The last embers turned into grey wings that fluttered away.

Mother and Father helped Wu-Lin down onto the grass. You weren't usually supposed to lie on the ground when you were wearing white clothes. There were a lot of new rules today.

They turned her so that her face was facing west. Stuck the lily better to her palm.

Father picked up the matchbox and rattled it. Met my gaze and pointed to the grass next to Wu-Lin.

I wanted to shake my head, but my body was completely locked.

"Come," he said. "You must lie together."

His eyes were black flint, just like yesterday morning when we found her. She was lying in her bed and couldn't wake up. Father spent a long time getting her eyelids up.

As he manoeuvred them, I said, "Maybe we should have called the doctor anyway."

It was the first time Mother had given me a slap.

I thought about it as I looked into the eyes of flint. The sharp heat on my cheek and the hug afterwards.

Above us, the sky had darkened. It was almost the same colour as the purple palace.

Family is the most important thing. Either you were a part of it or you were on your own. I swallowed a lump.

Then I lay down next to Wu-Lin.

CHAPTER 10

I pull the car's handbrake and adjust the rearview mirror so I can see myself. My eyes are big and opened wide, and I try to relax the facial muscles. I remove a bit of sleep from my eye and take a deep breath. I don't really want to admit it, but it's a relief to get out of the house. Away from the silence and the stench and the strange, distorted thoughts.

Since Steen became paralysed, I've only left the house to drive to the hospital or graveyard. Quick, hectic trips that were all about death. The conversation with the doctor about the autopsy. The crisis psychologist who sat with his head cocked, asking and asking while I watched the clock and pressed my nails into my palms. All of these I only attended to avoid more reminder letters and phone calls.

But now. For the first time in a long time, it's like I can breathe.

To strengthen the feeling, I open the glove compartment and find the lipstick I always have lying in there. I run it over my lips and press them against each other. Put some lipstick on my fingertips and dab it on my cheeks.

I turn my face from side to side in the front of the rearview mirror. The colour looks very red on my pale face and I imagine it's my blood pumping again. That something inside me is waking up.

You have arrived, repeats the GPS, which doubts whether I heard it the first time. I flip the rearview mirror back and step out.

My back is sweaty after the journey, even though it was less than twenty minutes. Every time an oncoming car passed, it gave me a start. The many days spent in silence at home have made me strangely sensitive to sound.

Maybe Klara is right that contacting Steen's mother like this is over the top. That it's a naive straw to clutch at. But I'll do anything to avoid handing Steen over to the hospital.

My heels click against the asphalt as I cross the car park to what must be the main entrance. The building is large and light yellow. *Psychiatric nursing home*, it says on a sign out front. I stand there for a long time, looking at the words. Then I gather myself and push open the glass door.

Inside, the air is dry and sharp. There is nothing on the walls. There are smoke alarms on the ceiling every five metres. I look up at them as a nurse in white plimsolls leads me down to a dayroom.

"She's painting," she says. "But they'll be finished soon. You can sit and wait here in the meantime."

"Painting?" I ask.

"We have many creative activities. You can look at the brochures over there if you're interested." She smiles at me. Says she will come and get me when Steen's mother is back and that I can help myself to cordial and coffee if I want to.

Her white plimsolls disappear down the hall and I look around the dayroom. Black leather sofas and light wooden chairs. A trolley with thermoses. A rollator with a box of mashed potatoes in the basket.

There's no one else in here. Only the television sends a mumble into the room. All the furniture is facing it.

The leather creaks as I plop down on a sofa. I look absent-mindedly at the television showing an old murder mystery. Give up trying to follow it.

I flip through one of the brochures.

Down the hall I can hear someone vacuuming.

He must have a reason for not wanting to see her.

I take out my liquorice and chew quickly. Try to breathe through my mouth. The dayroom smells of the same cleaning products as the hospital. Every time I inhale, I slip back into the syrupy feeling. The baby's lifeless body. Steen's lifeless body. The feeling of everything merging.

I get up and pour a glass of cordial. It's thin. Completely pink. I'm taking a sip. It tastes of water and hospital. The midwife's facial expression. The way she patted me on the arm.

Go home and get a good night's sleep, and see you again tomorrow.

The feeling of sleeping with a lifeless child in the womb. I kept getting up and looking in the mirror. My stomach hung so weirdly.

The next day, the contractions wouldn't start. My body clung to the baby and I was struck by a horrible feeling that we were both dead. The baby and me.

"Eva?"

The nurse is standing in the doorway of the dayroom.

"Would you like to come with me?"

We walk down the hall with all its many smoke alarms.

"She'll be delighted with your visit. She doesn't get that many anymore."

"No?"

"It's mostly television and what have you. And our activities, of course. She made that herself."

She stops in front of a door with a large painting of a tiger. "They're not actually allowed to put anything up here, but we've made an exception."

The tiger is painted with neat brushstrokes. The teeth are very long.

"There's an alarm cord hanging by the window," she says. "Just so you know."

"Okay?" A nervousness tingles over my skin. Alarm cord?

"Would you like some coffee?" she asks.

"No, thank you. It's fine."

"She usually has tea herself."

The nurse knocks on the door and a sweet scent flows out of the room as she pushes the door open. Spicy tea, perfume, and withered flowers.

An elderly lady is sitting in front of an old-fashioned box-shaped TV, watching *Antiques Roadshow.* The sound is turned up high.

The sight of her causes a restless sensation to run through my body. Reinforces the suspicion I got when I unfolded Torben's note.

Steen has always told me he's adopted. So why is his mother's name what it is? Why does she look so much like Steen?

50

Her long hair is twisted up into a knot with two chopsticks. Despite it starting to go grey, it's clear it was as black as Steen's. She has the same flat face and slanted eyes.

"Wu-Pei?" calls the nurse. "You have a visitor."

Steen's mother doesn't respond. Just sits watching the TV.

The nurse enters the room, takes the remote control, and turns it off.

Steen's mother jumps. She looks around. When she discovers us, she takes her glasses off.

"Who is that?" she asks, pointing at me.

"Your daughter-in-law," says the nurse.

"Daughter-in-law how?"

"Steen's wife," I say.

"I don't know anyone named Steen."

The nurse gives my arm a squeeze. "The paths of memory are mysterious. But she wouldn't harm a fly."

So why is there an alarm cord then? I think, but I don't want to seem nervous.

"Thanks for your help," I say, sending a smile as a sign that I can take it from here.

The nurse says, "Have fun," her footsteps disappear down the hall, and then we are alone. Wu-Pei and me.

My palms sweat as I pull the door in behind me and walk into the small, overcrowded room. There are things everywhere. Vases with artificial flowers and feathers. Plastic jewellery and gilded sculptures. A little tile-topped table with teacups and a teapot.

On the walls hang open fans, framed photos, and masks with goatees, slanted eyes, and sneering mouths.

"Well," I say. "You were just painting?"

She's wearing a coat, even though it's warm in here. Colourful glass stones glisten all over the fabric. It's clear she sewed them on herself. The stitches are large and coarse.

She points to an armchair facing her.

I unzip my jacket and sit down.

"Have a cup of tea." She points to the table. "It's Panyang Golden Needle."

"Thank you."

The teapot is tubby, of floral red porcelain with Chinese characters on the side. The sight of them makes me think of the open grave.

I hold the lid as I pour tea into one of the matching cups. Reminds me to ask Torben if they found out what the Chinese characters meant.

"Shall I pour some for you, too?" I ask.

She raises her hand in a defensive gesture.

I sip the tea. It's cold and very bitter, as if it's been brewing all day.

"Panyang Golden Needle is grown in the Taimu Mountains of China," she says. "When it steeps for a long time, it turns red. Red is the sacred, life-giving colour. That is why the Chinese flag is red."

"I thought it symbolised revolution."

She shakes her head. "The colour red means life-giving. It must be drunk strong."

I force myself to take a sip before setting the cup down.

"It's good to meet you," I say. "I apologise for not coming before now."

"Who did you say you were?"

"I'm married to your son."

"Which one of them?"

I look at her in surprise.

"How many children do you have?"

"Three in all. The youngest lives in a beautiful purple palace. A girl."

"So Steen has a little sister?"

"My two sons are my yin and yang. Do you know yin and yang?"

"Light and darkness?"

She nods. "One of my sons lives in pomp and splendour in his imperial residence. The other has sunk into darkness. I don't hear anything from him anymore. It worries me greatly."

"He's fine. There's just been a lot going on."

She looks at the turned-off television as if she has lost her concentration.

I can't fathom how far removed from reality she is. At least, I've never heard of Steen having siblings.

"Well." I drain the last of my cup and put it down. "I don't know how much you know about me. Perhaps nothing. But, well, my name is Eva. I met Steen eight years ago and we got married six years ago. At the town hall in Herning. Just the two of us. I come from there, Herning, originally."

I pause briefly, waiting for her to say something, but she just sits there, watching the turned-off television.

"When Steen took over your house, we decided to move. I thought it might be a bit deserted here, but the house was lovely. I would have moved to the moon with him if I needed to."

I stop. Remind myself why I came.

"I need your help," I say. "Do you know if there are any hereditary diseases in your family? Something that can lead to paralysis?"

She shrugs.

"I don't know anyone named Steen."

"Tell me about your son who lives in pomp and splendour."

The thought makes her smile.

"My son has continued the honour of his imperial lineage. He lives with his family in a magnificent palace. He often calls and tells me about it. The flower garden. The tea parties and the children. My other son, however … I don't know what happened to him. Several days have passed, and when I call, I get the answering machine."

I think of Steen's lifeless arms in the bed. How he has to yell at me when the phone rings. Sometimes I intentionally move slowly because I can't bear to talk to anyone.

"It's a shame they're not in contact," she says. "My two sons. We are a strong lineage, but we are also fragile. They could benefit from each other."

"I would like to contact your other son," I say. "What's his name?"

"Twins are a sacred gift from God. Two separate parts that are one. Do you understand?"

"Are they twins?"

"A sacred gift," she repeats, straightening the chopsticks in her hair.

My pulse starts racing. Does Steen have a twin brother?

"Maybe I could get his phone number?" I say. "Or his address, if you have it?"

She takes a pen and writes something on a piece of paper. Hands it to me. Two addresses. One is ours. The other is an address in Hvide Sande, not far from here.

"Is this where your sons live?" I ask.

The glass stones clink as she gets up and walks through the small nursing home apartment.

"Would you take this to him?" She hands me a thick book. The cover is burgundy and faded. On the front page is written *Grimms' Fairy Tales.* As I flip through it, I can see that it has to be an ancient edition given the language in it.

"It was his," she says. "Better to return things while you can."

She supports the small of her back before sitting down.

"You mean your son in Hvide Sande?" I ask.

"It's from a shop of secondhand books. Do you know the fairy tales?"

I nod.

"My husband was like a dragon when I said that our children were to read Danish fairy tales."

"Grimms' fairy tales are actually German," I say.

"That book is not German."

"No, not the translation, but ..." I give up.

"By the way," I say instead, "I have a message for you, too. It's about your husband."

"Yes, I know. He was here last night."

"What?"

"He misses me so much. He came last night to take me to the realm of the dead."

I open my mouth, but no words come out.

She leans forward in the chair and lays her hand on my knee.

"You don't need look so scared. I would probably do the same if it was me lying in a coffin all alone."

"The same?"

"He wanted to kill me. Over there." She points to a narrow, white bed with blue metal legs. "He tried to get my pillow from me so he could put it over my face. I explained that I wasn't ready yet."

"You explained it to ... your husband?"

"But he didn't listen."

"Then what happened?"

"Then I called the night nurse and he ran away."

Her hand is still on my knee.

"He said he would come back and that next time he would make sure the porter couldn't stop him."

"Okay?"

"I warned the night nurse. But he's like an empty melon."

I look at the alarm cord. Try to sound calm. "I'm sure the staff have everything under control."

"My husband is stubborn. Once he has decided something, then that is how it will be."

She tightens her grip on my knee. "Do you hear me? He's going to *kill* me."

I wriggle free.

"Well. I'd better get going, too."

Before she can answer, I edge past the many pieces of furniture and close the door behind me. Stand for a moment, getting my breathing under control.

The long corridor is deserted and I look up at the smoke alarms as I walk back to where I came from.

In the empty dayroom, the murder mystery has been replaced by the news. Torches flickering over graves, police reflectors glowing in the dark. At the bottom of the screen is a chyron with the word *Cemetery Mystery*.

The door to the staff room is ajar. I knock gently before opening.

At the table is the same nurse who showed me down to Steen's mother.

"Hi," she says.

"May I come in?"

She closes the diary she's writing in.

I sit down next to her.

"I'm sorry," I say. "This may sound strange. But she says someone was in her room last night?"

"What?"

"She sounded the alarm?"

"Well, that's correct. At this morning's handover, the night nurse said she called for help around midnight."

"And had someone been in her room?"

"Not as far as we know. If there was, they'd have gone in while the night porter was on rounds."

"Is that possible?"

"It is not a closed ward. In principle, people can come and go as they please."

"So, there may actually have been someone?"

She shrugs. "It's more likely that she saw ghosts."

I nod. Very apt expression.

"May I ask something else?" I say.

"Ask away."

"It's because … She said Steen has a twin brother."

"Yes?"

"Do you know him?"

"He used to come here a lot. It's been a while since we've seen him."

"She says he lives in an imperial palace?"

She laughs. "You could say that. He's well-off at least. As far as I know, he's a successful businessman. He was always very neat and well-dressed when he came here. The type who always wears a tie."

"And he lives with his family?"

"Mm. As far as I'm aware, neither of the sons has any children."

"What about a little sister? She said she had a daughter, too?"

"We have no information about anyone else other than those two."

Something beeps. The nurse checks the alarm on her belt.

"I have to go," she says. "Take the door there and you'll come straight out into the car park."

I follow her with my eyes as she runs out into the corridor. Can still hear the words: *He's going to kill me.*

I slam the car door behind me and lay my head back against the headrest. My body feels even more tense than when I came. Why did Steen lie to me?

My hands shake as I unfold the paper with the addresses. Ours and Steen's brother.

A twin brother.

I look at Wu-Pei's intricate handwriting for a long time. It all seems so far-fetched. I should forget about it all and drive home to Steen and Klara. But the uneasy feeling I got when I saw Steen's mother is still there. The feeling that nothing is as I thought.

I take a deep breath and type the address into the GPS. Look at the psychiatric nursing home one last time before hitting *Start route.*

CHAPTER 11

The pink snowflakes of the cherry tree fell through the darkness and landed on me and Wu-Lin. Every time I tried to get up from the grass, Mother held me down. Her face looked like a Jing mask before it was painted. White and stiff.

"Mother?" I called. "Mother!"

She didn't answer.

The sky was completely black now. I couldn't see a single one of the gifts up there.

It was forbidden to cry anymore. I had to use all my strength to abide by the rule.

Father stood with the matchbox looking at us.

"In the beginning, everything was chaos," he said. "The world was shaped like an egg that contained yin and yang. The whole universe is created from these two opposing forces. Light and dark, life and death, butterflies and moths. White ghosts and hungry spirits."

It was a long story today. About Death in a silk kimono that came flying down from a mountain on the back of a dragon. About artificial flowers and eternal life.

It was hard to concentrate. Every time he paused, I thought the story was over.

What was going to happen when the story was over?

Father fell silent.

I had come to do what was forbidden. I hurried to wipe my eyes.

"Yin-Yin," he said. "Do not be afraid."

He walked away, leaving us with Mother. There was silence in the garden. It lasted a long time.

The grass was cold against my back. I wanted to take my little sister's hand, but I didn't dare move.

Then something happened. Mother picked up the wooden fish, hit it faster and harder this time. The dragon's head was huge with red eyes and a forked tongue. It danced through the garden as Mother banged the wooden fish. Dancing around me and Wu-Lin.

It looked so different from the metal dragon in the front garden. Soft and alive. Mother had sewn it from small pieces of fabric in shades of green. As it moved, the fabric resembled the scales of a giant reptile.

The dragon's front legs were wearing Father's shoes, the back ones were wearing my brother's. The back ones were constantly lagging behind, so the dragon's green body looked like it was going to crack.

The last time I saw it was at the Moon Festival. Wu-Lin had been wearing a blue dress and her hand was warm in mine while we watched the dragon dance in the garden. Mother had baked moon cakes and poured red tea into fragile cups. The full moon was large and round over the cherry tree, and Wu-Lin looked at me as she sang. As if the words were to me.

When the night has come and the land is dark

Her voice was so light and nice. I wanted to catch it like a butterfly. Attach it to a piece of Styrofoam so I could own it forever.

No, I won't be afraid, I whispered every time she reached the chorus.

Paper houses to real houses. Feathers to birds.

Could you take music to heaven, too? How?

The dragon stopped in front of us, took its head off, and looked at us with Father's eyes. At the Moon Festival, he had been dishevelled and grinning when he took his head off. Now he was just dishevelled.

Father pushed my brother forward, and he walked slowly, tucked something under Wu-Lin's palms. Coins of silver paper. They were large and flat. I tried to make eye contact with him, but he kept looking down at the ground.

"There you go," said Father. "Enough money for a long and happy afterlife."

He bent down and laid a hand on my shoulder.

"Remember we do not say goodbye, only *see you again*."

"Okay."

"Say it."

"See you again."

Father nodded. He took my hand and pulled me up from the grass. My body was completely stiff. Father placed me in the white garden chair. Patted me on the head.

Then he lifted the petrol can and splashed petrol over Wu-Lin. The white dress got dark spots and her hair got wet. Father was thorough. Petrol rippled down her face, her feet, over both arms.

It hurt in my stomach. She looked tiny on the lawn, and I got up from the garden chair and lay down next to her.

"Not alone," I said.

Father's chin moved strangely. He put down the matches and was stronger than ever. I slapped his shoulders and arms as he lifted me back up into the white garden chair.

I tightened my grip on the chair's arms and looked at the lily in my little sister's hand. Looked only at that as Father struck a match and her body turned into fire.

CHAPTER 12

My hands are clenched around the steering wheel as I drive through the flat, yellowish landscape of Hvide Sande. To my left, the North Sea is clamouring. The beach is a mess of rocks, seaweed, and broken crab shells. It's low tide, making hidden things appear. Broken glass bottles, dead jellyfish, and lifeless fish. A wave hits the beach, crabs scuttle sideways across the sand, and two large, hooded gulls take off from a half-eaten trout.

The surface of the sea is vast and dark and I think of all that is concealing itself in the cold water. Swaying seaweed forests and stinging jellyfish pulsing like detached hearts with long threads hanging after them.

A twin brother and a little sister.

In 150 metres turn right.

Lyme grass and long grass rustle against the sides of the car as I turn onto a narrow gravel road. There are no houses. Only withered wild roses and dark spruces standing in scattered clusters, as if waiting for something.

It doesn't seem like anyone lives here. Maybe she made up the address?

Pebbles hit the car and I slow down. On the seat next to me lies *Grimms' Fairy Tales*. I try to imagine what the brother looks like. A Steen who can still walk. With a shirt and tie and no nappy.

In 200 metres you will arrive at your destination.

I lean forward in the seat, peering between the tree trunks and bushes. The gravel crunches under the car's tyres, and branches scrape against the windows. The path turns, and a building comes into view ahead of me.

I slow down. The spruces recede, and a large, windswept grassy area opens up in front of me.

In the middle of the dunes is a four-winged farm. Yellow bricks, white-washed plinths, and a thatched roof. So big that it looks more like an inn than a home for one person.

I glance at the clock on the dashboard. Had somehow hoped that Steen's brother lived farther away, so there would be a good reason for why we'd never seen each other. But this place is thirty-five minutes at most from where we live.

In front of the courtyard are two cars. A black Audi and a blue pickup truck. So he must be home. I drive towards the cars and park. I sit a moment with the engine running, taking in the courtyard. It looks newly renovated. Everything is neat and well kept. The flat landscape stretches out on both sides. The long dry grass has settled down in the wind, and the Danish flag is fluttering on a flagpole.

I turn off the engine and a silence follows that is reminiscent of the one at home. A shovel is leaning against one gable wall. Otherwise, there is no sign of life. No flowerpots. No toys. No pram or trampoline.

I take out my phone and write a text to Klara.

How is it going at home? Has he eaten lunch?

Almost a whole slice :-) He's having a nap now. Are you coming home soon?

Can you stay a little longer?

Of course

I put the phone back in my pocket and look around the courtyard again. What if his brother is dangerous? Nobody knows I'm here. Maybe I should have asked Klara to come out here with me.

I shake off the thought.

I haven't told Steen why I stopped seeing my parents. He could probably feel the bad chemistry between him and them. Must have noticed how they always cancelled if he was there. Klara explained it away by saying they're just old and have always lived in isolation, unaccustomed to meeting different people.

When they cancelled coming to our wedding, I'd had enough.

Fortunately, Steen has never tried to dig into my past, and I've never tried to dig into his.

Not until today.

The salty wind beats against me as I get out of the car. It smells of conifers and rotten seaweed. Seagulls hover over me with hoarse screams, as if to warn me of something. I pull my coat closer around me and walk over to the two parked vehicles. The black Audi looks brand-new. The seats are of light leather, and the body is shiny and clean, except for a little gravel dust. There's a suit jacket on the passenger seat. On the back seat is a brown leather briefcase. In the cup holder is a cardboard cup with a plastic lid and the text *Simply Great Coffee*.

The blue pickup truck looks more used. The tyres are muddy, but inside it is vacuumed and tidy. Behind the driver's cab a thick, black tarpaulin is stretched over the pickup bed.

I touch the edge. Feel like lifting it to see what's under there.

Above me, seagulls scream loudly. I release the tarpaulin and look up at the sky. The gulls' white abdomens and the clouds, which are moving quickly.

I breathe into my hands and rub them against each other, turn my back on the vehicles, and walk up to the front door.

On the doorstep is a black rubber mat. There are remnants of soil and mud on it. There's no name on the door or letterbox. At the top of the door is a small, matted window. The kind you can look out through but not in. I step up onto the doorstep and ring the doorbell. The gold-coloured bell is half rusted and resists when I push it all the way down.

I can hear the ringing inside the house. Behind me the North Sea swells. There must be a nice view from the farm's many rooms. The North Sea on one side and Ringkøbing Fjord on the other.

I ring again. Hold the button while I look at my blurry mirror image in the frosted pane.

Still nothing.

The door feels cold as I put my ear against it. There's no sound inside.

Carefully, I try the handle.

It's locked.

I step down from the doorstep and go to the nearest window. Look into a large kitchen. It looks old but well-maintained. Plenty of cupboards, thick wooden counters, and white lace curtains. Next to the stove is a jar of olives with a long spoon in it. On the toaster are two slices of baguette.

I continue along the main south-facing wing. Through the painted white lattice windows I can see into a large, bright room. It has a beamed ceiling and plank floor and select but expensive furniture. At one end of the room stands a long dining table on a dark red carpet. In the middle of the table is a candelabra with eight burnt-out candles that have dripped onto the tablecloth. The chairs have high backs. They're all pushed in, except one at one end of the table. In front of it is a glass of red wine and a plate of something resembling tapas. Bluebottles are crawling around on ham, dried cheese, and the stem of the red wine glass. The knife and fork rest on the edge of the plate. Next to it is a crumpled napkin.

On the walls hang strange, disturbing paintings of dragons with jagged tails and flared nostrils. On a chest of drawers is a large glass bowl with fruit and a swarm of fruit flies.

There's a rustling in the thicket behind me. I look out over the rolling sea of grass and the dunes behind. The cord on the flagpole slaps in the wind. Above me, the gulls circle in ever closer circles.

"Hello?"

My voice disappears in the wind. It's as if the North Sea is even noisier now. The wind must have picked up.

I look over the desolate landscape one last time, before moving on along the main wing and to what must be the east wing. It looks empty in there. I brush some spiderwebs away with the sleeve of my coat and press my nose against the pane. Two eyes look back at me and I abruptly pull my head away. Stand for a moment with a pounding heart.

Hesitantly, I lean against the window again. On a table, just on the other side of the glass, is a stuffed wild boar head. It is mounted by the neck on a large wooden plate that's leaning against a toolbox. The canines are white and smooth. Under the black snout, the mouth is half open, exposing the teeth in a way that makes it look alive.

As I look closer, I see that the wild boar isn't alone. Three stuffed birds are sitting on a branch, in a large, dome-shaped silver cage, hanging from the ceiling. An owl, a raven, and a dove. They sit close together. It reminds me of something. Those exact three birds in that order. Where have I seen that before?

The wind catches my scarf, making it flutter, and I look over my shoulder. All the while, I have a feeling of being watched, but it has to be my imagination—the landscape is desolate, except for the seagulls circling over me. I shake off the feeling and move on.

The north wing is empty, except for some stacked dining chairs, a floor lamp, and a box of empty lemonade bottles. There's a washing machine a few metres from where I'm standing, too. The door is closed, and as I look closer I can see that the drum is filled with wet clothes.

I walk around the corner to the west wing. It looks more worn than the others. All the windows on this part are covered with black bags. The bags are set up from the inside. It makes the building look mummified.

The door is made of thick, green-painted wood with small sash windows at the top. They are covered with bin bags, too.

I try the handle.

Locked.

Over the door hangs a wind chime, tinkling with its limp metal tentacles.

I walk farther along the wall and spot a narrow strip of light. There's a little gap between the bags, at most a few centimetres, but enough for me to look through. I put my forehead against the cold pane and fold my hands around my face.

The sight in there spreads an icy feeling through my body. The entire west wing is full of taxidermied animals. They stare into space with shining glass eyes. Stags. Deer. Squirrels and birds. Even a large reindeer. It's like a creepy still image. A Pompeii of animals.

Up against one wall is a large wooden workbench. Above it hangs a board with pliers, scissors, and knives. A lot of knives, and I come to think of the midwife's words when I asked for a caesarean section: *You can't remove grief by cutting it out.*

I feel dizzy. Think for a moment about the bitter, red tea. I can almost still taste it.

Next to the tools hangs an animal head with huge antlers. An elk.

To the right of it is a rifle on a hook. It's positioned so the barrel is pointing to the elk's temple. It looks macabre. Still, I can't stop staring at it.

I take out my phone and scroll down to Torben's number. Shudder from the cold as I listen to the ringtone.

After two rings he picks up.

"Eva? All okay?"

As soon as I hear his voice, my pulse drops. The animals behind the windowpane seem less sinister than before. What am I even ringing him about?

"Hi, yeah," I say. "Things are fine, thanks. I just wanted to …"

I'm the one who has blown things out of proportion, I think, and I can't bring myself to tell him where I am.

"Em," I say. "I just wanted to hear if you have figured out what the Chinese characters mean—the ones that were painted on the coffin."

"We have actually. One moment, I wrote it down." There's a rustling of papers. "I just have to be sure that I give you the correct wording. Yes, here." His chair creaks.

"The translator confirmed that it was the same characters written on both the headstone and the coffin lid. Same paint. Same handwriting."

"So what do they mean?"

"Family is the most important thing."

CHAPTER 13

I'm sitting on a blue chair with wheels underneath. Little feet without slippers run around me, and there are already both Brio trains and wooden bricks and dolls on the floor, even though the children are supposed to clean up before taking out something new.

On the noticeboard hangs a staff schedule, so you can follow which adults are here and when. We're all smiling in the pictures taken out on the playground.

Today is 14 September. Next to my name is: *On maternity leave.*

The words are crossed out with a thin, blue pen and replaced with *8:00–(13:00)*. The parentheses mean I'm allowed to go earlier if it gets too much.

I take the signing-in pen and look at the attendance list. Small boxes with kids I am to look after today.

Children who have lived long enough to start kindergarten.

I hold on to the signing-in pen, despite there being no more children to sign in. I hatch the A of *Alma,* wishing we had managed to give the baby a name.

I click the pen and put it down. I'm the only adult in the room. My armpits are wet with sweat even though I am sitting still. A child screams and my pulse beats faster. Okay, Lærke is just laughing. I concentrate on breathing slowly. When I look at my hand, it's holding the pen again. I put it down.

The time now is 9:11. I showed up at 7:56. So how long have I been here? I can't work it out. My body jumps every time a child shouts or drops something on the floor.

At ten o'clock another adult will come down. Then I can clean up. It's easier than asking the kids to do it.

I look around at the toys all over the floor. Crumpled dress-up dolls and teddy bears wearing tight clothes. Colourful bouncy animals that have lost air. Small plastic animals with limbs that can't bend. Horses, chickens, and elephants with black dots for eyes.

It feels like they're staring at me, and I think of the stuffed animals in Hvide Sande. The abandoned tapas plate, and *Family is the most important thing.*

There's a knock on the door, which is already open. Tanja from the grasshoppers smiles at me.

"Well?" she says. "I just wanted to see if everything was okay in here?"

"It's fine."

"Just say if you need a hand with anything."

"I will."

Her gaze glides over all the toys on the floor.

"If the older ones are being too noisy, I can take a few of them in with me."

"You don't have to do that."

She fiddles with a parrot hanging on the inside of the door. It has large, round plastic eyes with pupils that move and tiny wings that protrude from the sides.

"You're looking well," she says. "I didn't get to say it this morning. And it's great that you're back already."

I put a hand on my face.

"I hope you don't ..." She hesitates. "What happened at breakfast ..."

"It's okay," I say. "That's how children are."

"Still though."

"It's fine. They have to be told at some stage."

It's hard to keep smiling. As if everything weighs more than it usually does.

"It's probably best to tell the parents as well," says Tanja. "Like I said, we wrote that they should, you know … That it could seem a little overwhelming if they all came and talked to you here over the first few days. Even though it's well-meant. But it's not certain that everyone understands, so … you just have to say, right?"

"Will do. Thanks."

Tanja remains standing in the doorway looking at me. Her eyes are like an owl's eyes. Large and investigative.

"Okay. But … It's good to see you again, at least."

She raises her hand in an awkward wave and goes back to her own room.

I look at the plastic animals again. Think of the dome-shaped birdcage. The workshop table and all the knives.

Why is your baby dead?

The sound of cornflakes between little milk teeth. Tanja's nervous smile.

All right, Alma. Eat your breakfast.

The slice of cheese on my bread looked more and more inedible the longer I looked at it. It was up to me, Helen had said on the phone. Whether the children should know or not. But that was what they recommended. That was what the crisis guidelines said. I didn't even know what I wanted for breakfast. Just nodded when Tanja held out bread and cheese.

The time now is 9:17.

I pick up the pen again. Flick it back and forth between two fingers.

A plastic bag rustles, and Olivia takes a bite of a shiny apple.

"It's not fruit time," I say.

She takes another bite and chews with her mouth open. The apple is red and shiny, and I think of *Grimms' Fairy Tales* lying on the seat next to me as I drove home from Hvide Sande.

After putting Steen to bed in the evening, I sat down to look in the book, but I couldn't concentrate. I had to give up just at the table of contents.

When I got pregnant, I read about cell division, embryos, and morula for hours on end. Thick books with red and pink illustrations of growing life.

I can only manage the internet now.

Mirror twins: The personality of identical twins is reminiscent of yin and yang

Being fired while sick—these rules apply

Prison: Danish poacher caught with a stag in the car

The water is cold. I can feel it all the way down to my stomach. I set down the glass and look down into the sink. How did I get here? I thought I had just sat down.

I sit back on the blue chair with the wheels underneath.

Juice runs down Oliva's chin and I lean towards her.

"You have to wait until it's fruit time," I say, but my voice is just a whisper and Olivia takes another bite. A crunch. She has red cheeks and I think of Steen alone at home. All the times he read "Snow White" aloud to the baby in my stomach, I thought: *Why do the dwarves go to work? Every time they go, something terrible happens at home.*

I jump as a hand is placed on my shoulder.

"Sorry," Helen says. "Did I scare you?"

"A little."

"It's good to have you back."

"Thanks for the flowers. I completely forgot to write thank you."

"Don't worry about it. How are things going at home?"

"We can handle it."

She pushes some hair behind her ears.

"Yes," she says. "That wasn't so good."

"No."

A tall Duplo tower topples over behind us.

"Yes," says Helen. "I was a little surprised when you called yesterday. But I really understand. Sometimes it's nice to just get started again. And if that's what is right for you, we'll make sure it can be done."

"Thanks."

"It's the least we can do. We'll do our best to help you through this."

"Thanks."

She smiles. Seems relieved about the conversation. As though she had feared what it would be like to see me again.

"Yes," she says. "It's about looking ahead. Even if you're forty-three, it's not impossible to get pregnant again, right?"

I think of Steen's lifeless body. How we struggled for six years to get pregnant for the first time. The monotonous slapping sound when I desperately tried to give him an erection one evening. The feeling of the limp member that I put back into the nappy, and Steen's eyes that refused to meet mine for a whole day afterwards.

"Well," says Helen. "But the ten o'clock shift just rang. Unfortunately, someone else has called in sick, so I'm on my own with the goldfish. Bjarke is taking the ladybirds, and Tanja, the grasshoppers. I'll send Camilla down to you so you don't have to be on your own."

"Okay. Thanks."

I met Camilla for the first time this morning. A fourteen-year-old work experience student from the local school who didn't say a single word during breakfast.

"Just come down if there's anything," says Helen.

I nod.

In El Salvador, a woman was sentenced to twenty years in prison for giving birth to a dead child. I think about it as I sweep yellow beads up from the floor of the snails' room. I think I should be glad I'm at work and not behind bars.

Camilla sits at the drawing table, checking her phone in secret. Maybe she's already figured out that I'm unable to be the responsible one.

I empty the dustpan into the bin. The little yellow beads sound like a brief hailstorm as they land at the bottom, and I sit back on the blue chair with the wheels underneath. Flick the pen back and forth between two fingers and look up at the clock.

10:14.

Lotus has her hair in pigtails that bounce up and down every time she jumps on the sofa. Every now and then, she leans over to see whether I'm getting angry.

"No jumping on the sofa," I say, but so quietly that I don't know if she hears it. I inhale to have enough voice to drown out the noise in the room. But the air seeps out of me again as I look at Lotus's two pigtails. Her hair is shiny and black, just like Steen's. I can't stop looking at it.

Time goes strangely in reverse inside me, like an undercurrent pulling me back. Again, I hear the cries of babies from the other rooms, the screams of women giving birth, and grandparents with crackling cellophane around large bouquets of flowers, and I imagine pressing a pillow against their faces. Holding it tight until they are as lifeless as my baby and the image is so vivid that I have to look away from the kids in the snails' room.

"Are you on ironing duty today?"

Isabella stands in front of me with a bead pegboard depicting a panda.

I look around for the ironing board and iron.

"Mine, too." William shows me a pegboard with a blue flower. "And Lærke's and Noah's. They're on the green shelf."

"Of course." I smile at them.

Out in the corridor, the fluorescent bulb flickers on the ceiling. The door to the staff room is closed with a latch that the children can't reach. My jacket hangs on a row of hooks adorned with pumpkins. I find the box of Ga-Jol. Put some in my mouth.

A text comes in from Klara.

How goes it?

I move the liquorice from one cheek to the other while trying to get a feel for how I am doing.

Actually pretty well, I write.

Great to hear. I plan to be with Steen at lunchtime so we can eat together. I'll stay until you're finished.

Thanks. It's good you're minding him.

Two secs. Phone's ringing.

I put some more Ga-Jols in my mouth. Wait.

Meanwhile, I look at the words:

Actually pretty well.

CHAPTER 14

The shaver buzzes against my upper lip. The skin has to be completely smooth, otherwise it won't stay on.

I breathe on the double-sided tape and press it against my skin. The moustache is black and very long. I open and close my mouth. Smile and make faces to make sure it's properly attached.

In the box is a matching goatee. *Beard set, Chinese* is written on the front of the box. I hold my goatee up to my chin. It reaches all the way down to my shirt collar. It looks great. Still, I decide it's too much and put it back in the packaging.

The brush breaks the water surface, and a brown colour spreads in the plastic mug. I turn my head from side to side. Look at my mirror image while I think of larvae that get too big for their own skin.

The transformation starts from within. Long before it is visible to the naked eye, the larva has developed a support network for its wings.

I take the black one instead. The smell is sharp and the face paint feels cold against my skin. I raise my eyebrows. Lower them again. They're not exactly the same, but they are beautiful. Very strong.

The tie is black, too, and I carefully tie the knot. Pull it until it fits into the shirt collar. The tie length is perfect and I think about how certain butterfly larvae pupate for years. They're so quiet that you can easily forget they exist.

Until they suddenly unfold their wings.

Gently I lift the wig. Enjoy the tight feeling as I pull it down over my head.

When I was a kid, we had a butterfly hatchery. An old aquarium with a gauze lid. There were newspapers at the bottom and I remember the smell. Of plant remains and knockoff ham. I was fascinated every time I watched the process. Eggs that hatched and turned into larvae that hatched and turned into bigger larvae.

I remember how the larvae became restless and crawled around looking for the right place. How they kind of trembled, as if they were holding a secret.

It's the same unrest I feel now. An insistent tingling, like a song you can't get out of your head.

I use a comb. Concentrate on getting the side parting completely straight.

The glasses have tinted lenses. A bluish tint at the top of the field of view. I press them firmly on my nose. Feel an intoxicating lightness in the body.

I lace up my shoes and button my coat.

The sweet bag is big. I stand for a moment weighing it in my hand before putting it in my pocket.

CHAPTER 15

Actually pretty well.

I have been looking at the words for so long that they start to seem distorted. As if they are somehow misspelt.

Klara still hasn't replied.

I put my finger in the text box to ask if everything is okay, but get interrupted by the door opening.

"What are you doing?" Isabella is standing in the doorway. She still has her bead pegboard in her hand.

I put the phone back in my jacket pocket.

"Coming now." I smile at her.

Ironing board. Iron.

I force my body to move, push it like a heavy cart, out of the staff room and down the corridor.

On the wall hang watercolour drawings of snails with spiral-shaped houses, and it strikes me that it doesn't look like they're carrying the houses, but as if they are trying to escape from them.

I stop in the middle of the corridor. Have to stand there a moment before I remember what I'm on my way to get.

The little light on the front of the iron makes a click and glows orange. I gently run the iron across the pegboard. The smell of molten plastic causes me to glance over at the plastic animals still lying on the floor.

There's a knock at the door and Tanja from the grasshoppers sticks her head in.

"Will one of you take the playground? Camilla?"

"My trainers aren't waterproof," says Camilla, hiding her phone in her pocket.

"There are wellies and raincoats in the staff room. In your size, too." She gives a thumbs-up and winks at me.

Camilla pushes the chair back clatteringly and gets up.

"We'll go out then," she says sharply.

It takes a long time to get all the kids out to the cloakroom and I only manage to help with two pairs of boots. Keep bungling the laces.

Tanja pulls on a hat and catches my eye. "Just come out if there's anything, okay?"

"Okay."

"Otherwise, Bjarke and Helen are in the other rooms."

I watch the throng of children running down the corridor and disappearing out the door to the playground. Remain there until the door closes behind them.

In the snails' room, a naked doll is on the floor. Facedown. Pale plastic skin and arms at the wrong angles. I pick it up. Straighten its hair and put it on a shelf.

The echo of the children's noise still hangs in the air. Only Mads, who has a snotty nose, and Maya, who has again been dropped off without any rain clothes, have stayed in the room with me.

We sit on the floor and look out the window, out at the playground, where the children are jumping in puddles and playing on the climbing frame. Lotus is wearing a red rain jacket. The hood is pulled up and I can't take my eyes off it. The red hood.

My phone vibrates in my pocket.

I sneak a peek at Tanja out in the playground before taking it out. I don't recognise the number.

"One minute," I say to the children.

I watch them as I back away from the window and squat behind a bookcase with toys.

"It's Eva?" I whisper.

"Hello?"

"Yeah, hi," I say a little louder. "It's Eva."

"Hi. It's the stonemason. I'm calling to let you know your headstone is ready."

My hand around the phone. Plastic animals on the floor. The kindness of his voice.

"You ordered delivery and setup, too," he says. "But just to be sure, I always call people and ask if they would like to come once we've installed it."

I nod, even though he can't see me. Pull out a wicker basket and pick up a race car. Put it back in the basket.

"It's nice to be a part of it," he says. "And then you have more influence on where exactly you want the stone to stand."

There's a strange whizzing. As if he's talking from somewhere far away.

"Well, it's the least we like to offer. If you're interested?"

As I look at my hand, it's holding on to the race car again.

"Hello? Are you there?"

"Sorry," I say. "I'm at work. You can just go ahead and set it up. It's fine. Thanks for calling."

"No problem," he says. "We're driving out there now. It's turned out really nice, the headstone."

I nod again. A tiny movement, as if the muscles in my neck are petrified.

"The soother was a nice touch," he says. "It looks really good. You'll be happy with it."

My eyes burn. Maya turns around and catches my eye and I force a smile. She doesn't reciprocate. Looks questioningly at me.

"I have to go," I say. "Thank you for calling. Thanks."

Then I hang up. My thumb holds the button in, the phone turns off completely.

The floor feels porous as I walk back to the window. I sit next to the kids. Mads puts a hand on my knee and it makes me jump. I move away from his small, warm body.

I stare out at the playground without seeing anything. The rainy weather has turned everything foggy.

She would have been two weeks old today.

"My dad says that when it rains, it's God crying," says Maya.

"I thought he was peeing," says Mads.

They laugh, and the metal chains holding the swings up begin to sway. Two pairs of wellies dangling between them. Laughing mouths and little hands holding on tightly.

I look away.

A withered leaf swirls past the window and lands in the sandbox. There's an empty blue bucket. Next to it is a shovel with a split blade. It was there when I felt her kick for the first time. While I was standing on the edge of the sandbox, imagining the colour of her snowsuit when she was about to start kindergarten. Her laughter and little hands digging moats.

A new gust of wind whirls through the playground and the blue bucket overturns.

I hold my breath and feel how my insides tighten. The contractions. The burning sensation of her head penetrating through me. The hope that she's breathing. That everyone made a mistake. It feels like it happened only a few minutes ago. Like it's happening right now.

My shoulder shakes. Only after a few seconds do I realise it's Maya and Mads who've found some books.

I rub my temples and get on my feet.

We sit on the sofa that Lotus was jumping on earlier. Maya on one side and Mads on the other. I can feel how they breathe, their breath and their pulse. I clear my throat and open the book they've put in my lap.

Camilla has red cheeks, and she smiles at me as she sits across from me in the lunchroom. She looks completely different from when she showed up this morning. More alive, somehow.

I pour water into an orange children's mug and drink. Feeling different, too. As if I have wrestled off a tight jumper.

"Did you forget your lunch?" Camilla nods at my empty plate.

"It's okay. I'm not that hungry."

"You're welcome to some of my pasta salad if you like?" She pulls the lid off a plastic tub and pushes it towards me.

"Thanks. That's nice of you."

I get a fork and push some pasta salad down onto my plate. It smells good, of lemon and parsley.

"Check out the pasta," she says. "It's made from squash. Isn't that smart?"

She empties the rest of the tub onto her own plate. "*Squashgetti*. It's so easy. My mum has a machine and it's just *bam*! The vegetables are pasta."

"Smart."

"You can make them out of beetroot, too. The only problem is that your pee turns red afterwards. I always think I have my period when that happens."

She laughs and I remember that I completely forgot to change the sanitary towel.

"Have you done that?" she says. "Peed red?"

"We're not really eating so many vegetables at the moment."

"I can ask my mum where she bought the machine." Camilla picks up her phone and starts dialling. It's amazing how alive she is after being in the playground with the kids. There's something contagious about it that makes me straighten up in the chair.

"That's sweet of you," I say. "But the kindergarten is actually mobile-free. Except for the staff room."

She looks at me.

"No problem." She puts the phone back in her pocket. "I can ask her tonight and tell you tomorrow."

"Do it."

A finger pokes me on the shoulder.

"Will you open this for me?" Maya holds out a plastic bag.

The knot is very tight. On the front is a drawing of a smiling face and a heart.

"Yes," I say. "It's definitely well tied."

"My dad is too strong to make packed lunches."

I smile at her. Try not to ruin the bag or to think of amniotic membranes bursting. Small steaming bodies and lungs that don't breathe.

"There," I say, handing the bag back to her.

"You're my favourite adult in the whole kindergarten."

Her big eyes barely blink as she looks at me.

I give her hand a squeeze. Clear my throat to remove the lump.

"I'm glad to be back, too."

I sit a little with her hand in mine before releasing it.

"Are you coming tomorrow, too?" she asks.

"Yes. Definitely."

She smiles.

"It's sad for you that your baby died."

The lump in my throat returns and I nod. Nod, at least, I think.

"Eva and Camilla!" Helen is standing behind us, looking out over the tables. "Where's Lotus?"

I follow her gaze. Only now do we realise that Lotus isn't there.

Maya's rabbit shoes bob their ears as she walks back to her seat.

"Oh, I know," says Camilla. "She was picked up early by her grandad."

"Which grandad?" asks Helen.

"He didn't give me his name."

"Did you check the file?"

She chews her lip.

"Didn't I tell you to always check before handing a child over to someone? Only those in the file are allowed to collect a child without a prior agreement."

"Sorry."

"I'll ring her mother to ask if they have an arrangement we don't know about."

When she's gone, Camilla catches my eye and grimaces.

"Oops."

"Don't worry, everyone makes mistakes in the beginning. On one of my first shifts, I spilt a whole jug of black currant juice over a girl wearing her favourite dress. One of those lovely, white princess dresses. It was like a bloodbath."

Camilla giggles. Gets serious again.

"Why did the grandad ask me, anyway? He could see that I'm new here. I can't even pump up a football."

"Did he just come into the playground?"

"No, he stood behind the fence, waving at me. Tanja was on the other side of the building, so I went over on my own, and then he pointed to Lotus and said she had won a half-day."

Helen returns with the phone in her hand and red blotches on her neck.

"This is not good. It's really not good."

"Mum knew nothing?" I ask.

Helen shakes her head. She closes her eyes and presses two fingers on the bridge of her nose.

Bjarke and Tanja come over to us.

"What's going on?" asks Bjarke.

"Lotus has been collected by a man. No one knows who he is," says Helen.

"Just now?" asks Tanja.

"A few hours ago. While you were out on the playground."

Tanja throws the rest of her sandwich on the table. "I'll run out and look for her."

"I'll go with you." Bjarke kicks off his slippers. "If you look by the stream, I'll take the forest."

They leave the lunchroom quickly, and as soon as they're outside, I can hear them running off.

"I'll lock the doors in the meantime." Helen hurries out into the hallway. I can hear her turning the locks and pulling hard on the door handles.

She comes back in with the phone in her hand and sweat on her upper lip. Looks up at the clock.

"Her mum will be here in a little while. She left home as soon as I told her."

"What should we say?" asks Camilla.

There's a bang behind us as a plate falls onto the floor. A child begins to cry.

"I'd better get that," I say, getting up.

"Thanks." Helen doesn't look at me as she says it. Just stands, drumming the staff phone against her thigh.

"I'll call the police," she says.

CHAPTER 16

Some animals are more complicated than others. But with training, you can stuff all kinds of vertebrates.

In the beginning, it's a good idea to practise on something small. A hamster, for example. It's easy to flay, and a towel is all you need to wipe up the blood.

I think about that while washing off the face paint.

I think of everything that was said to scare me.

Ghosts, flames, and hungry spirits flying around the streets like bats.

Carefully, I put the glasses with the blue-tinted lenses back in the case. Think about being chosen or not being chosen. About inheriting an entire house or not inheriting anything.

I lay out the things. Scissors. Cord. Duct tape.

A scalpel with a teeny tiny blade, intended for cutting paper.

Art knife, it says on the packaging. I like that name.

Again, I think of the butterfly hatchery all those many years ago. How we carefully lifted the gauze lid and stuck in our hands to catch the hatched butterflies. It had to be done gently but firmly. A wrong move could ruin their beauty.

We never said it aloud, but, in reality, I think all three of us preferred them when they were dead. All their fluttering and insanity made me nervous. Only when they had succumbed in the jam jar with ethyl acetate did I dare to really look at them.

Father taught us how to guide the needle through the chest and farther down in the foam board sheet. It was important to hit the large flying muscles so the butterfly was firmly attached. Afterwards, we fastened the lower body with several needles so the animal didn't twist when the wings were unfolded. It was about finding a position that looked natural. As if it was the butterfly's own choice to sit there.

When it was completely dry, it was ready and it was put down in the box with the other butterflies. With two fingertips, Father held the needles and drew circles in the air. *Once upon a time*, he said, and the dead butterflies flew again. They became monkey kings, pigs, emperors, and twin brothers.

The stories always ended unhappily. Caused me to lie awake for hours after Father said good night.

I pull the scalpel out of the packaging and hold it up to the light. The shaft has grooves, so it's easier to hold. I make some cuts in the air. Practise doing it without my hands shaking.

With a firm grip on the scalpel, I walk to the closed door. I push it open and can hear a rustling sound. A restless scraping as if from a small animal.

I turn on the light and go over. Squat down.

The crumpled cloth is now wet with saliva. I gently peel it out of her mouth. Tell her to be quiet, even though she's not making a sound.

Her lips are chapped. She keeps her mouth open.

I want to caress her cheek, but suppress the urge.

"Little butterfly," I whisper.

She stares at the scalpel in my hand. I close her lips and press down a piece of duct tape.

My heart beats faster, and again I am thrown back in time. I think of dancing dragons, silver coins, and Death wearing silk kimonos.

The stories became eerier and eerier over the years.

My story is to be the opposite. And she is going to help me.

This time, there will be a happy ending.

She squints. Follows the scalpel as it approaches her face. She's still wearing the red raincoat.

CHAPTER 17

The blue lights from the police cars alternate between hitting the swing set, the play tower, and the window to the staff room. The swing set, the play tower, and the window to the staff room that I am so close to, my breath mists the glass.

They have called in backup. Two officers are putting plastic tape on the wire fence around the playground. Long red-and-white ribbons flutter in the wind. Somewhere farther away I can hear dogs barking.

The air in the staff room quivers, arm sweat and rapid footsteps. Helen keeps pacing back and forth behind me. Camilla is sitting on the sofa, tapping a foot up and down.

The time now is 13:09. Lotus has been gone for almost three-quarters of an hour.

Every muscle in my body tenses as I watch the officers. I can't hear what they're talking about. Can only see their mouths moving as they tie off the plastic tape.

I don't understand what is happening. My first day at work. My very first day and now the time is 13:10.

I wipe my breath off the pane. A moment later, it's there again.

The sandbox has been cleaned. No shovels or buckets, just the damp, grey sand, and I press my thighs against the radiator under the window. Keep trembling, just like the air.

The time now is 13:11.

I take my jacket down from the peg with the pumpkin. Put it on and zip it up.

"Are you cold?" says Helen.

"It's a sort of nervous thing," I say.

She follows my gaze out the window. The blue lights hit her face and disappear again.

"I just don't understand ..." she says to Camilla. "How did Lotus react to being collected by that man? What did she say?"

"Not much." Camilla's legs keep tapping up and down. "She was just happy to get the bag of sweets he had with him."

"Shit. Shit." Helen drums the staff phone against her thigh. Starts pacing back and forth in the little room again.

I remember that my own phone has been off since the stonemason rang. I take it out and turn it on.

Klara has called twice. A message has been left on the machine, too.

"It's your turn next." Helen nods at my phone. "You ready?"

"Of course. I'm just writing a quick text to my sister."

Hi Klara. I'll be a bit delayed. Explain later.

"I'm really sorry you have to go through this," says Helen. "I wish I could send you home. But it's not allowed."

"No problem. It's okay. No problem."

The door to the staff room opens, and Bjarke and Tanja enter, gasping for breath and with windblown hair.

"So, what now?" says Bjarke. "Why did we have to come back?"

"The police want us all to be here," says Helen.

"Where are they?"

"My office. They want to talk to us one at a time. Lotus's mother is in there now."

"How is she?" asks Tanja.

Helen shakes her head. Looks like she's been beaten. "We have to find her. We just have to find her."

"What about the kids?" says Tanja. "It's so quiet here."

"We've gathered them in the TV room and put on a film. Edith is with them." She points to the corridor where Edith's cleaning cart is parked up against a wall. "We'll go in shifts and help. But only those of us who feel we can. We can't have anyone breaking down in front of the children."

Camilla hides her face in her hands.

"Sorry. Sorry! I had no idea ..." The rest of the sentence disappears in sobs.

Tanja sits down next to her. Strokes her back.

"It's just ..." Camilla removes her hands again and wipes her nose. "He looked so nice. And he looked like Lotus, so I didn't think there was anything suspicious about it."

"Like Lotus?" Tanja looks at her, confused.

"What is it?" says Camilla.

"Lotus is an adopted child from Korea and doesn't look like her mother or her father. And as far as I know, there are no grandparents."

"No, there are no grandparents," says Helen. "It is almost only Henriette who comes here. The mother. They divorced shortly after the adoption, and the father moved to Herning. The mother has sole custody. They had a rather problematic relationship. But the father gets Lotus for one night a couple of times a month."

"Maybe it was the father who was here?" says Bjarke. "You hear of these things. Divorce problems and then a kidnapping."

"But the father doesn't look like an older Korean man," says Tanja. "Have you never seen him?"

Bjarke shakes his head.

"He's a tall man." Tanja shows us with her hand a good distance over her own head. "Mousey-brown hair and glasses. Doesn't look in any way Asian."

"Maybe he got someone to help him?" says Bjarke. "I read about a father who persuaded a friend to go to his daughter's school and get her. And he was in the car, waiting. Maybe Lotus's father knows an older Asian-looking man?"

"Stop," Helen says. "We can't start accusing everyone. Did anyone other than Camilla see the man?"

We shake our heads.

Camilla bites a nail. Out in the playground, the officers have finished with the plastic tape. One of them is talking on the phone. Shortly afterwards, they walk out the door and disappear from my field of vision.

A blackbird lands on the wire fence. It sits for a moment, turning its head from side to side, as if looking for something. A gust of wind sweeps through the playground, causing the red-and-white plastic tape to move.

"In a way, it's even worse if it's not the father," says Bjarke. "Who the hell is it then?"

I look at the blackbird while I think of Lotus's black pigtails. How she looked at me as she jumped on the sofa.

"You look pale, Eva," says Helen. "Do you want to go outside and get some fresh air?"

I look away.

"Isn't it my turn next?" I say.

"We can just change the order a bit."

I nod slowly. Look at the blackbird again.

"In that case, I'm going out for a bit, too," says Bjarke. "Being in here is unbearable."

"Okay," says Helen. "You go out and get some fresh air. We'll call when it's your turn."

The air outside is not fresh. It stinks of car exhausts and cigarette smoke. Bjarke inhales deeply and holds the smoke in his lungs for a long time before exhaling.

"Today is a day for not giving a fuck about the smoking ban," he says. "Do you want one?"

I shake my head. Pull my hands up inside the jacket sleeves and let my eyes slide along the wire fence and up into the grey sky. The sun is gone.

Bjarke kicks a rock and sucks so hard on the cigarette that I can hear the crackle of the glowing tip.

"I just don't get it," he says. "Tanja was right on the other side of the building. And all the rooms have windows facing the playground. I don't understand how no one noticed anything."

"No."

He walks over to the stone he kicked before. Kicks it again.

I think of the stonemason. I think about my phone. I think the man who took Lotus came at just the right time. I think: *Maybe someone helped him?*

Another police car pulls up outside. The front doors open and Torben and Dagmar get out. They walk along the fence and I move closer to the wall. Press my back against the cold bricks and hold my breath.

Bjarke takes one more drag, as he also follows the officers with his eyes.

"What are they looking for?" I say.

"Clues, right?"

"But other officers have just been here. They looked out here already."

He shrugs. Throws his cigarette on the asphalt and stamps it out.

"Knowing my luck, I'll get a smoking fine on top of it all," he says.

I look at Torben's full, red beard, trying to decode his facial expression as he walks along the fence and turns the corner.

"And what about you?" says Bjarke.

"What about me?"

"Weren't you out on the playground, too, before? I thought I saw you out there."

"When?"

"Before lunch. While the children were out playing."

I think. Can remember the blue bucket that overturned. How Mads and Maya breathed while I read. Their warm breath and Camilla's squash pasta. My thoughts are like the toys in the snails' room. Scattered everywhere. What did I do between reading them the story and lunch?

No matter how hard I try, I can't remember.

CHAPTER 18

I pull out my car key and rub my face. It's almost half-past three and I was supposed to have been home a long time ago. Helen wouldn't let me go until I had talked to the crisis psychologist, and I barely know what I said in the police interview because everything blurred together strangely in my head. Lotus. Playground. Alive.

The wind hits my face when I get out of the car. There are dead insects on the windshield, flies and daddy longlegs with their wings bent out to the side.

Despite me wearing a winter coat and scarf, the cold penetrates me and I shiver. I shouldn't have gone to work. I wasn't ready. I *told* Klara I wasn't ready. The more I think about it, the more I shiver.

I knock on the door. Three quick raps. Three slow.

Through the windows I can see that the light is off inside the house. In the distance, I can hear dogs barking and a helicopter circling the fields.

Down in my pocket my phone beeps.

Did you get home okay?

I stand for a moment, looking at Helen's message before writing *Fine, thanks.*

I bend and stretch my fingers while I wait for Klara to open the door. There are still no lights inside. The ivy leaves on the wall of the house move, making it seem like the house is breathing. I've never cared for ivy. The roots bore into the brickwork, enveloping the house like a hedge of thorns. Like a parasite living on the outside of its host.

But you can't remove it without destroying the bricks. You can't cut out the grief.

I knock again. Three fast. Three slow. Three blinks. *It's okay.*

Klara still doesn't open the door. Maybe she's changing Steen's nappy?

I pat my coat pockets. Can't remember where I put the house key. Did I even bring it with me this morning, or did I just slam the door behind me?

My bag rattles as I search it. Headache pills, an empty water bottle, Ga-Jols. Postpartum pads and the way the blackbird sat turning its head.

Somewhere above me, I can hear the helicopter approaching. It flies slowly over the stubby, black fields, and I give a start when my phone rings.

Torben.

For several seconds, I hold the beeping phone as I look at the *Decline call* button. Then I take a breath and put it to my ear.

"Eva? Hi. I'm calling from the kindergarten. Can you talk?"

"What is it?"

"I'm ringing because … we found something. On the fence to the playground. At first we just thought it was rubbish, but when we looked, we could see it was origami."

"What?"

"The art of paper folding. I think that's what it's called. I didn't know the word, either. It was a small bird. Attached to the fence with steel wire."

"Okay?"

"And you're probably wondering why I'm ringing you." There's a faint scratching sound as if he's running his hand over his beard. "Well, because when we unfolded the paper, we discovered that some Chinese characters had been written inside."

I hold my breath.

"Yeah," says Torben. "It was our painter again. *Family is the most important thing.* Do you have any idea why that would have been put there?"

"No."

"Who was the girl who disappeared? Did you have a special relationship?"

"She was in my group. Otherwise, I've no idea … I've been on sick leave. It's been ages since I've even seen the kids."

"So what was it like to see them again? The kids?"

"Why do you ask?"

"Just thinking … It must have evoked some feeling. Am I right?"

Again, I feel the time rushing backwards, babies crying and bouquets of flowers, women screaming without having anything to scream over. My hands pressing a pillow against the little faces of the kindergarten children.

"It went fine," I say.

"Okay. Good to hear."

There is an expectant silence on the other end.

"What?" I say.

"That's good to hear. That it went fine."

I can't figure out his tone. Why does he sound like he's waiting for something?

"So," I say. "So, if there's nothing else …?"

"That's all right. Ring if you think of anything."

After we hang up, I stand for a moment with the phone in my hand and a strange restlessness in my body. The blue lights on the police cars. The smell of Bjarke's cigarette breath when he asked if I was out in the playground.

Was I?

No matter how hard I try, I can't remember what I did between reading the story and lunch.

"Eva!"

A car brakes in front of the garden gate. Klara looks breathless as she slams the driver's door and runs up the driveway. The brown vet bag bumps against her hip. She stops and puts her hands on her thighs.

"Sorry. There was an emergency callout—a cat was having convulsions and was almost unconscious."

"What?"

"I stopped by this morning to tell Steen that I'd be able to be here in the late afternoon. I was as quick as I could."

"What about his lunch?"

"Like I said, it was an emergency call."

"So he's been home alone almost all day? Without anything to eat or drink. Is that what you're saying?"

She steps forward to lay a hand on my arm.

I take a step back. Turn my bag upside down and everything falls out, clatters on the doorstep.

"There was no one else who could take it," she says. "What was I supposed to have said?"

"You promised you'd mind him today. You *promised*."

My hands shake as I rummage through the things. A lip balm without a lid, a bent metal clip, two paracetamol tablets, bag lint. I don't understand why Torben sounded like that, why I got so nervous about his call, why Lotus had to disappear the one day I was at work.

"Eva?"

Klara puts a hand on my shoulder and I straighten up abruptly.

"Why didn't you call me?" I say.

"I did. But you didn't answer."

I press my palms against my temples. Give up trying to find my keys and walk over to the bird table.

At the top is a ledge that the birds can't reach and that burglars would probably never guess is a hidey-hole. A trick Steen learned from his father.

I stick my fingers in, grab the spare key, and stop. Stare at the key chain's advertising logo, which I have a habit of always turning down. An uneasy feeling fills me.

Klara comes over to me. She pushes my hair behind my ears and looks at my face.

"Are you okay?" she asks.

I turn away from the bird table tersely. Try to shake off the unrest.

"What do you think?"

I stare at her until she lowers her eyes.

"I'm really sorry," she says. "I tried to call, but you didn't answer."

She has already said that, and I don't bother to answer.

The helicopter makes a noise over us and I watch it while Klara takes the extra key out of my hand and goes to unlock the door. The clouds are heavy and grey. Autumn has come early. As soon as the calendar changed from August to September, the summer turned off as abruptly as a sunbed whose time had run out. I can feel the cold creeping underground and up through my body.

"So ..." Klara pushes the door open. "Come on, sis."

I push her aside as she tries to go inside.

She steps down from the doorstep. Throws out her arms.

"Shouldn't I take a look at him?"

"Just go."

"Sorry, Eva." She grabs my arm.

"Leave me alone." I wriggle free. "Go home to your children who are alive and your husband who can walk."

Then I close the door in her face.

Steen is asleep. He has sweat on his upper lip. In the V of the pyjama shirt, the skin is ruddy and moist.

I lift the duvet. The nappy is heavy with urine and faeces. I caress his hair, but he doesn't respond. With two fingers I feel the side of his neck. His pulse is fast and intermittent.

I pat him on the cheek. He moans faintly.

"Steen!"

I pat him again, harder.

"Leave me alone," he mumbles. "I won't."

His eyes are white and upturned under the half-closed eyelids.

"Steen! Sweetheart?"

I end up patting him so hard that it feels like giving him a slap. His face contracts. Slowly, he opens his eyes and looks at me. His gaze is distant, as if he doesn't see me properly.

"Eva?" he whispers. "Is that you?"

"Who else would it be?"

"I don't know. Maybe it was something I dreamt."

"What do you mean? What have you dreamt?"

"I'm not sure. I'm so thirsty."

"Tell me. What did you dream?"

"Just … it was like there was someone in the room."

"In here?"

One blink.

"Are you sure it was a dream? Could you see who it was?"

"I don't know. I'm so incredibly thirsty."

I look towards the window. It's closed and the blinds are pulled down. I go and check the latch. Check the child lock. Everything is as I left it.

I stick two fingers in between the blinds and look out. The shadows are getting long. The drizzle is lying like a glistening coat over the grass and the stack of boards that were to have been a porch roof for the pram. The helicopter is a black dot on the horizon.

The blinds crinkle as I release them. I screw the curtain rod to close them as tightly as possible before I sit down on the edge of the bed.

I get a wet wipe and wipe the sweat off Steen's face. Hold the feeding cup against his lips and let him drink.

"Sorry I left you," I say. "I don't know what I was thinking."

My phone rings.

Klara.

I put it on silent.

Neither of us says anything while I see to him. Somewhere above the house, I can hear the helicopter flying closer, and I hum to drown it out. Can't make myself tell him what happened in the kindergarten. He doesn't need to worry, my little sweetheart, and I hum louder as I unbutton his pyjama shirt and pull it off. I wash under his arms. Put my palm on his chest to feel his heart in there. His strong, living heart.

The freshly washed pyjama shirt smells of fabric softener as I unpeg it from the clotheshorse and I lift his arms one at a time to get the sleeves on. Close the buttons and pull the duvet up around him.

"So," I say. "As good as new. And dinner will be ready in a little while."

I've cooked the chops from Klara a little too long and I have to saw with the knife for a long time before I can lift the fork. Steen opens his mouth and I try to follow his pace.

At first, I keep lifting the fork up to his mouth before he has finished chewing. At other times, I'm too slow or get lost in my own thoughts so there are some awkward seconds where his mouth hangs open and I fumble to get the next mouthful ready.

Things are a little better today. I concentrate on being present. Not think about Lotus anymore. Don't respond when the display on my phone lights up. Just sit here with my husband.

The ticking of the wall clock amplifies the silence, and I imagine that one day he will lose his voice and have to speak through a robot. A machine that detects the movements of his mouth and always pronounces the words in the exact same way. I always thought there was something creepy about that. As if the machine was more alive than the person using it.

"Does it taste okay?" I say.

One blink.

"A little gravy might have been good," I say. "Or some vegetables."

I think of the aroma of lemon and parsley. Of peeing red and the police's fluttering plastic tape, and my gaze wanders to the blinds. The smell of meat and urine hangs heavily in the bedroom, but I don't dare open the window to let in some fresh air. Can't let go of the thought that someone was in here while I was away.

When I look at Steen again, his mouth is open like a baby bird.

"Sorry." I hurry to get the fork to him.

He chews faster than usual. Shortly afterwards, he swallows and opens his mouth again. It's been a long time since he's been hungry like this, and I stick the fork in another piece of meat. Feel a jab of guilty conscience for leaving him. That I know how easy it is for me to choose something other than this.

"Maybe tomorrow we could have some vegetables for dinner?" I say. "Doesn't that sound delicious?"

One blink.

"We should be eating healthier in general," I say.

Steen opens his mouth again. Usually, it looks like he has to work hard to eat. Now, he opens his mouth so wide that I can see his uvula and I stab a new piece of meat.

I think of the helicopter and of mothers playing aeroplanes to make their children open up. Put the fork in his mouth and watch him chew.

"Don't you want something, too?" asks Steen.

"Maybe later. I ate at work."

He swallows. His Adam's apple moves under the pyjama collar.

"It's so loud," he says.

"What?"

"Eating on your own."

He finishes chewing and I put the cutlery down.

"I've extended my sick leave," I say, putting the plate away. "It was no problem."

"Oh really?"

I look towards the window. Listen for the helicopter.

"Did something happen?" he asks.

"It was just too early. It was stupid of me to go."

I let my finger follow his jawline. The stubble of his beard feels like tiny thorns, and I imagine the ivy on the house growing and growing, so that it's impossible to get out of here in the end.

"Sorry, sweetheart." I kiss him on the forehead. "I'm sorry I listened to Klara. Going to work was a crazy idea."

He blinks three times.

"It's not okay," I say. "I promised I wouldn't leave you. I understand if you're angry."

"I'm not angry. I'm grateful you still come home to me."

"Do you mean that?"

"The most important thing is that we are together. I can do without everything else. Just not you."

I look at him in surprise. Can't remember when he last spoke to me like that.

"I've been thinking about it all day while you were away," he says. "Being bitter doesn't help. I no longer have control over my body, but I still have control over my thoughts."

His black eyes look into mine. The bushy eyebrows and the short, dense lashes.

"The paralysis hasn't settled on my brain," he adds.

I feel a warmth flow through my body and we look at each other for a long time. His beautiful eyes. The hint of a smile on his lips. For a moment, everything is almost like it once was.

"If I could, I'd give you a hug," he says.

It makes the warm feeling inside get stronger and I stroke his hair away from his forehead.

"Explain it again," I say. "You just decided not to be bitter anymore?"

"Just and just. This isn't exactly easy. But ..." He sighs. Seems to be searching for the words.

"I always thought that if she wasn't here, then I didn't want to be here, either. So there was nothing to get up for. And I may never be able to convince my body otherwise. But I can, at least ..."

His tongue makes a dry sound and he shoots his lips out. I take the feeding cup and let him drink.

"Thanks." He holds my gaze while I dab his lips with a baby wipe.

It's been a long time since he's said so much to me at once, and his mouth seems completely out of shape.

"When we got married, I promised you I'd be a good husband," he says. "That promise still holds true."

"How can you be so strong? I can still walk, but I ..." I fiddle with the armhole on my cardigan. "It feels like my body is the only thing working and that everything inside is broken."

"It'll get better," he says.

"Do you think so?"

"I promise."

The bed creaks as I lie down beside him. I roll over onto my side and look at his profile. The fine nose. The arch of the upper lip.

I take his arm and put it over me, try to position us so we're holding each other.

"Do you still want me?" I say. "If you could ... would you like to ...?"

"Of course."

I kiss him on the cheek. Put my lips to his ear and whisper, "I once saw a movie about a man who was paralysed from the neck down and who was aroused by having his earlobes fondled."

"Okay?"

"Does that sound crazy?"

"I don't know."

I press my lips against his ear. Can feel my exhalation on his skin. Very gently, I let my tongue slide over his earlobe. Up along the edge of the ear. Slowly. He tastes salty, of man.

"How does that feel?" I say.

"Nice."

"Should I keep going?"

"Only if you want to."

"But do you like it or what?"

"Yes. It's nice."

It looks like he's holding his breath.

I roll back onto my back and look up at the ceiling. Wish I hadn't tried. I wish I could stop thinking about his muscles and movements inside me. His gentle, gentle hands.

After only three months as a couple, we threw my contraceptive pills on the barbecue grill and set fire to them. It smelled awful and the smoke was probably toxic, but I loved him for having those kinds of ideas. We stood there together, watching the blister packs sizzle and crumple, and as I look up at the ceiling now, I sense our baby here somewhere. She's lying between us. She rolls down to the end of the bed, falls on the floor with a small bump.

I close my eyes, but she is there, too. Her soft, cold legs. The tip of her nose. The bloody stump of the umbilical cord.

I rub my face hard and reach for my Ga-Jols. Chew until the taste of laughing gas and thin, red hospital cordial disappears.

"The vicar has called several times," I say. "She asked if we were interested in having a chat. I don't know if it was stupid to say no."

"God let our daughter die. What do we have to talk to the vicar about?"

"I don't know. It's just ..." There's a daddy longlegs hanging from the ceiling. It's not moving.

"I just always wanted to be left in peace, too," I say. "But now ... I don't know."

The screen light of my phone casts shadows on the wall.

"Who keeps ringing?" says Steen. "Shouldn't you take it?"

"I don't know. I'm just going to the bathroom."

I plonk down on the toilet seat and pull the postpartum pad out of my knickers. There's no more blood, and even though that's a good sign, it makes my stomach clench.

I close my eyes as I pee. Hold my breath so as not to inhale the smell. It's gotten worse. My urine. My body. The strange smell is everywhere. Of bacon and dust, a bit smoky and musty.

A bluebottle lands on one of my knees. I look at it for a long time before pulling my phone out of my pocket.

There are four missed calls. All from Klara. Helen has sent the number of a crisis psychologist, who everyone in the staff group is welcome to contact. I close the message and open Google.

Central and West Jutland Police are looking for a five-year-old girl who went missing earlier today from her kindergarten in Hemmet. The girl is described as about one metre tall and of Korean descent. She is wearing a red raincoat, grey trousers and

Sorry. Ring! Lots of love, Klara

I delete her message without replying.

Losing a child is every mother's nightmare. "It felt like I was losing a part of myself," says the author of the book Angel Children, *which has just been published on*

I'm going to keep trying until you answer. Love, Klara

I delete that message, too.

Klara gave birth on all fours, I was told. Pushed out her kids with the same force as one of Dad's sows. It's only because Alfred used his veto that they stopped at three children.

It keeps dripping down into the toilet bowl. Like I'm leaking.

Klara still hasn't bought a new washbasin, so I had to use the pink one with the flowers again today. It's on the floor bottom-up to air dry. Steen forbade Klara from putting it and the things from the front garden down in the basement. He said he didn't want more baby stuff down there. That the basement shouldn't resemble a burial chamber. His whole head turned red from the exertion of saying so much at once.

I replied that if he wanted to check what was down in the basement, then he had to get up.

Just get up.

I lean forward and rub my eyes. It scares me that I'm starting to feel this way. These sudden outbursts of anger.

Klara calling.

I tighten my grip on the vibrating phone. Squeeze it until it is silent.

My legs feel strangely stiff as I get up from the toilet and go to the sink. I don't look at myself in the mirror as I wash my hands. The synthetic hand soap from the supermarket foams between my fingers and I scrub them thoroughly. Scrub and scrub.

The bedroom door is open. I stand behind the frame and peer inside. Steen has his eyes closed. I look at the pink feeding cup with the flowers. His bare feet sticking out from under the duvet. The sleeping pills.

For some reason, I can't bring myself to go in there. The sight of his lifeless body makes me think of the stuffed animals in Hvide Sande. When I think back, it all seems surreal. The farm, the rifle, the wild boar's head. Like a dream I had.

The smell of Bjarke's cigarette. *I thought I saw you out there.*

I gently pull the door closed. Lay my palm on it and close my eyes.

Rissoles. Bacon. Schnitzels. There are dewdrops on Klara's handwriting and I look at it for so long that the freezer starts beeping.

I take out a random bag for dinner tomorrow. Close the door again and place the meat in a bowl to thaw. It's pale under the plastic and I look at the bedroom door. Like so many times before, I imagine the handle suddenly being pressed down. That he spreads his arms and smiles. It's getting harder and harder to imagine.

Is it because I actually don't want him to get up?

I shake off the thought.

The sofa cushion has a mark in the place I usually sit. I pull my legs up under me and turn on the television. Zap between channels.

The citizens of Hemmet are holding their breath after a kindergarten child today ...

... Chose to put in all available resources into finding the girl who, according to kindergarten headteacher and director, Helen ...

I turn off the television again. Pull my legs even closer to me and look around the quiet living room.

On the coffee table is the book of *Grimms' Fairy Tales.* The sight of it makes it all come flooding back. Steen's lips against my pregnant belly. His loving, whispering voice. He read to my bump every single day. Even after her heart had stopped beating, he still read to her.

I lean forward and pick up the book. Hesitate for a moment before turning on the reading light and flipping to the first page. The table of contents is long and closely written. That's what got me lost in my own thoughts last time. All the memories.

I flip on. Concentrate on keeping my breathing calm.

The pages are bulging and smell faintly of tea leaves and dust. The letters are old-fashioned and intricate, and over each fairy tale is a small black-and-white illustration.

In times past there lived a king and queen, who said to each other every day of their lives, "Would that we had a child!" and yet they had none.

I flipped to the next fairy tale.

There was, once upon a time, a little girl whose father and mother had died, and she was so poor that she no longer had a little room to live in, or bed to sleep in …

I flip further on.

There once lived a man and his wife, who had long wished for a child, but in vain. Now, at the back of their house, there was a little window which overlooked a beautiful garden full of the finest vegetables and flowers; but there was a high wall all round it, and no one ventured into it …

I try to concentrate on reading. To surrender to the story.

People never get older in literature. You can take a book off the shelf, blow off the dust, and all the characters are exactly the same age as when you last read the book.

So it is, too, with death.

If a child dies, it continues to be a child while everyone else ages.

I flip back a page. There's something confusing about the page numbers. There's something wrong. The page numbers. The frayed pieces of paper protruding between two chapters.

Twenty-four pages have been torn out of the book. An entire fairy tale is missing.

I flip to the table of contents to see which one.

"Snow White."

The entire "Snow White" story is gone.

Again, I think of the dwarves going to work and coming home to a lifeless body.

What's with that fairy tale?

I pick up my phone and find a free version online.

It was the middle of winter, and the snowflakes were falling like feathers from the sky, and a queen sat at her window working, and her embroidery-frame was of ebony ...

I hold on tight to the phone while my eyes run across the lines. It is completely quiet inside the bedroom. Somewhere above the house, I can hear the helicopter circling.

And they made a coffin of clear glass, and they laid her in it and wrote in golden letters upon it her name and that she was a king's daughter. Then they set the coffin out upon the mountain and one of them always remained by it to watch.

At the next line, my eyes freeze. A chill runs through my body as it dawns on me. The three stuffed birds in Hvide Sande.

An owl, a raven, and then a dove.

The three birds that sit by the dead Snow White's glass coffin and weep.

CHAPTER 19

The double bed creaks as I sit on the edge.

Steen looks at my folded arms. Then at my face.

"What is it?" he says.

"Why did you never tell me you had siblings?"

"What?"

"Your mother says you have a twin brother and a little sister."

"Have you been talking to my mother?"

"You never tell me anything."

"Stay away from them, Eva. I mean it."

"Do you have your brother's phone number?"

Two blinks.

"You don't have a number for your own twin brother?"

"I deleted it when we broke off contact."

"Why?"

"I don't want to talk about it."

"But I want to."

He looks up at the ceiling.

"Hello?" I wave my hand in front of his face.

He continues looking up at the ceiling. His jaw muscles are working under the pale skin.

"What happened to all your fine talk about being a good husband and not shutting yourself inside yourself?" I ask. "What happened to your *apology?*"

"I don't have my brother's number. Okay?"

"What am I not allowed to know?"

"The less you know about him, the better."

"I went to his house."

Steen stares at me. There's fear in his eyes and I hate doing this to him. I had decided to keep it a secret, to protect him, but now I can't hold it in any longer, and everything comes out. That I have visited the psychiatric nursing home and his brother's farm in Hvide Sande. That his mother thought her husband had been there that night. That he came to kill her. That his brother's farm looked as if it had been abandoned in a hurry.

Steen doesn't say anything in the meantime. Just grinds his teeth harder and harder.

"You went behind my back," he says.

"What do you expect me to do? I'm dealing with everything on my own, and you ..."

"What? ... are just lying here?"

"You're lying to me. You're not adopted, are you?"

"We agreed to put the past behind us so we could concentrate on our life together."

"But we don't have a life anymore. The only thing here is death and more death and more ..." My voice cracks.

I take a deep breath and laid a hand on his shoulder even though he can't feel it.

"Sweetheart," I say in a higher tone than intended. "It would make me really happy if you would tell me about your siblings."

"You don't always get what you want."

His eyes are completely black. As if he has rolled up a tinted car window.

"So you're refusing to tell me anything, or what?" I say.

One blink.

The feeling of powerlessness makes my body tremble and I let go of his shoulder again. Have to make an effort not to raise my voice.

"Fine," I say. "Then you get some water yourself if you get thirsty. And when your nappy gets too full, you can change it yourself, too."

With an abrupt motion I get up and leave. Slam the door behind me.

It's been a long time since I've been in Steen's home office. There's something scary about being here again. Like stepping into the estate of a deceased person.

On the walls hang football diplomas and certificates from various IT courses. A poster of Manchester United. A framed photo of Torben and Steen standing in a football stadium, each with a draught beer. They look as if they are singing or shouting something in chorus. Steen is squinting as though bursting with laughter.

On the desk are two computer screens and a keyboard. I push the mouse. *Password* appears in a text box on the screen.

Below the keyboard is a writing pad depicting a world map. I lift it up. Lower it again.

Everything in here is neat and tidy. Apart from the thin layer of dust that has settled on all the horizontal surfaces, it looks as if the room has just been cleaned.

I sit down on the office chair, swing back and forth a little. Above the desk hangs a framed picture of me. I look young. Young and happy.

This is really unfair. Just walking away from a man lying paralysed. But right now I can't bear to go in to him again.

The arm of the desk lamp creaks as I straighten it and direct the light down on the floor.

Under the desk is a bin. There's something down there. A crumpled bit of paper. I fish it up. Glance at the door before unfolding it.

Hold your christening in our beautiful venue offering the best views of West Jutland. We can cater for parties of up to 120. The perfect place for a day in …

I crumple the paper again. Throw it back into the bin and turn around.

Torben meets my eyes. I look away from the picture and go to the bookcase of ring binders. They stand dead straight next to each other. Broad white spines with years written on lined labels. I pull one out and flip through it. Accounts. Invoices. Receipts. I push it in again. Pull out a new one. More accounts. I push it into place. Pull out all the ring binders in turn and flip through them.

The dust whirls up and settles in new ways and it's like my thoughts follow suit. Detached images begin to accumulate. Snow White in the glass coffin. Steen in bed. A vague connection that's slowly becoming clearer. Stuffed animals. Steen's scared eyes when I got home. *It was like there was someone in the room.*

I wipe my palms on my trousers. My heart beats faster and I turn away from the bookshelf.

On the shelf above the desk are three file boxes. They are heavy as I lift them down. In one, there are payslips going back several years. In the next is a members' magazine from the football club. The last one contains cables and wires.

I put them back in place and go to his other bookshelf. More invoices. Contracts and budgets. Magazine racks with transport documents. I don't quite know what I'm looking for, but as the dust swirls in the air around me, I become more and more confident that the twin brother has something to do with everything that has happened. But what? And why is Steen hiding him?

I think of the blue pickup truck and the stuffed animals. *My two sons are my yin and yang.*

An owl, a raven, a dove.

Lives in pomp and splendour in his imperial residence.

I pull out the desk drawers in turn. Rummage between papers and folders. Printed spreadsheets. Computer codes. A headset. Batteries and clips.

The bottom drawer sticks and I pull it. The drawer half opens and I sit down on the floor. Stare at a picture of smiling parents with small babies in their arms. Over them hover chubby angels with trumpets and huge wings.

Parent and baby church choir.

Carefully, I pick up the brochure. It's from our local church.

The parent and baby church choir is good for baby's language and motor development. You don't need X Factor potential to participate. Baby always thinks mum's and dad's voice is the best.

The pages are filled with open mouths singing and smiling at the same time. Apples cut into wedges, homemade cake, and babies in romper suits.

The parent and baby church choir meets every week during autumn. The course ends with a toddler service where family and friends can come and see what the babies have learned.

I put the brochure away and spot a pamphlet with a baby seal on the front. *Welcome to the Kattegat Centre.*

As I search deeper, I can see that the entire drawer is full of that sort of thing. Fathers' group at the library. Museum Silkeborg. Harrild Hede Nature Centre. Bork Viking Harbour Museum.

There are also four weekly magazines, still wrapped in plastic. It rustles under my fingertips as I slide them over a smiling family in a garden. Red strawberries and green grass, sunshine and a cream-coloured pram under a parasol. The man has a hand on the woman's pregnant belly. He's wearing a short-sleeved T-shirt. Looks strong.

The plastic makes it look like there's a window between us. A transparent membrane, and the hot splash as they poked holes in me and the amniotic fluid gushes down my bare legs.

A fly lands on the side of my neck and I brush it away with a violent motion. *Our Children*, it says in big yellow letters, and I breathe in all the way up to my throat.

The idea that Steen has bought these magazines. That he requested all these brochures. *We parents. How to get an annual pass to Jyllands Park Zoo.*

Only when a tear hits the cream-coloured pram do I realise I'm crying.

I rub my eyes, and it runs hot and wet, tears and amniotic fluid, and the fly settles on my neck again. It crawls up to my ear as if it wants to whisper something to me, and this time I let it be. Sit stock-still with *Our Children* in my lap.

I think of everything locked in the basement. Cradle. Changing table. Rocking horse. I don't dare go there. Haven't been in there at all since Klara carried the stuff down there. She managed it all in the week that passed from the birth to the funeral. Went patiently up and down the basement stairs while Steen lay paralysed in bed and I sat freezing in the living room.

Baby duvet. Bathtub. Changing table. *Go home and get a good night's sleep, and we'll see you again tomorrow.*

I hold my breath and the taste is there again. Laughter gas and thin, red hospital cordial.

They lifted the baby up and laid her on my chest. Her tiny limp body.

I didn't dare look at her. People say that labour hurts terribly. People have no idea what pain is.

The midwife came in with a tray. There was no flag on it.

The fly takes off buzzing and flies away. I gather magazines and bro-chures in a pile, try to remember what order they were in before. I don't worry about whether it makes any difference. Whether Steen will ever come in here again.

The drawer still sticks even when empty. I push it in and out a few times. There's a crackling noise.

I get down on my knees and look into the bottom of the drawer. There's something sitting on the back of the drawer. Something glued on? I reach in my arm and feel for it. It feels thicker than paper. The drawer is too dark for me to see properly, but I can feel that sticky tape along the edge. I scratch with my nail to get it free, keep going until it loosens.

A padded envelope.

I turn it over and over in my hands. The edges have ripped a little from the tape, but otherwise it looks like an ordinary white padded envelope. Nothing is written on it, neither on the front nor the back. I gently press it. There's something hard in one corner. I lean towards the door. Listen for sounds.

With one finger I pop open the envelope.

At the bottom is a USB stick. It looks old.

I sit for a moment with it in my hand. Think of Steen in the double bed. His dismissive look and the way he looked up at the ceiling. Then I tighten my grip on the USB stick and get up.

CHAPTER 20

The bathroom lock clicks as I turn it. I stick two fingers in between the blinds and look out. Listen for approaching cars. Everything is quiet. Even the sound of the helicopter is gone. I release the blinds and sit on the toilet seat with my laptop.

The start-up sound is replaced by a mountain landscape. I haven't uploaded a new background image after deleting the photo of the scan.

I insert the USB stick and a file folder appears. I double-click it. A moment passes as the computer loads.

Below me, water runs in the toilet. A quiet, trickling sound.

I lean back against the cistern until the computer is ready. The folder is full of photos. Hesitantly, I move the mouse up to the first one and click. It shows a garden. There's a large cherry tree. On the lawn is a football. There are no people in the picture.

There is something familiar about the garden. It's like I've seen it before. And yet, also not so.

I shake off the thought and click again.

The next photo is of a kind of buffet. Spring rolls, noodles, and something I don't recognise. In the middle of the table is a bouquet of flowers that looks strangely dead. As I look closer, I can see that they are made of paper.

The next pictures show food, too. Each bowl is zoomed in on. Finely plated vegetables and deep-fried king prawns. All served with thought and care.

I keep clicking.

The photos must be in random order because this seems to have been taken earlier in the day.

A small man with a red tie and sharp side parting stands on a lawn, resting his hand on a garden chair. Above him the sky is pale pink, as if the sun is about to rise. In the background, I can see hollyhocks and a Danish flag.

The man is in the next picture, too. Standing with a silver bell in each hand. He smiles, but it's a sad smile.

I continue clicking.

A skinny boy standing with a younger girl in his arms. They are wearing nice clothes. A tie and a dress and … A cold sensation runs through me as I notice the girl's face. I zoom in on her and the cold feeling worsens.

Her skin has purple discolourations and her jaw is open. Her arms look strangely stiff, like on a Barbie doll.

Fuck.

There's a bang as I push the bedroom door open.

"What is this?" I turn the computer screen towards Steen.

His eyes flicker.

"What is this?" I say. "What are these photos?"

"Have you been going through my stuff?"

I sit on the edge of the bed. Hold the computer right up to his face.

He blinks several times in a row. Looks at them reluctantly.

"My brother sent them to me. It was a long time ago."

"Why didn't you tell me about it?"

"I didn't want to worry you."

"About what?"

He closes his eyes.

"About what?" I say.

"I don't want to talk about it."

"Then I'll have to go to your brother's house and ask him."

His face tenses. As if he is trying to lift his body with his facial muscles alone.

"Do you know what the only good thing about of all this is?" I say. "It's that for once you can't leave in the middle of a conversation."

His face winces.

"Sorry," I mumble.

He meets my eyes and there is a pain there reminiscent of the afternoon we stood bent over her little transparent cradle in the hospital, unable to figure out how to say goodbye.

"I'm just trying to protect you," he says.

"I know." I lay a hand on his cheek. "But you can't shut me out anymore. Not with everything that has happened."

The screen has gone black. I press a key and the children appear again. The girl's open mouth and the boy's strained smile. The frightened eyes and blood vessels that clearly stand out on the back of his hand as he holds her up.

"Tell me about it," I say.

He looks away.

Keeps looking away despite me staring at him.

Then he blinks twice.

No.

I clench my fists. Feel the sense of powerlessness scratching inside my eyes.

"They were taken here, at home, weren't they?" I say. "The photos."

The thought makes me sick.

"The dead girl," I say. "She was here. In our house."

Even though he doesn't answer, I know it's true. That was how I recognised the garden and the living room, too, despite both the wallpaper and furniture being different now.

She lay dead in this house, just like our baby.

Two dead girls in the same house. As if the place is cursed.

Steen still doesn't say anything. I am alone with the eerie speculations and uncertainty.

The scratching sensation in my eyes increases and I lift my chin.

The more a woman breastfeeds, the more milk she produces. Maybe the same goes for crying. Tears run down my face and Steen emits the same tormented sound as when Klara and I turn him in bed.

"Please don't cry," he says.

This time, it's me who avoids his eyes. There's something liberating about surrendering yourself to crying. I disappear so much that I barely hear him.

"Okay," he repeats, a little louder. "I'll tell you."

We look at each other.

"And your brother's phone number?" I ask.

He looks desperate and I'm ashamed to use my tears against him.

"Yeah," he mumbles. "I might have it somewhere. From the old days. I don't know if it's still in use."

"Where?"

"In my contacts on the phone. At the bottom. Under *WC*."

I raise my eyebrows.

"I couldn't help it," he says. "I know it's petty."

I check his phone and there it is. At the very bottom is a mobile number hidden under the initials *WC*. My pulse quickens as I look at it.

I copy the number onto my phone. Wipe away the tears.

"Good," I say. "So tell me."

I turn the computer so we can both see it. Steen takes a breath before looking at the screen. His face contracts. As if he's getting one of his old tics, but only his facial muscles can react.

"Who's the girl?" I say.

"It's ..." He hesitates. "It's our little sister."

"What happened?"

"She died."

"But how? She's so young."

"She started coughing."

I look at him questioningly.

"Maybe it was just whooping cough," he says. "I don't know. She never went to the doctor. Father didn't believe in them."

"He didn't believe in doctors?"

"He crushed nettles and made tea and bought huang qin plants online. He peeled the needles out of the butterflies and gave her acupuncture and ... And one morning she was dead in her bed."

Her eyes are still open. Black and empty in the little face, and I can hardly bear to look at her.

"Who's the boy?" I ask.

"It's …" He hesitates again. All the muscles in his face look as if they're fighting the conversation. "That's him. My brother."

I look at the photo for a long time. The secret twin brother and the dead sister.

"Why is he standing with her like that?"

"They're getting married."

"What?"

"They got married," he repeats, mumbling.

My stomach churns. A living big brother who gets married to a dead little sister. A mother and a father celebrating them.

"That's sick," I say.

"Where my family comes from originally, it's quite common. It's called a ghost marriage."

I look at his brother's stiff smile. The tie and his shiny patent leather shoes.

"So you think this is okay?"

"I was a child."

"But you think it's okay?"

He's quiet for a moment. Then he says, "I've become more understanding with time."

I zoom in on his brother's face. Look at the flat bridge of the nose and the lips that turn down with a little curl on each side. He and Steen are identical. In the old childhood pictures, it's almost impossible to tell the difference between them.

"What's his name?" I say.

"Wu-Chao."

"Wu-Chao? And your name is Steen?"

He takes a breath. Looks like it's hard to talk about.

"I was once called something else," he says.

There's a moment's silence.

"I needed to start fresh. Distance myself from my family."

"Why?"

"A lot of things happened."

"What was your name before?"

"I'd rather not talk about it."

There's a pain in his voice that makes me look at the computer screen again.

The twin brother with the dead sister.

"Isn't there a picture of him as an adult?" I say.

"The most recent one I have is from when my father turned fifty. It was the last time the whole family was together. If you scroll down, you'll see it."

I press the arrow key and get to the bottom of the folder.

Steen's brother is standing with his arm around his father. He has the same razor-sharp side parting. Same small, slender body.

They're the spitting image of each other.

My stomach drops as I realise.

My husband was here last night.

CHAPTER 21

The screen light of the computer goes out and the image of the dead bride and the living groom disappears.

"Unfortunately, the person you are calling cannot be reached. Please leave a message after the beep."

"He's still not answering," I say.

"He must be busy."

Steen looks exhausted. The light in his eyes has faded, and I should let him sleep now, but I can't let go of the thought that his twin brother has something to do with all the eerie things that have happened. That he is somehow the key to it all.

"What kind of business does he have?" I say.

"Something to do with imports-exports."

I slap the phone against the palm of my hand a few times.

"We've been trying for over an hour now," I say.

"He's probably just at work."

"When I was at his place yesterday, he wasn't there, either. And there were two cars parked in the front courtyard. Unless he owns *three* cars, he'd gone for a walk. And given how deserted it is where he lives, I doubt it."

"Maybe he's away. He may have taken a taxi to the airport."

I think of the washing machine of wet clothes. The glass of red wine and the plate with uneaten tapas. The fruit bowl with swarming fruit flies.

"It looked more like he'd left the farm in a hurry," I say. "Like he'd fled?"

"On foot?"

I shrug. "Maybe the police called by late at night while he was eating a midnight snack. And so he panicked and fled through the back door."

"That would be just like him. To run away."

"But why hasn't he returned to the farm?"

"He must have his reasons."

I think of the deserted area, the long shadows of the trees and the silence.

"Maybe he's hiding in the woods?" I say. "Like a war veteran."

"He's never been to war."

"No, but ..." I shrug. "Some experiences are so traumatic that you're no longer able to be part of society."

I call the number again.

"Unfortunately, the person you are calling cannot be reached. Please leave a message after the beep." I hang up without saying anything.

"How long has it been since you saw him?" I ask.

"Six years."

"When we got married?"

One blink.

"So you broke off contact when we got married?"

One blink.

"But ... why?"

"It got out of hand."

"What?"

Steen looks at the black computer screen and a few seconds pass before he answers.

"A few days after the wedding with our sister ... He claimed that he wasn't the one who'd touched my hamster. But there was something in his eyes. Something scary. It was lying completely stiff in the cage and I tried to wake it up. And suddenly, he was standing in the doorway of my room looking at me and smiling."

I press a computer key to get the screen back. Look at the boy with the red tie and tense expression.

"I couldn't prove anything," says Steen. "But a few months later, I was going to an important football match. I had trained really hard, and then … just before we left, my brother pushed me down a flight of stairs and broke my arm."

"Seriously?"

"Things started to disappear from my room, too. Everything I really liked."

"And it started after that wedding?"

One blink.

"I stopped taking girls home. If they went to the toilet or to get a glass of water, they always came back completely white in the face and said they had to go. I have no idea what my brother said to them."

"And you don't think it was something you imagined? Maybe you were more affected by what happened to your sister than you knew. Maybe you were overanalysing?"

"Maybe. But you should've seen that hamster. Its eyes were completely dilated. As if it had seen a ghost."

He emphasised the last word and I look over my shoulder at the door. Have a sudden feeling that we're being watched.

I shake off the feeling. Remind myself that more than thirty years have passed since that wedding.

"But if he was like that," I say, "why did you first cut off contact when we got married?"

"He was still my brother. So I tried. I was also afraid that he would do the same to you as he had done to the other girls."

"And you haven't seen him in six years?"

"Not on purpose, at least. I'm pretty sure I've seen him drive past our house. And he can just ring all of a sudden. That's why I've changed my number so many times. But he always ends up getting it. And it's hard to be anonymous when you want customers."

"What does he ring you about?"

"Unpleasant things. He can get really angry. And when you got pregnant …"

"What?"

"Just stay away from him."

"When I got pregnant, what?"

"He has never had a girlfriend, and I don't know if it was him who didn't want one or our parents who forbade it. Either way, he continued to wear the wedding ring after our sister was buried."

I look at the boy's slender hand. The thin ring on his finger. The girl is wearing a similar one.

"He became strangely silent and closed off," says Steen. "When I asked him why he didn't take the ring off, he said: *Til death do us part.*"

A cold shiver runs down my spine.

"That was after that wedding," says Steen. "His perception of what was normal seemed to be shattered."

"He's dangerous," I say.

Steen frowns, as if trying to find the right words.

"I just think we should stay away from him. Don't contact him."

"You're not afraid of him at all?"

"Not anymore."

"But he sounds so ..." I circle an index finger around my temple.

"Don't worry. He's had a tough time, but he would never do anything to anyone. All that was years ago. I'm sure he's moved on."

"But you said yourself that when I got pregnant ..."

"Yeah, that. That was hard for him."

"Hard how?"

"We should just stay away from him."

Steen looks at the computer until the screen turns black again.

"It ruined everything," he says. "That she died. That they got married."

I think of the dead hamster and the broken arm.

"My brother became so jealous," says Steen. "Everything I had, he wanted, too."

Somewhere inside me I can feel something take shape. An unnerving connection that's still foggy.

The sound of the doorbell pulls me from my thoughts. The clock on the wall says 18:57.

I close the computer, pull my cardigan closer around me, and go out into the hall. My hand rests for a few seconds on the handle before I open the door.

Outside is Lotus's mother. Her blond curls are wet from the rain and she's not wearing a jacket.

"Sorry for the inconvenience," she says. "I just wanted to ask you something."

"What?"

Her blue eyes flicker around the garden and out onto the gravel path behind us.

"Can I come in for a moment? Just five minutes?"

I think of the clotheshorse, the cloth nappies. The packet of incontinence pads and the pink washbasin.

"Give me just two seconds."

I put the door on the latch. Leave her in the rain and try not to make too much noise as I move the baby things into the bedroom.

"What?" whispers Steen from the double bed.

I put my finger to my lips and close his door. Pull the handle an extra time to make sure it won't open again.

Out on the doorstep, Henriette has taken out her phone.

"I'm sorry if it doesn't suit," she says.

"It's fine. Come in."

We go into the living room and sit on the couch. She sits right on the edge. There are small beads of sweat on her upper lip. She wrinkles her nose and looks around.

"Does it smell weird in here?" I ask. "Sorry. We had ... damp in the basement."

"Okay."

"Would you like something? A cup of coffee?"

"No thanks."

"A glass of water?"

"Are you home alone?"

"My husband is asleep."

"Okay." She looks towards the bedroom door. Keeps looking at it as she wipes her lip.

"You wanted to ask me something?" I say.

She nods. "They said he looked Asian. The man who took her. Did you see him?"

"No."

"What about your husband? He's Asian, too, isn't he? Do you think he knows anything? Maybe it's someone he knows?"

"Not every Asian all over the world knows each other."

"But still. It's not exactly crowded with them here. Maybe we could go in and ask him?"

"If he knew anything, he would have told me."

She rubs her eyes. When she opens them again, they are shiny and she shakes her head.

"I'm sorry, I'm just so … desperate. I've been driving around all day. Right up until it got dark. Then I went home. But I couldn't bear to be at home. All her stuff is everywhere."

"I thought you were at your mother's? Isn't that what you told the police?"

"I had to say something to be allowed to go. I've been looking everywhere for her. Her favourite playground. By the river. In the forest. All the way up and down the coast. Then I thought she might have gone home, but …" She shakes her head again.

"There's a reason they recommend people not to be alone," I say.

"I just couldn't stand being with the crisis psychologist. Just sitting and talking. I just couldn't."

She picks up her phone and turns on the screen light. "The police say they'll call when there's news. But they don't. I've been driving around for hours. I've been everywhere. *Everywhere.* And then I remembered. About him, the man."

"And that's why you came here?"

She nods. Looks towards the bedroom again.

"What about the girl on work placement?" she says. "I tried to google her, but there are hundreds of Camilla Hansens. Do you have her number?"

"You'd have to ask Helen about that."

"I've already spoken to her, but she won't give me the number. She says I should contact the police. But I just want to talk to her, you know?"

"We've all given a statement. I'm sure the police will find out what happened."

"Maybe I could try asking him? Your husband?"

"I understand. But I assure you he doesn't know anything."

I pat her on the arm.

She pushes my hand away.

"You don't understand a thing. You don't have any children."

It feels like I'm being electrocuted. My hand falls back into my lap and my throat tightens.

"Sorry," she mumbles.

I try to nod.

"Sorry," she mumbles again.

I have a hard time getting the air through my constricted neck. Can't bear to stay sitting.

"I think I'll go out and make that coffee," I say.

As the water runs through the coffee machine, I take out my phone. There are a number of messages from Helen. Something about an extra parent-teacher meeting. Something about my sick leave and some formalities we need to keep track of when we get a chance. *Hope you're okay?* it says several times.

The coffee machine is full of limescale. The water runs slowly and with difficulty and I think of Steen's blood and bodily fluids. I think about the delivery room and the baby's little cold body. The placental abruption. The lack of oxygen. The absence of symptoms. Lotus's pigtails bouncing up and down.

I rub my temples. It's all merging together, like when you put things in a blender.

My phone vibrates on the table.

Baby 14 days: Remember vitamin D.

I stand for a long time looking at the reminder I wrote for myself in the calendar. There's a little red alarm bell next to it.

I tap the screen. Hold down my finger.

Delete.

Neither of us really wants the coffee after it's poured. Henriette keeps picking up her phone and looking at it.

"I just feel like I should be doing something," she says. "Something. Do you know what I mean?"

I nod.

"I called her father, but he didn't answer. I don't know if I should drive to his house and check whether she's there."

"I'm sure the police have already been there."

"I don't trust him. I called his work and they said he hadn't come in today."

"Where does he work?"

"In Herning. At the Great Wall of China. I mean, the restaurant."

Something moves inside me.

Maybe he got someone to help him? Maybe Lotus's father knows an older Asian-looking man?

"When you rang the restaurant," I say. "Did they say if anyone else hadn't turned up for work?"

"Why?"

"Just …" I hesitate. "Sorry, that was a strange question."

I look out into the garden. Up at the grey sky.

"I'm sorry," she says. "About before. I shouldn't have said that."

"It's fine."

"I can't imagine what that must have been like. I'm so scared … so horrified that my daughter is dead and you saw your own …"

"It's fine. You don't need to say anything."

She nods several times in a row. Puts her hands on her thighs.

"Well, I won't take up any more of your time, either."

It's a relief to get up.

We go out to the hall together, and Henriette buttons her coat crookedly.

I open the door for her and my stomach drops.

A police car has stopped at the end of the driveway. The engine hums as if it has just arrived.

"Oh no." Henriette's hands go to her mouth.

The police car shuts off the engine and the doors open. It's Torben and Dagmar again.

They push the garden gate open and catch sight of us in the doorway.

Torben raises a hand in greeting. It's a limp hand, and Henriette's breathing increases.

"Oh no," she says. "Oh God."

The officers walk through the front garden, up to the house. They shake both our hands.

"How did you know I was here?" asks Henriette.

"It isn't you we've come to talk to," says Dagmar. "It's Eva."

CHAPTER 22

The wrought-iron gate creaks in its hinges as I push it open. The smell of box-wood and wet flowers is pervasive, and I wince as the gate slams behind me.

Klara opens it again. Fumbles with her car keys.

"Wait for me," she says, but I'm already on my way down the gravel path.

While Torben and Dagmar were talking, it felt as if my trachea was constricting more and more, and I pushed the chair back before they were finished. Staggered out to the car. My baby.

My hands shook and the driveway was floating and I didn't dare start the engine. Instead, I called Klara and asked her to drive me. I couldn't breathe.

I can't breathe.

The drizzle makes the graveyard shine in the glow of the many candles and lamps. An almost full moon has appeared above us, making the evening appear silvery and illuminated. Klara's wellies crunch against the gravel behind me. She has a bouquet of flowers and an umbrella that she's trying to hold over me, but I'm walking too fast. Can't get the inhalations into my lungs properly. It's as if my chest is being crushed, like the baptism gown that was laid in a flat, hard box and put down in the basement.

Police tape has been set up around the grave. Red-and-white-striped plastic, just like at the kindergarten.

All the solar lamps are lit. The tiny flames flutter from side to side behind the glass, illuminating the piles of flowers.

The newspaper crackles as Klara unpacks the bouquet. She stands with it in her hand for a moment, looking around the grave. All the vases are full. Buried metal cones with yellow marigolds and brown rainwater along the edge. Square granite vases with roses in different stages of decay.

Klara lays her bouquet on the ground. Blue-purple asters and white hemp-agrimony that she must have picked in a hurry before leaving home.

"I didn't bring anything with me," I say. "I didn't even think of it."

"They're from both of us."

I put my hands in my pockets. Take them out again. Can't figure out how to be in my body. Some of the flowers on the grave look fresh. The thought that someone must have laid flowers on an empty grave makes my blood vessels feel like they're filled with cold shards of glass.

"Were you in the middle of dinner?" I ask.

"No, no. It's fine."

I nod.

"Thanks for driving me."

"Of course."

"I had promised Steen I wouldn't leave him again, but the thought of staying at home …" I shake my head. "And I couldn't stand Dagmar and Torben staying with him. Even though it was thoughtful of them to offer."

"He'll be fine," says Klara. "We're not that far away."

We stand in silence for a moment. The red-and-white police tapes move every time the rain falls on them.

"So it was the stonemason who discovered it?" she asks.

I nod.

"They were here early this morning," I say. "With the headstone. They had to move some of the vases to make room, and then they saw that something had been written on the ground in red paint."

"What had been written?"

"Torben said it was impossible to decipher, but that it looked like Chinese characters."

The grave goes blurry in front of me and I tilt my head back. Feel the heavy, cold drops of rain hitting my face.

Klara asks about something I don't hear. It takes all my strength to stay upright. Breathing. Can't see it. Deserted night. Earth being moved. The tiny coffin.

"Eva?"

There's sound again. Klara is holding me by the shoulder.

"Shall we find a bench?" she asks.

I shake my head.

She releases my shoulder slowly. As if making sure I can stand on my own.

We look at the grave for a long time without saying anything.

"It's a nice headstone," she says.

I nod. The stonemason was right. It has turned out beautifully. The little silver-plated dummy is so detailed. The granite is coarse-grained and is the same colour as salmon tartar. Truly a stone for a princess, as Steen said when we found it among the samples on display.

In engraved, black letters stands *Our much-missed daughter*. Below are two dates with a hyphen in between.

The same date twice.

"We should have given her a name," I say. "*Our daughter* ... it could be anyone."

"We know who it is," says Klara. "Isn't that the most important thing?"

I shrug again.

Beside the headstone is a little metal windmill that's not turning. I can smell the piles of wet compost and stagnant puddles, the light green moss and the soil.

As always, I try to guess where her face is, which way her body is turned down there, underground.

But there is no body.

Klara strokes my arm.

"They'll find her. The police know what they're doing."

I nod. Think of how I said exactly the same thing to Lotus's mother. That I said it without believing it.

"They're setting up surveillance now," says Klara. "In the graveyard. Whoever is exhuming people, it's going to stop here."

I push the windmill. It rotates slowly. Stops again.

"Doesn't it look a little creepy?" I say. "That the same date is written twice?"

"Do you think so?"

"It's not even true, is it?"

"Something had to be written."

"But if you didn't know, would you not think that the child was born alive? Would you not think that the child didn't die until after birth?"

"I don't know."

"I would."

The most accurate would have been to write the date of conception and the date of when the heart sound disappeared. But Steen didn't want that.

"I think it looks fine," says Klara.

"You're just saying that so as not to upset me."

She moves the umbrella over into the other hand and puts an arm around me. Pulls me into a side hug that makes our rain jackets crackle against each other. We stand for a moment, leaning against each other, listening to the raindrops falling into vases and onto the wet ground.

"It's a nice grave," she says. "A very nice grave. Just like she would have wished."

I want to say something, but my mouth is completely dead. I look at the silver-plated dummy and the black letters. Try to breathe properly and not just in the upper part of my chest.

"You should have put wellies on," says Klara. "Aren't you freezing?"

I shake my head.

"You're always freezing. Even I feel cold today. I'm usually always sweating."

"You don't have to constantly find something to say."

The gravel crunches as she changes position.

I look towards the stand of green watering cans. The other day, I started doing something straightaway. Pulling up weeds, raking and watering, removing spruce needles and dirt from the lanterns. Making noise.

People often stand so petrified at the other graves that I feel like pushing them in the same way that I feel like pushing Steen.

Today I'm the one standing like that.

"Did you know," I say, "that in some places in Greenland the ground is so hard that it's impossible to dig? That's why the coffins are placed directly on the ground."

"Eva, sweetie …"

I stuffed my hands in my pockets again. Try to imagine a graveyard of coffins in the open.

From the corner of my eye, I can see Klara looking at me. I can feel her gaze like a little nervous insect. I have to stop telling her what I've been googling. Only Steen understands.

We stand in silence under the umbrella's black plastic sky and look at the empty grave. Above us, dark clouds pass over the sky like ragged cobwebs. The moonlight flickers before illuminating the graveyard again.

"Torben said it was written on the coffin, too," I say. "Chinese characters similar to those found at Steen's father's grave."

"So the same person did it?"

"Looks like it."

"Do the police have any suspects?"

"Not as far as I know. But they probably can't tell us anyway."

"But Torben often tells you more than he should, doesn't he? Because he's friends with Steen?"

I shrug.

The forensic team made an effort to leave everything as it was. Except for the police tape, the grave looks like itself. Still, everything looks wrong. Like when a home looks different after a burglary.

Again, I think of Greenland and the hard ground. When I read about the bare coffins, it gave me the same feeling as when I think I've forgotten to lock the door at home. I thought of vandalism and graffiti and drunk teenagers climbing around on things, and kleptomaniacs and a thousand other scary things that only the sleeping pills could stop.

But she was taken from me anyway. Even though she was buried deep into the ground, she was taken from me a second time.

"It's so creepy," says Klara. "An old man and a newborn. Who is that sick in the head?"

I look at the many flowers. Their cut stems.

According to the Malagasy Christian faith, man is not made of dust and ashes, but of the bodies of the ancestors. Once a year, the graves are opened and the dead are carried out into the open, where they are wrapped in silk, and the families dance around the corpses until they are again lain in the grave. It's a way to show respect. Taking the lonely bodies out of the cold earth and giving them love.

This time, I don't tell Klara what I'm thinking.

"Lotus's mother came to our house tonight," I say. "She was there when the police arrived."

"What did she want?"

"Just to hear if I knew anything."

She strokes me on the back and I can't help but count. It has only been six days since the funeral. She must still have skin and lips and eyelashes and …

Klara's hand stops on my back.

"Sis?" she says. "Should we not go? You're as white as snow."

"I want to stay a little longer."

"You're soaked to the skin."

"I don't care. And I'm not going to back work, either. Whatever you say."

She takes a breath.

"We'll stay here," she says. "We'll stay here until you are ready."

The rain streams down over her black umbrella, hangs on the edge for a moment before the drops fall.

"But I really have to pee," she says. "Is it okay if I just run inside?"

She points to the church and I nod.

"You take this while I go in."

She hands me the umbrella and I accept it. Listen to the crunching sound as she walks. The rain sounds louder now that I'm on my own. It makes holes in the surfaces of the puddles. Slams against the umbrella, making everything seem porous.

My dad says that when it rains, it's God crying.

Again I feel the sucking sensation of time going backwards inside me. The rain drums on the empty grave and down into the washbasin as the midwife washes the baby's tiny, motionless body. She does it slowly and carefully, and I wonder whether she checked the temperature of the water, or if she just turned on the cold tap because it doesn't matter.

We were allowed to keep her for twenty-four hours. The midwife put on a little white hat, just like the one the living children got. Steen placed her gently in the carry-cot and took her out of the hospital. I stumbled along behind them as I leaned on the wall. The pad between my thighs felt huge.

When we got home, we put her in the cradle. Sat next to each other, as we both held on to the edge of the cradle.

The house was so quiet. I'd read stacks of books on how to make your baby stop crying. And now she was just lying there.

We agreed to go for a walk. It had taken us days to find the perfect stroller, and there was something nice about using it. That it wasn't a complete waste.

We drove around along the fields and down to the beach. It was so strangely quiet, the whole thing. I kept expecting her to start crying.

I suggested that we drive to Herning. A place with more sounds.

The sky was very blue that day. People were sitting outside drinking coffee and there was a man playing the accordion. We bought two soft ices with sprinkles. Steen was wearing a yellow T-shirt and we took turns pushing her.

As we walked through the pedestrian street with the buggy, people smiled at us. Steen took my hand. Held it tight.

In the evening, she sat in the baby bouncer while we ate. Neither of us said anything. Not even while we were rinsing off the dishes and putting them in the dishwasher. Outside, the late summer sky grew darker, and we put on her pyjamas. Sang "Hush Little Baby" with voices that kept disappearing.

The next morning, we drove back to the hospital in silence. I could see her in the rearview mirror. The little head with the white hospital hat. Steen turned on the car radio. Turned it off again.

At the hospital, we were given an hour and a half to say goodbye. I don't know why it was just an hour and a half. I don't know why they said that in advance. I kept looking at the clock while we were alone with her.

It was now we were supposed to cry and kiss and say goodbye. But we didn't do anything. Stood completely stiff like two switched-off bodies.

The door was opened and the nurse came in. She said that in a little while a psychologist would come and talk to us. Then she rolled the little cradle out of the room and closed the door behind her.

We didn't wait for the psychologist. We opened the door and walked down the long corridors, stood silent in the elevator, walked through the flickering lights of the parking garage, and drove home. We didn't say a word to each other on the road.

When we locked ourselves in the house, Steen said, "I'm going to go to bed."

He went into the bedroom and closed the door behind him. He stayed in there for a long time.

I looked up at the sky. I looked at the cradle that was empty, wishing I could sleep.

I made food even though I wasn't hungry. Pasta. Cream. Leeks that weren't rinsed properly. I called Steen.

I called again.

I pushed the chair back and went into the bedroom. His body lay in a strange position, and his eyes were flushed with fear.

"Sweetheart?" I said.

"I can't move," he whispered. "I can't move at all."

There are footsteps in the gravel behind me, and I detach my gaze from the headstone. Look around the rain-soaked graveyard.

A man in a black raincoat is standing at the water's edge with his hood pulled up. There's something familiar about him.

I squint and look at his stooping figure. He has his hands in his pockets and is looking in the direction of the unrecognisable graves. Raindrops fall from the hood of the raincoat. He makes a groove in the gravel with the tip of one shoe, covers it again.

Maybe he can feel my eyes on him, because he looks up and towards me. The hood casts a shadow over his face, hiding it. Still, I sense that we make eye contact. We stand staring at each other like that for a nerve-racking moment. Then he pulls his eyes away and starts walking towards the exit.

I feel like calling after him, but don't know what to say. Don't know whether I know him or not. The gate creaks as it falls in behind him.

At the same time, Klara comes walking over from the church. Her rain jacket crackles every time she swings her arms.

"Typical," she says as she reaches me. "There's never any toilet paper. Just as well I had Kleenex in my bag."

"Did you see him?" I ask.

"Who?"

"The man who was just here. He was standing by the watering cans. When he noticed us, he hurried out."

Klara looks towards the water cans. Then towards the exit.

"I didn't see anyone," she says.

"Right there." I point.

"Sis." She puts her forehead against mine and her skin is warm against my cold. "Come on, Let's go home."

"Are you sure you didn't see anyone? A man? Over by the unmarked graves?"

She follows my gaze. Shrugs.

"Not really. Maybe. I was focused on coming over to you."

I look towards the church. The worn white tower and the cross up there.

"Here, let me hold that again." She takes the umbrella from me and holds it over us.

"Why were you gone so long?" I say. "Didn't you just have to pee?"

"Sometimes nature demands more of us." She pats her bag. "Long live Kleenex."

She smiles, but I don't return it. Can't get rid of the eerie feeling of having overlooked something.

"I think someone is after us," I say. "It can't be random, all this."

"After you how?"

"The teddy bear is gone, too."

"Which teddy bear?"

"The one that was on her coffin in the church. A brown teddy bear with a pink satin heart that said *Love you to the moon and back*. Don't you remember it? After the funeral, I put it there." I point to the grave.

"Oh yeah, that one," says Klara.

"Last time I was here, it was still there, so …"

I stop. Stare at the grave where I spot something.

Between the many full vases, half hidden behind some cut roses, is a paper flower. The stem is made of steel wire, inserted directly into the ground.

I bend forward and pull it up. It's neatly folded. The paper is half dissolved by the rain, but I can still see how carefully it is made.

Origami, I think, turning the flower in my hand. A line of black letters stands out on one of the small, white petals.

My heart beats fast as I pull out the wire stalk and unfold the paper. It's hard not to do it without breaking it. Petal by petal, I open the flower until I end up with a piece of paper in my hand. It looks like it's been pulled out of a book.

I hold it up to the light and feel as if cement is solidifying around my feet as I read.

Oh, that I had a child
As red as blood and as black as ebony.
Not very long after, she had a daughter

"What's wrong?" says Klara.

"It's from 'Snow White,'" I say, showing her.

CHAPTER 23

"Colder. Very cold."

The dress rustles around her legs as she changes direction. She edges in between furniture and things. Tries to look behind them but has a hard time bending over.

"Still cold."

She turns around. Goes the opposite way. Her nostrils flare every time she draws in air.

"Warmer. Warm on your hair."

She looks up. Notices the protruding paw. The weight makes the lampshade hang crooked, and she stands on her toes. Can't reach up due to the rope around her wrists.

I do it for her. Take hold of the teddy bear's arm and get it down from the lamp.

It's dusty from lying up there, so I brush it off. Stroke a finger over the pink satin heart. The lyrics on the heart echo the song I can't get out of my head.

And the moon is the only light we'll see

"You must not cry," I say. "You found it."

I hand her the teddy bear, but she can't accept it. The blood rushes inside. I'm so tense it's hard to maintain my composure.

I help her back into place. Look forward once again to the place I have found for us. We won't be disturbed here. The light is dim and everything is quiet. Only the chest freezer emits a deep, friendly hum.

For now, she has to lie on the floor, but it's only until I get the last piece of furniture in place.

She's still crying.

I put my index finger against my lips.

"Remember," I say. "In fairy tales, all wishes can come true. Listen for yourself to what the teddy bear is saying."

I hold it up to her ear. Change my voice and whisper, "Are you ready to meet your little sister?"

CHAPTER 24

We drive home in silence, Klara behind the wheel and me next to her. Her car smells of dog. On the floor are a kid's storybook and the wrapping from a dried fig bar. I follow the windshield wipers with my eyes, thinking of the nappy I'll need to change when I get home.

"Anyone could have put that paper flower there," says Klara.

"Maybe."

"And why on earth would he spy on us afterwards?"

"I don't know."

Her gaze alternates between me and the road. I can feel it even though I keep looking at the windshield wipers.

"Sis ..." She lowers her voice, speaks to me in the same way as when she has to get people to let go of their dying pets.

"With everything that's happened, I understand that your head is probably reeling, or whatever they call it. But you have to keep yourself together. For Steen's sake."

I nod slowly. I look at the raindrops flowing together on the windshield and have an uncomfortable feeling that my cells are doing the opposite. Flowing farther and farther away from each other.

The baby's tiny body in the cradle. On the autopsy table. Naked skin against steel. The doctor didn't share any details afterwards, but I pictured

134

it quite clearly. Strange hands in rubber gloves dissecting her as though she were a fruit. A beautiful paper flower that was folded backwards, back to nothing.

"Have you given any more thought to calling the hospital?" asks Klara.

"Not really."

My mirror image drips with the rain down the car window. Klara switches on the headlights and the surroundings emerge from the darkness. In a meadow, the sheep raise their heads as we drive past. Their eyes light up.

The headlights catch a sign pointing the way to a stone dolmen, and I think of all the dead down there, under the dolmen. Of how long it must have taken to pull the heavy stones.

"Things can't continue like this, Eva."

Klara turns up the speed of the wipers.

"You need help. Someone to talk to. Especially now that …" She shakes her head. "Are you sure I shouldn't talk to Steen about being admitted?"

"Things are actually going a little better."

"How?"

"He's started talking more to me. Today, for example, before I rang you, we talked more than we ever have before. He told me about all kinds of things from his childhood. Things I never knew."

"Okay?"

"About his parents. About his family. He was open in a way I've never experienced before."

"Okay?"

"What do you mean by *okay*? *Okay*? Do you not think it's a good thing or what?"

"Of course. It's just …"

"What?"

"Nothing."

Klara drives up to the front of the house and turns off the engine. We stay in a car that is no longer running. My mouth feels dry.

"Sometimes I wonder if it was a bad idea that we took her home," I say. "Maybe it would've been better if they'd kept her in the hospital. A plaster needs to be ripped off quickly, right? Maybe we made things worse for ourselves. I mean … Before that day, Steen was okay, right? He was upset and shocked when we were told the baby was dead in my womb, of course.

But he still got out of bed. He could open his own computer and go to the toilet himself. We still had a normal life, you know?"

"That's what they recommended you did," Klara says. "To take her home as part of the grieving process."

"But they also said it was our decision. That it was a matter for each individual what felt most right."

I look out the window. Swallow without having anything to swallow.

When the Egyptians mummified their dead, it was about getting all the moisture out of the body. It's the moisture that makes us rot and I should stop googling so much. Now I can't stop thinking about mummies and what a baby looks like after six days underground.

Klara opens the seat belt and pushes the door open. Stops.

"Hey," she says. "What's happened to your broom?"

We stand next to each other, in the shadow of the shed, looking at the two brooms without handles. They lie in the grass like heads after decapitation. It looks like someone tried to push them under the red currant bush but was interrupted.

"Someone's been here," I say.

Klara looks like she wants to repeat her thoughts about me having to keep myself together. But she just stands looking at the broom heads.

"I agree," she says.

The keys clink in my hand and we keep our jackets on as we enter the house. Klara turns on the lights. Her rain jacket says *scritch, scritch,* and the police are still looking for the five-year-old kindergarten child who this morning ... I point the remote control at TV 2 News and the screen turns black. Silence descends over the living room, and I look at the clotheshorse of cloth nappies, the bucket, and *Grimms' Fairy Tales.* The darkness outside makes the room seem smaller, and I get the same feeling as at the grave: Everything looks as it usually does, but something feels wrong.

"Hello?" I say.

Klara walks through the living room checking the window latches. The house is completely quiet, except for the uneven buzz of a bluebottle.

In the bedroom, Steen is sleeping with his mouth open. Enough light is coming in through the door so I don't have to turn on the ceiling light and risk waking him up.

I stroke his hair gently. Stand for a moment looking at his eyelids and the open mouth before I go back to Klara.

She pulls on the patio door. Shakes her head and goes out into the kitchen.

I remain standing in the living room looking at the bookshelf. The picture above the fireplace. Our smiling faces in the sunshine in front of the town hall, and it's like a spot-the-difference.

But I only see our living room.

Klara comes out of the kitchen again, dusting off her hands.

"There are no signs of a break-in," she says. "No broken doors or windows."

"Wait," I say.

The bottom drawer of the writing bureau isn't closed properly. I pull it out and my heart beats faster.

"There." I point to the drawer. "The box of long, white candles is gone."

"Do you not think maybe you've just forgotten using them?"

"I haven't lit candles since Steen's paralysis. I'm also sure there were two boxes of matches."

"Okay, so two broomsticks, a box of candles, and some matches are gone. But the television and your jewellery are still here."

She looks at me and I think the anxiety in my eyes infects her.

"What do we do?" she says. "Should I call the police?"

I look down at the drawer without answering. The cat plays with the mouse. Dad always held me back when I wanted to stop one of the bony farm cats in their brutal game. The cat pawed the mouse so it fell down and nudged it to make it get up again. When the mouse was about to give up, the cat let it run, let it sense its flight and freedom. Only then was it killed.

"If you're sure those things are gone, we have to ring them," says Klara.

"I don't want them here again. When they came to tell us about the grave, Dagmar was ready to call Doctor Møller. She said Steen should be in treatment. Torben said so, too. I don't want them in my home again."

"But this could be an opportunity to actually get him treated. At some point, he's going to *have to be* looked at again. And ..." Her eyes flicker. "And maybe he's worse than we realise."

"What do you mean by that?"

She runs the zip of her raincoat up and down.

"What, Klara?"

"Nothing. It was just … Nothing."

"Out with it."

"I was just thinking … When we were sitting in the car and you told me that things were going better with Steen. That he had started talking more and stuff like that."

"Yeah?"

"Yeah, I just thought … I've heard that when a traumatised person suddenly livens up, it can be a sign that … well … that the person has decided to put an end to their life."

I stare at her.

"It's just something I've heard," she says. "That when a person is really in shock, they're paralysed to act and out of danger. But as soon as their mood improves just a little …"

"Steen is paralysed in case you forgot. How was he supposed to … at all?"

"Of course," she says. "It was just a thought."

"A pretty ill-considered thought."

"Yeah, it was. Sorry."

I look in the direction of the bedroom door and think of *paralysed to act. Paralysed.*

"Sorry," Klara says again. "It was stupid. And, of course, it's you who decides what we do. I wouldn't ever call the police if you didn't want me to."

I picture how he lay in bed. His closed eyes and open mouth. Did I even listen to see if he was breathing? Maybe he bit off his tongue and choked? Maybe he … I get up abruptly and walk to the bedroom door. My heart is pounding as I step into the semidark room.

He's lying like before, with his eyes closed and his mouth open. I lay my ear on his chest. He's not breathing.

A panicked feeling consumes me and I'm about to shake him as I hear him inhale. Then exhale. His breathing is calm and regular and I start when Klara puts her hand on my shoulder.

"I can sleep here tonight if you want me to?" she says. "I just have to see to a few practical things, but then I can come back. And I can bring a midnight snack. Pork chops. You can always eat those, can't you?"

Steen's chest is hot against my ear. I can't stop listening to his breathing. How could I not hear it before? How could I even believe ... I look at Klara. Look at her with a new look. Her wide, rough hands that kill animals. That can unlock Dad's barn door without shaking. Hands that pull pigs into life and push others into death.

"Eva?" she says. "Do you want me to come by later?"

"You don't have to do that."

"Are you sure?"

One blink.

"What?" she says.

"Yes."

She looks at me and Steen in turn.

"If you want me to ring the police for you, just say, won't you? Or if there's something else I can do. Anything."

One blink.

"And forget what I said before, okay? About Steen."

I don't answer. Keep looking at her hands.

"Just forget it, okay?" she says.

One blink.

She looks at her watch.

"I have to go. Will you be all right?"

I get up from the bed and we go out into the hall together.

"Thanks for taking me to the graveyard," I say.

She gives me a hug that smells of fresh air and hand sanitiser.

"Of course," she says. "Like I always say: No animal is as faithful as a sister."

I stay standing by the living room window and watch her wave from the car before she drives off. One hand on the steering wheel, one in the air, and I keep picturing them long after she's driven off. Her wide, strong hands that have gradually come to touch my husband as much as my own.

The afternoon he lay suddenly paralysed in bed, I didn't know who I was supposed to ring. That annoys me now.

I look towards the shed. Look at the two broom heads that someone left on the lawn.

I think about how long Klara was in the toilet while we were at the graveyard. My sense of time is not the best at the moment, but I think I must have been alone for at least twenty minutes. Maybe longer?

As long as there was no one in the toilet?

I think of the taxidermied animals in Hvide Sande.

Dead animals. Veterinarian.

Dad who handed my wedding invitation back and said they wouldn't be coming.

Klara, who was sitting next to him and joined in Mum's silence. No matter how much I raised my voice and said that they had bloody well only met Steen twice. That you shouldn't judge a person so quickly, and if they refused to see him, then they wouldn't be seeing me again, either.

"So be it," muttered Dad, and a little later all three of them got up. Left me sitting alone at the dining table while Mum washed up and the other two put on wellies.

I think of Dad and Klara alone in the pigsty. Their whispering voices. Their calm while they selected which pigs were to go to the slaughterhouse.

I think of all the times I stood with my back to Klara as she examined my husband. All the medicine in her bag. Strong medicine intended for horses and pigs. I think you can easily make it to the house from the graveyard and back in twenty minutes.

The Ga-Jol box rattles as I shake out a handful. I eat them while I wonder. Rub my face hard.

Steen is still lying in the double bed with his eyes closed. I sit on the edge of the bed and let my fingers slide through his hair. It's getting greasy because it's been so long since I washed it.

I put my ear to his chest. Listen to his breathing. He's still asleep. That's nearly all he does now. As if he's getting more and more tired. A heavy, lifeless sleep.

As I listen, his breathing seems to disappear again and I press my ear harder against his chest. Harder.

"Eva?"

My body jumps. I straighten up and meet his eyes. He looks asleep.

"Sorry," I say. "Did I wake you up?"

"Are you back?"

"Klara's headed off again. Was everything okay here?"

One blink.

"Was anyone here while we were gone?"

"Who?"

"I mean, did you hear anything? Any noises?"

"I was asleep."

I straighten the edge of the bed-wetting sheet. "Do you think we could get by without Klara if we had to?"

"If we had to?"

"If we asked her not to come anymore."

"Why would we do that?"

"I don't know. I'm just so …" I rub my face again.

The bluebottle rubs its head with its forelegs. It's sitting in the middle of the back of my hand. The bathroom light makes the large, blue body shine metallically. Again and again, it cleans its eyes and mouth. As if there is something it can't get off.

Zinc ointment, washcloths, plastic bags. I take things down from the bathroom shelf and change Steen's nappy while I think of Klara's bouquet of flowers and the man by the unmarked graves.

Oh, that I had a child.

Things can't continue like this, Eva.

Feel so exhausted that it hurts my body.

When I'm finished changing him, I sit on the edge of the bed.

"Can I lie with you for a while?" I ask.

One blink.

I crawl under the duvet and lie down in the same way as him. On my back with my arms down along the side. The daddy longlegs is still hanging on the ceiling. Hasn't moved at all.

I listen to the silence. Steen's breathing. The rotating drone of the police helicopter still flying around the area.

"Maybe we could turn her room into a guest room?" I say.

"We never have guests."

"No."

I want to say something more, but my throat contracts. It feels like I have a hole in my stomach that the cold is whistling through, like a smashed window.

I think of the two broom heads and the bottom drawer of the writing bureau that was open. The feeling of having been robbed.

I roll over onto my side and look at Steen's face.

"Are you sure there was no one here while I was gone?"

"Why are you asking me that again?"

"I just want to be sure."

He looks like he's thinking about it.

"Well …" he says. "Maybe."

"Maybe what?"

"I did actually think I heard something at one point."

"Something?"

"Footsteps."

"Where?"

"In the living room, I think. But it was dark. And I was half asleep. I'm not sure."

"Why didn't you say something before?"

"I didn't want to worry you."

"I get more worried when you lie to me."

"But I don't even *know* if anyone was there or if it was just a dream. Everything blurs together so strangely when you're just lying here."

A chill runs through me.

"The key," I whisper.

My pulse beats faster and I look towards the door.

"Our spare key," I say. "The one we keep hidden in the bird table. I'm sure it was in a different position when I got home today."

Suddenly, it all makes sense.

"Of course," I say. "Your father taught you that a bird feeder was the perfect hiding spot. Your brother was able to find the key like this." I snap my fingers.

Only when I see Steen's shocked face does it really dawn on me what that means.

"Your brother, who wants to ruin your life, has had free access to our house."

I raise my voice, frustrated at being so thoughtless.

"Your brother, who kills animals for fun and has a huge rifle hanging up, was able to just wander into our house whenever he wanted!"

"Maybe you were looking at the key the wrong way?"

I get up abruptly. Pace back and forth in the bedroom with quick steps. "Do you know that I take a double dose of sleeping pills? I hear nothing at night. He could be standing right here in our bedroom, aiming at us without me noticing anything."

"Why are you yelling at me?"

"Sorry."

I sit back down on the bed. Run my fingers through my hair and tighten the knot.

I think of earlier today when I came home from work and Steen was lying with his turned-up eyes, mumbling *Leave me alone, I won't*. His distant gaze and the way he said *Eva? Is that you?*

"He *must* have been the one who was here," I say. "He must be out to get you somehow."

I think of the fairy tale torn out of the book. Wu-Pei didn't say anything about the book being ruined. Maybe because it was actually intact when I got it.

"It was the middle of winter, and the snowflakes fell like feathers from the sky," I say.

Steen looks at me with a confused and frightened look and I look at his feet sticking out from under the duvet. His pale skin and black hair. As white as snow, as black as ebony and ...

"The glass coffin," I whisper.

"What?"

"Maybe your brother paralysed you?"

"How?"

"Like in the fairy tale. Snow White lies in a glass coffin, unable to move."

"She's dead."

"Everyone *thinks* she's dead. But if you're dead, you can't wake up again, can you?"

"That makes no sense. How was my brother even ...?"

"He was with your mother at night. A place overflowing with strong medicine. Maybe he poisoned you?"

"With an apple?" he says disbelievingly.

"Or with a pork chop? What do I know? If he has access to our home, it would be easy for him to put something in our food."

"That Mother claims that someone was with her isn't the same thing as there actually being someone there."

"She *saw* a man. And the staff confirmed that she pressed the alarm. I believe her."

I think of the long, quiet corridors. The unlocked doors. The night porter rising from his seat to go round.

"He must have snuck in without anyone seeing him," I say. "Why would he do that if he wasn't up to something?"

Steen stares at me. His eyes are even more frightened than before, but I can't tell whether he's frightened because he believes what I'm saying or because he thinks I'm crazy.

"You yourself said you cut off contact because he was trying to ruin your life," I say. "Maybe he still wants to ruin your life."

"Wouldn't he just kill me then?"

"Maybe that's not enough for him. Maybe he wants you to see him destroy everything you have without you being able to do anything."

I look at Steen's lifeless arms.

"That would be the ultimate nightmare," I say. "To be in full consciousness, but unable to move while your whole life is being destroyed."

Again, I see the images of the dead sister and living brother. I think about how the dead were made alive and how the living came to seem strangely dead.

Isn't that what has happened to Steen now, too? A living death?

The thought is far-fetched, but I can't let go of the little nagging feeling that something is starting to take shape.

My brother became so jealous. Everything I had, he wanted, too.

I look towards the window and the rolled-down blinds. Think of the matches, the candles, the broom handles.

"I think he's trying to tell us something," I say. "The things that are missing. They're a sign somehow. He wants to tell us something."

"What?"

"That's what I can't figure out. There must be something I've overlooked."

I get up from the bed and go back to the living room. Look at the bookshelf and the pictures of our smiling faces while I think of the taxidermied animals. An owl, a raven, a dove. The dead sister in a wedding dress. The paper flower in her hand. The paper flower on the grave. The fairy tale of "Snow White" torn out of the book.

What does he want?

I look in the writing bureau again. Rummage through the drawers, but apart from the candles and matches, everything looks like it usually does.

I go to the coffee table and pick up *Grimms' Fairy Tales*. Sit on the sofa and slowly flip through it. My eyes search the pages. Running over the crooked letters and curved page numbers.

"The Wolf and the Seven Goats." "The Juniper Tree." "Godfather Death."

The farther into the book I get, the more my hope fades. Everything looks normal. "Snow White" is the only fairy tale that's gone.

Then I notice something. In the fairy tale of "The Brave Little Tailor," some of the words are underlined with ballpoint pen.

There he let one <u>stone</u> after another fall on the chest of one of the giants. For a long time the giant was quite unaware of this, but at last he waked up and pushed his comrade, and said, "What are you hitting me for?"

It's hard to read the old-fashioned, slanting letters. Still, I quickly identify the pattern.

They composed themselves again to sleep, and the tailor let fall a <u>stone</u> on the other giant.

I flip a little farther on. Can see that the same word is marked on every single page.

Stone.

… Stone … Stone …

Sten in Danish.

Steen.

CHAPTER 25

The tiger with the long teeth keeps an eye on me as I straighten my hair and look at the handle. Behind the door, I can hear music. It's a slow number. A deep male voice. As I put my ear to the door, I can hear that it's an old version of "Stand by Me."

I rap my knuckles against the door and wait.

No one opens. There's only the scratchy music and the tiger's eyes.

I knock again. Can't bear any more waiting. I didn't dare leave Steen alone today, so I had to wait to come out here until Klara was free. The time is 17:25 and I have a nagging feeling that time is running out. That if I don't figure out how it's all connected soon, it'll be too late.

The song in there gets louder. Maybe she can't hear me knocking?

I grab the handle. None of the residents have a lock on the door, the nurse said. For security reasons, it must be so they can always gain access. *Security.*

Paper flower. Broom handles. Snow White. Lotus, who has now been missing for twenty-eight hours. He has to be hiding somewhere, the brother, and right now Steen's mother is my only chance of finding out where.

My phone beeps in my pocket and I take it out. It's a message from Klara. *Is it the pork tenderloin that's in the red bowl?*

I squint at the tiger on the still-closed door before answering.

Yeah. Hope it's thawed. Took it out of the freezer yesterday. And thanks again!

No prob. Thought it was just what you needed

I answer *Say hi* and put the phone back in my pocket.

After the funeral, the vicar recommended that I come to the weekly midnight service, and there was something about the silence of the night and the organ music, the darkness and the candles that bestowed a calmness I hadn't felt for a long time.

Klara insisted I go there again tonight. She even suggested that I attend the communal dinner at eight o'clock followed by coffee and bingo, too. I'd never have asked her to mind Steen for so long myself, but I felt a sigh of relief when she did. The mere thought of sitting in the quiet church, watching the flickering flame, soothes a little of the unrest I've felt all day.

I gently push down the handle and open the door. The sweet aroma of tea and perfume flows out to meet me. Wu-Pei is standing by an old gramophone with her back to me. She's still wearing the coat with the glass stones. Sways from side to side and appears to be far away.

I clear my throat.

The needle bumps up and down, and she moves in her own rhythm, as if she's hearing a different tune to the one coming from the gramophone.

"Excuse me?" I say. "Wu-Pei?"

She turns around slowly. There's something distant in her gaze, as if she doesn't see me properly. As if she's looking at *anything* other than me.

Then she blinks. Raises her eyebrows.

"Well?" she says. "So you came to save me anyway?"

"What?"

"From my husband."

She turns down the music and nods to the bed with the blue metal legs.

I open my bag and take out *Grimms' Fairy Tales*.

"Have you ever thought that it might not be your husband who was here? But your son?"

"My sons do not live in the realm of the dead. Why would they want to send me to a place where we cannot be together?"

"I don't know. But I'd like to show you something. Can we sit down?"

She remains standing. Looks at the record rotating on the gramophone.

"My daughter had a beautiful singing voice. Like a thousand nightingales."

"Really?"

"That was her favourite song."

"It's a good one."

"King made it."

She takes a photo down from the wall and shows me it. A little girl is standing with a microphone and I shudder as I recognise her. The dead little sister. She looks happy and alive.

"Moon Festival is the fifteenth day of the eighth lunar month," says Wu-Pei. "The whole family unites for a magnificent party with songs and moon cakes in the light of the moon. Both the living and the dead attend."

I look at the girl's smile and thin ankles under a blue dress. The red cheeks and the little hand around the microphone.

"My husband had rented a sound system," says Wu-Pei. "We set it up in the garden under the cherry tree."

"Really?"

"You should have heard her. The air was full of nightingales. We so wanted to catch them. Lock them in a golden cage, like the blue-breasted quail they got for their wedding. So we could listen to her forever."

She lifts the needle and moves it. The song starts over.

When the night has come
And the land is dark

"Then it turned out there was a recording button on the sound system. So I could record her singing."

"Yeah?"

"I do not know where those recordings are now. I took such good care of them. But one day they were gone."

"That's a pity."

"Moon cakes are made from salted duck eggs. Have you tasted them?"

"No?"

"The woman in the moon cannot return to the earth and those she loves. Only when the moon is full can we see the loved ones we are separated from."

"Okay. But, like I said, there was something I would like to show you."

"Is it about my husband?"

"More about your son."

She turns off the gramophone and closes the glass lid. Points at the green velour chair where I sat last time.

"Would you like a cup of tea?"

"No, thank you." I take off my coat and we sit down.

"What about my son?"

"Well, I can't get hold of him. Every time I call, it goes to the answering machine."

"There is a reason it is called the Forbidden City. Not everyone is allowed to go in."

"I see?"

"But I can tell you the way."

She takes a red fan and waves it in front of her face.

"To enter the Imperial Palace, go through the Qianqing Men, the Gate of Heavenly Purity."

"Does he not live in Hvide Sande?"

"It is tradition to write your greatest wish on a piece of paper and hang it on the gate. Perhaps you wish for wealth, beauty, or a magnificent horse. It is best if you write it in Chinese hanzi."

My body grows more and more tense as she speaks.

"From the gate, you enter the private chambers of the imperial family. This is where they hold their wonderful tea parties, where the entire family is gathered."

The fan makes her hair flutter. It's wispy and has a touch of grey, and I think: *You can tell how an animal is doing by looking at its fur.*

"If you see a dragon with five claws, you know you are going in the right direction," she says. "For it symbolises the emperor."

"Does it have anything to do with fairy tales? Here, if you look at this." I flip through the old book and hold it out. "See how some of the pages have been torn out. And words have been underlined elsewhere."

She nods slowly.

"Fairy tales were our secret language."

"How?"

"It takes a long time to learn a new language."

"I'm a fast learner."

She narrows her eyes and looks at me.

"In that case, get the box over there."

She points to an old bookcase with vases and sculptures. On the bottom shelf is a cardboard box, twice the size of a shoebox. It's surprisingly light when I lift it.

I carry it over to her and sit back in my chair.

She lifts the lid of the box and takes out a foam sheet. Puts it on her thighs.

"Once upon a time there was a mother and a father …" She takes something else out of the box. Two dead butterflies, each on their own needles.

"The mother and father wanted a child so badly." She sticks the butterflies into the sheet of foam.

"One day a nightingale flew out of the mulberry tree and threw three mulberries in front of them. The berries grew and became three beautiful children." She reaches back into the box and takes out three new butterflies.

The children were called Peacock Butterfly, Scarce Fritillary, and Mazarine Blue. They were so dainty and so lovely."

She flutters them around.

"No one but the father was allowed to touch them. The father was always afraid that something would break. That something would be lost."

She sticks them in the foam sheet.

"The mother flapped around all alone and wanted to get close again. She had to put on her best Jing mask. She had to play on wooden carp and dance with dragons. The mother butterfly loved the father butterfly so much, and the father butterfly told them fairy tales. About sacred mountains and Death walking through magnificent gardens, his silk kimono blowing around his back, and …"

She sits for a long time looking at the dead butterflies as if she has lost her train of thought. She shakes her head.

"No," she says. "He was better than me. That was not even the one who used to play mother."

She pulls the butterflies out of the foam sheet and puts them back in the box. Closes the lid.

"Was that how he told fairy tales?" I say. "With butterflies?"

"He knew so many."

Her eyes glaze over and I try to imagine it. The father sitting with his children, playing puppet theatre with dead butterflies. It is at once beautiful and eerie.

"So you had to play along?" I say. "With his stories?"

"There were once ten suns in the sky. Such was the children's father. Filled the whole sky. He told fairy tales about monkey kings, turtles, and demons. I read aloud from Grimm and H. C. Andersen. I said: 'You must not lock the past in a cage. You have to set it free, like a bird.' He said that sometimes freedom was more frightening than a cage."

"The past?"

"It can be so great. Like a whole mountain."

She sits for a while looking at the gramophone that's no longer playing.

"Your daughter ..." I say. "What happened to her?"

She picks up the fan again. Waves it with rapid movements.

"If you were to tell it in fairy-tale language?" I say. "Then maybe it would be the tale of 'Snow White'?"

She waves faster.

"Snow White dies," I say. "Then a prince comes and kisses her and they get married."

She keeps waving. Doesn't say anything.

"The prince," I say. "Was it your son? The one who lives in the Imperial Palace?"

For a long time, there is only the swift movement of the fan. Then she nods. Dries under one eye.

"My little prince," she says. "He was so scared to go to sleep. We read until we were completely blue in the face."

"Why was he afraid to sleep?"

"Because then the old emperor came."

"The old emperor?"

"That is what we called him. He had a long, black beard; a long braid; and a silk kimono with an embroidered gold dragon. He snuck in at night to kill my son."

She sits a little in silence, as if she's remembering it afresh.

"My poor boy. Almost every night he fell asleep and woke up with the sensation of the emperor's cold hands around his neck. The emperor was strong, and the worst thing was that my son could not move."

The words send a chill through me.

"Couldn't move?"

She shakes her head.

"He wanted to push the emperor away, but his arms did not work. He was wide awake while his body was still asleep."

"What was wrong with him?"

The sound of a text message interrupts us and I fish out my phone. Klara again.

Would you mind giving me a ring?

Wu-Pei sighs. "I told you."

"What?" I put the phone back in my pocket.

"I told you, he is coming to kill me, and yet you do nothing."

"Has he been here again? Your husband?"

"I would not be sitting here if he had, would I?"

"No ..."

"No," she says. "So not yet. It has been quite quiet here. Except for when the police were here this morning."

"The police?"

"Something about a pickup truck parked at the graveyard, precisely when ... Yes, I do not remember how they put it. But they also wanted to talk to my son. They had called and called his phone."

"There was a pickup truck at the graveyard?" I say, feeling something cold run through my body. "What colour? Can you remember?"

She nods.

"Blue."

CHAPTER 26

I turn the paper over so the underside is revealed. Repeat the folds on this side. I make an effort as I pull the bottom tip toward the top and press down. Still, it ends up crooked and I wipe my forehead. Set down the half-finished paper flower.

"Stop stressing me out."

I get up. The children are lying with the teddy bear between them.

They look scared.

I stroke their hair. Shush them soothingly.

But the stressed feeling persists.

There's something in the little one's eyes. Something wrong.

With their fingers, too. It's all so fragile.

I try to pretend that everything's okay, but I know full well that too much time has already passed.

I think of needles.

Brown Hairstreak Butterfly, Cryptic Wood White, Emperor Butterfly.

Musty eggs and candied fruits.

My hands shake as I pick up the bottle of sleeping pills. I crush a pill with the back of a teaspoon. I do it carefully. Sweat as I'm doing it.

With scissors, I cut the top of a carton of juice, sprinkle the tablet down there, and stir it around.

The big one shakes her head, but I get her to sit up. She's close-lipped behind the duct tape and it's difficult to get the straw through the small hole I've cut. *Art knife.* I delight in the words. Rejoice at how perfectly the hole in the tape fits.

I finally get the straw in.

I focus on the swallowing movements of her neck instead of on her eyes.

When she's drunk it all, I help her back into place. Sit for a moment looking at them. The children. The teddy.

Proper tools are important. Although it's risky, I have to go back to the farm.

I wipe sweat off my upper lip. Look at my watch.

Behind me, the chest freezer buzzes.

Now she closes her eyes.

Shortly afterwards, her breathing slows down.

I check that the rope around her wrist is still tight. Tie her slender ankles together, too.

I get up, go to the window, and look out. Above me, the Heavenly Dog has swallowed the sun. The black sky makes me hard inside. As if my body is preparing for what is about to happen.

In my mind's eye I see butterflies. Colourful, patterned wings that open and close. Slower and slower until they stop at the bottom of a jam jar.

I go back to the children. Pinch the big one on the arm. She doesn't respond.

The teddy bear smiles. Its mouth is sewn from red yarn that always curves upwards. With its red smile, the teddy bear kisses the children, one after the other.

I lay a blanket over the big one. Stand for a moment cracking my knuckles before I bend over the little one.

Gently I lift her in my arms. Like a doll, like a bride.

She is tiny and cold. I want to say something. Something about the universe and eternity.

"Do not be afraid."

That's the only thing I can think of.

I say it again.

"Do not be afraid."

I wrap her carefully in a blanket. Roll it around her tightly.

A little support network for wings.

No I won't

be afraid

I hum to reassure us. Rock her back and forth as my voice cracks constantly.

Oh, I won't

I stop.

I stand still for a moment to get control of my breathing.

I'm wearing a tie. I can do this.

Gently, I pull the blanket down over her face and go out into the increasing evening darkness. The area is deserted and quiet. I look over my shoulder, anyway, before putting the carry-cot in the car.

My hands are wet with sweat as I put them around the steering wheel. I turn my head to one side until it cracks. Then I turn the key and head back towards Hvide Sande.

CHAPTER 27

The full moon is low and makes the sea surface look like tinfoil. It's completely round now. I think about how it illuminated the graveyard last night. How it has grown into a perfect circle in a single day. It takes the moon as many days to orbit the earth as it takes a woman to go through a menstrual cycle.

I've always thought of the full moon as being pregnant.

Beneath it, eelgrass and seaweed glisten on the shore. There are no other cars on the road. Not a soul in sight. Only the sea and the moon on one side and tall, dark spruces on the other. Steen and I often talked about how it was so child-friendly here. All that air, all that nature.

A loud rattle tears me from my reverie and I pull the steering wheel. Get free of the edge of the ditch and back onto the asphalt.

My heart beats fast. I straighten up in the car seat and blink hard. The moonlight is so bright that I can almost feel it. It's almost physical, and I hear Wu-Pei's words.

Only when the moon is full can we see the loved ones we are separated from.

I look sideways at the luminous circle out there, over the ocean. It's been a long time since I've seen a moon that big. Despite its beauty, it gives me chills.

My stomach rumbles and I think briefly of the communal dinner in the church, which starts in just under an hour.

I find my phone and put it in the holder on the windshield.

This time, Torben answers.

"Eva," he says. "Sorry. I was just in the shower."

In the background, I can hear running showers and resounding voices.

"Are you at football?" I say.

"A match. We lost three–one. You have to get Steen back on his feet again."

"I'm working on it."

"Anyway, what can I do for you?"

"The blue pickup truck that was parked by the graveyard … I know whose it is."

"How do you know a pickup truck was parked there?"

"It's Steen's brother. He lives on a farm in Hvide Sande. I can send you the address."

"We've already been out there."

"What? You didn't tell me that."

"You're not part of the investigation team, in case you've forgotten."

"But what happened? Did you talk to him?"

"No one was home. So we left again."

"You just left again? Can't you get a search warrant, or whatever it's called?"

"Only if we have concrete evidence."

"Isn't the car proof?"

"It's not illegal to go to the graveyard."

"But still."

"You go there yourself every day, don't you?"

The tone of his voice makes me nervous and I tighten my grip on the steering wheel.

"If he's not at home," I say, "then where is he?"

"That's what we're trying to figure out."

"I think you should go out there again," I say. "To the farm. I think you should head out there right now."

"On what grounds?"

"I think he was at our house."

"What?"

"Things were stolen. I think it's him."

"Why would it be him?"

"Because of the things that are gone. We had an extra key on our bird table. That must be how he got in."

"What was stolen?"

"Two broom handles and some candles. And some pages were torn out of a book, too."

There's silence on the line.

"Lots of things, Torben. Okay?"

"Is that an engine I can hear? Where are you?"

"I know, it sounds weird. And I understand if you think I've gone mad. But I really think you should go out to the farm again. I think he's going to kill his mother."

"Let us do our job now. Don't do anything stupid."

There's a bang in the background; Torben cheers and shouts *"You shit!"* There's laughter.

"I have to go," he says. "Now you won't do anything stupid, will you?"

He hangs up.

I chew the inside of my cheek. Press harder on the accelerator and drive through the moonlit landscape of Hvide Sande. I feel like I'm viewing a 3-D picture that one has to look at a certain way before the image emerges.

But nothing emerges. Only lyme grass, thorny bushes, and the long shadows of the pine trees.

158

CHAPTER 28

The tie hits me in the face as I get out of the car in Hvide Sande. I push it back into the tiepin, wipe my sweaty palms on my trousers, and pat my pockets. I left so quickly I forgot both my driver's licence and money and everything. It annoys me. The nervousness. That I'm exposing us to risk.

The Heavenly Dog has swallowed the sun, but a full moon has been lit. As though in my honour. A large, round lamp illuminating the farm-yard for me.

I look around before gently lifting the small body up from the carry-cot in the back seat. The wind is strong and for a split second, we make eye contact. My heart pounds as I pull the blanket down over her face again. I look around quickly before crossing the yard with long strides.

Even though it's cold, I continue to sweat. The thought that we could have been stopped by the police. That the missing driver's licence might have made them look in the car. That a small, stupid oversight could have ruined everything.

I get the key from the bird table and let us in. Stand for a moment between the animals, try to breathe more slowly. *Focus.*

The North Sea is so loud that I can hear it even though I am inside. It's cold in the west wing. That's perfect. The colder, the better.

I carry her past the animals. Hold her in one arm while I turn on the desk lamp with the other.

Everything looks the same as when I left.

I put her on the workbench. Roll my head from side to side to release the tension.

There are still a lot of tools and things lying around, so I have to stand at the opposite end of the table. I feel like I'm being watched, but don't like to move anything.

No I won't
be afraid

My humming is hoarse as I roll up my sleeves and disinfect my hands.

A crow looks at me with its black glass eyes. It sits on a crooked branch and is made so well that it seems it could spread its wings and flap away at any moment.

My eyes run over the board with tools. A bag of cotton wool hangs on a nail. I take it down and tear off a bit. Stand for a moment clenching the soft, white clump.

Carefully, I open the blanket.

The crow looks at me with its glass eyes as I roll the cotton into two small balls and stuff them into her nostrils. A lot of blood can run out that way if you're not careful.

I don't actually know if there is any liquid blood left in a body after it's been buried. But I dare not take any chances. The mere thought of how much of a mess there was last time I stood here makes nervous sweat trickle down all over my body. I couldn't bear it if any of her dripped on the floor, that I might step on her.

The bag of cotton sticks to my palm as I hang it back on the nail. I wipe my sweaty hands on my trousers again. Breathe deeply and try to relax.

I carefully lay out the tools. The small, sharp knife I need to loosen the eyeballs. The tweezers. Needle and thread. The bucket.

I had pictured it as I wrapped her in the blanket. Like slow-motion shots of flowers blooming. Delicate, red poppies opening up and exposing their insides.

How I would pull the skin into place afterwards, hard but gently, like when pulling a tight jumper over a child's head.

Outside, the North Sea sounds like a wolf trying to blow the building down. I rub my forehead with my sleeve, pick up the knife, and put it down again. Tense and stretch my fingers.

I think of the phoenix. Of high flames and the smell of petrol.

I had imagined it all. But now that I'm standing here with my tools, my hands are shaking. This colossal dizzying fear of ruining something. That it would, somehow, hurt her.

I roll my head again. My neck cracks and I take a breath.

I have to start with the eyes.

The eyes are the most important.

I pull out drawers until I find them. They clink. Staring glass balls in different colours.

I choose a pair that is black, like the crow's. They shine as I hold them up under the desk lamp.

They're a little too big, but now that they've looked at me, I can't find it in my heart to put them back in the drawer.

I think of pink cherry blossoms losing their petals. I've always wanted to pick them up and glue them back on the tree.

My thoughts are interrupted by a door creaking.

I hurry to turn off the desk lamp. Turn around slowly.

The darkness in the wing is dense and dizzying, and I can't see whether anyone is there. Whether it's just the wind, or whether I'm being interrupted once again.

With my hand clasped around a hammer, I walk to the door. Stand for a moment holding my breath before pushing it open.

Outside, the full moon illuminates the landscape. The treetops are swaying in the wind and I narrow my eyes. Look across the lawn and to the forest behind. The sea's silvery surface and the narrow path meandering up and down hilltops.

Nothing.

I exhale.

My hand has become sweaty around the hammer. I move it over to the opposite hand. I straighten my tie and am just about to go back to the workbench when I spot them. Out in the distance, faintly glimmering between the trees of the forest.

A pair of approaching headlights.

CHAPTER 29

The gravel crunches under the car's tyres as I drive up in front of the brother's four-wing farmyard.

There it is. The blue pickup. Parked in the same place as last time.

But the spade that was leaning against the gable is gone.

I sit for a long time looking at the yellow bricks and the whitewashed plinth that the spade leaned against two days ago.

The brother must have been here in the meantime.

Maybe he's still here?

A cover of clouds grows dense on the horizon. I follow it with my eyes as it rapidly fills the sky. Shortly afterwards, it slides in front of the moon, and it's as if a switch is turned off.

My heart beats faster and I stay seated with my hands on the steering wheel while the wind whistles and the sharp, white light of the headlights makes shadows dance. The sudden darkness is as dense as fog. I listen to the rhythmic rumble of the sea and the dry rustle as the wind sweeps through the lyme grass and the long grass. Somewhere in the distance, a sleepless seabird calls.

I struggle with the seat belt, stumble out into the raw wind, and find my phone. I activate the torch function and aim it at the ground in front of me. Sand crunches under my shoes as I walk up to the front door. The beam of light zigzags in front of me. In my other hand, I clench the pepper spray I bought online when I found out I was pregnant.

The west wind carries with it a sharp smell of seaweed, marsh, and seagull droppings, as well as the cold from the sea. The farmyard is a silhouette in the dark, and my steps resound loudly in the silence. I shine the light on the door.

A long-bodied cellar spider sits on the doorbell like a leggy, eight-fingered hand. It crawls away when I ring the bell. The sound echoes inside the house, and I grasp the pepper spray while I wait.

Above me, the gulls keep the air in motion, flying in circles like a creaking ceiling fan.

The adrenaline makes me dizzy and I really just want to run back to the car. But I remain standing. Ring the bell again.

Still nothing. I try the handle.

Locked.

I look out over the flat landscape. The wind rasps and I think of the taxidermied animals in the west wing. Stiff-legged and with glass eyes, lined up like toy soldiers. I can feel their eyes. How they stand waiting for what I'm going to do now.

A rosehip bush grabs my trouser leg as I squeeze through a thicket. I keep my eyes fixed on the bird table that I spotted in the dark.

When I get there, I see it has an extra shelf just like ours at home.

I carefully stick my hand in. Pat around the wood.

Nothing.

I pull my hand out again and go back to the front door. Rub my face hard.

Ants and woodlice peep out as I lift the mat to see if there's a key. I stand on tiptoe and let one hand run over the top door frame. A large, black spider darts over the brickwork and disappears.

There are lights in several of the windows. Were they on the last time I was here, too? I try to remember but can only recall it was daytime. Maybe I wasn't able to see whether the lights were on or not.

I go to the kitchen window and peer inside. There are still two slices of baguette on the toaster. The jar with the olives and the long spoon are also standing in exactly the same way.

Still, I have the feeling that someone is here.

There's a loud flutter when a magpie lands on the thatched roof. It spreads its black-and-white wings, and the light from my torch makes its metallic blue-green plumage shine. It turns its head and looks at me with its black eyes. For several seconds, we hold eye contact, then it flies up over the house and lands in a tree so the branches move.

I stand for a while watching it before going to the living room window. The chandelier above the dining table is still on. I put my hands on the glass, look in at the high-backed chairs and the long dining table with the candelabra. Everything is as it was when I was here two days ago. The glass of red wine. The plate of tapas. There are even more flies than last time. Heavy, black bodies that crawl, take off, and land.

Maybe I'm wrong. Maybe he hasn't been home at all. But what about the spade that's no longer standing outside?

I click away from the torch and find the number I copied from Steen's phone. I put it under *Twin brother*. My finger hesitates briefly before pressing call.

Somewhere in the dark, I can hear a faint ringing tone. I press the phone closer to my ear and look around. Silhouettes of swaying trees and long grass changing direction with the wind.

"Unfortunately, the person you are calling cannot be reached. Please leave a message after the beep."

I call again. Listen to the faint ringtone. It's hard to hear where it's coming from.

The magpie flaps away from the treetop, hangs over me like a black silhouette, and I turn on the torch again. Hold tight to the phone as I walk along the yellow bricks and whitewashed plinths. My steps crunch and make it sound as if someone is walking behind me. I shine it on the grass and up on the house wall, and every time the torch hits a window, my reflection appears so sharp and suddenly that it gives me a start.

Everything is as it was last time in the east wing, too. The wild boar head with the bared canines. The cage with the three stuffed birds. An owl, a raven, a dove.

I look at the birds as I call again. Stand still in the dark, listening.

The ringtone is louder now. I hold my breath and a chill runs through me as it dawns on me. The ringtone is coming from the west wing.

With the phone in one hand and the pepper spray in the other, I slowly move closer.

Black garbage bags are still taped to the windows. Old spiderwebs hang from the thatched roof, waving like ghosts in the wind.

I walk along the outer wall, following the sound of the ringing telephone. It gets louder and louder as I approach.

In the grass, in front of the door, is the spade. There's earth on the blade. Someone must have thrown it away before they entered.

I step over it and take the doorknob.

Locked.

Inside, the ringtone stops.

"Hello?" My voice sounds hoarse. "Hello, is anyone there?"

A gust of wind sweeps through the lyme grass and pushes the wind chimes, which send their lonely clinking out into the silence.

The darkness seems closer now. As if it's watching me.

Gravel and twigs crunch under the soles of my shoes as I walk away from the door and out between the birch trees. I find a stone, stand with it in my hand for a while, and look at the black sacks.

I breathe in. Feel how my lungs fill with the smell of heather and grass and sea. Then I throw the stone at the lattice window of the door. The sound of shattering glass is loud in the silence and I take a step back. If anyone is hiding in there, at least now they know they're not alone. I stand for a moment and wait. Imagine the brother rushing out with his rifle.

But no one comes. The darkness is quiet around me.

I stick my arm in through the broken pane. The glass teeth tear my jacket sleeve, making the skin inside sting. I hear Torben's voice.

Don't do anything stupid now.

I should go, leave it to the police. But something makes me ignore the pain and edge my hand down towards the lock. Something deep inside me, where my baby lived.

There's a stabbing pain in my arm, as if teeth are biting, as if the window has actually closed its jaws around me. I twist my arm farther in and grab the lock. Turn it.

The hinges creak as I give the door a push. It opens and hits the wall with a little thud.

I step forward and stare into the darkness. A dusty, lingering odour seeps out from inside. From the ceiling hangs a large lamp that looks like something from an operating theatre. I reach in and pat the wall. Find the switch and press.

Nothing.

I press a few more times.

A sound makes me stiffen. A crackle and a rustle, as if someone is flipping through a newspaper. Hesitantly, I lift the phone's torch and shine it in the direction of the sound.

I jump as a mouse darts out the door. It runs close past me and disappears into the darkness.

Then it's quiet again.

I support myself against the doorframe and get my breathing under control. Wish I could call Steen and ask him to come.

The shards of glass crunch under my feet when I step inside. The torch flickers around, hitting brick walls and furry tails, wings, and hooves mounted on wooden plinths.

I'm sure the sound of the brother's phone came from here. So, where is he?

The stuffed animals stand like silhouettes in the dark. Glass eyes twinkle every time the light hits them. Dusty squirrels, foxes with bared teeth, crows, and falcons.

It looks like it was once stables. As if the old stalls have been torn down but left their mark on the wooden floor and in the brick walls. Animals are everywhere in here now. Standing all around me, emitting a rancid, bestial odour.

Farther inside the wing, it looks like some of the stalls have been preserved. Someone could easily be hiding in there. Waiting for me to come closer.

Outside, the cloud cover is briefly ripped and the full moon shines in through the windows. The mullions cast barlike shadows on the floor and over the animals' fur and feathers.

My skin feels damp as if from a feverish sweat. A badger with dusty glass eyes looks at me. Next to it stands a marten, its fur filthy and reddish-brown like rust.

Then the clouds slide in front of the moon again, and the darkness descends closer than before.

The floor creaks under my shoes as I walk farther into the room. Dust swirls up from the floor, spins around in the light cone, and the musty animal odour grows stronger. But there's something else, too. Something sharp. Somewhat fermented. Sauerkraut and smoked serrano ham. A smell that reminds me of something.

I look around at the silent squirrels, the stag, and the fallow deer, and it feels as if my body temperature is falling below freezing when I notice it.

The rifle is gone.

The hook protrudes from the wall in the same way as the teeth of the stuffed wild boar.

My rapid breathing makes the smell in here even more penetrating. Serrano ham and old jam jars and I give a start when my phone beeps.

Did you see my message about ringing? Huge fire on a farm. Will only be back when you come home from the midnight service. Sorry.

I look at Klara's message. Then at the empty hook.

Driving home now, I write.

I click back to the torch function and am just about to turn around. Then I notice something lying on the workbench. Something that makes my heart pound. I slowly move closer and I nearly slip.

I've stepped in something.

When I turn the sole of my shoe upwards, a lump is stuck. Something full of dust, but I can't see what it is. I wipe the sole off on the floor.

Under the board with the tools is a desk lamp and I find the switch. It lights up with a click, illuminating the floor.

There's something down there. A dark puddle, as if something has dripped down from the tabletop. It has run over the crooked wooden planks, and I squat down. Gently touch it with a fingertip. It's dried solid.

I straighten up again and look back at the workbench. I point the lamp there, and an icy sensation spreads from my neck and up the back of my head.

On the table are three eyes.

My heart beats faster as I stare at them. I get the creepy feeling they're staring back at me.

Something about them is so wrong.

Are they from animals?

I don't think so.

Slowly I let go of the lamp. Recall the feeling of stepping on something, and the icy feeling intensifies.

Did I just step on a … human eye?

CHAPTER 30

The cold of the west wing penetrates deep into me as I gape at the macabre find. Three eyes on a workbench.

Their blank stares are turned towards me, as if someone made an effort to put them that way.

The rest of the bench is covered in tools, steel wire, and safety pins. A crowbar smeared in blood. Heaps of something white that make the table look like a grotesque Christmas landscape.

Two of the eyes are small, as though from a child. The third is larger. From an adult?

All three look shrunken and dry. Like they've been lying here for a while.

Their irises are covered with a matte, pale membrane. The severed optic nerves protrude from the back.

I shudder. Can't let go of the thought that I might just have stepped on a human eye. I consider picking it up from the floor and laying it on the workbench with the others. But the mere thought of touching it makes me feel sick.

Outside, the chimes are clinking in the wind, and I imagine that whoever cut the eyes out is on their way to me right now. That soon there'll be six eyes, and I flinch when a loud sound breaks the silence.

The brother's phone again.

I point the torch at the corner where the sound is coming from. The light is reflected in bare teeth and silent beaks. The rest of the pale ray of light fades into darkness. I slowly move closer as I shed light on the direction of the sound. Then I stop.

The ringing sound is coming from a bin.

Hesitantly, I head over to it. It's a large metal bin with a lid. I lift off the lid.

At the bottom are some crumpled clothes. Light canvas trousers, a light blue shirt, a black tie. There's blood on everything.

The phone is still ringing. I hold my breath and take the trousers out of the rubbish. Find the phone in a pocket. It goes quiet.

The screen says: *142 missed calls*.

CHAPTER 31

The double-sided sticky tape on the beard no longer works. Though it doesn't matter this time.

I lift the scissors and cut into the air. Listening to the blades sliding against each other.

There's nothing left of the rope I tied the girl up with, so I look for something else. Open and close metal drawers and old plastic boxes, while the deep hum of the chest freezer forms a sound curtain.

My shirt is still wet with sweat after the hurried car ride from Hvide Sande. I had to cut across fields and through bushes so as not to be spotted by the approaching car.

I try to shake off the stressed feeling. Cut with the scissors in the air again and look at my watch. I'm so close to my goal. Nothing can go wrong now.

On a shelf, I find a roll of clothesline made of blue plastic. I put the scissors around a piece of it. Press hard but can't cut through.

Still, I put the scissors in the backpack. Feel a childish delight, like when I first defied Father and stole one of the dead butterflies. This dizzying mix of fear and euphoria at being able to change the world order.

The pliers are cold and heavy when I pick them up from the box. They make a small, soft sound as I cut the clothesline.

Perfect.

I put the pliers in the backpack.

In the box with painting gear, I find an old cloth and scrunch it into a ball. Open my mouth and assess the size ratio.

The smell from the cloth makes me grimace. I put it in the backpack and go over to the mirror.

The tie is freshly washed and I lift my chin as I tighten it. I like to look nice when I can. It's a way to show respect. Like when Father turned fifty.

Red-letter days are important.

The small plastic container is drying on a radiator. I refill it with fresh, red paint. Screw on the lid and hold it up to the light. It's a happy colour.

I put the container in the backpack.

Some special days come to an end. Others arise. The thought makes me whistle.

It's windy outside. Still, I sweat in my jacket and gloves, which I put on to avoid leaving any prints. The full moon, which shone so brightly earlier in the evening, has been swallowed by clouds. The sky is dark grey and restless. I increase my pace. My shadow grows and disappears every time I walk under a streetlamp.

I had parked on a side road. Now I approach the building with a pounding heart and my backpack on my back. I stay hidden and count windows. Find her.

A flickering light leaks out from inside. As I move closer, I catch glimpses of her. She's sitting in a chair watching television. The sight moves me.

It looks like she's waiting for me.

Once I'm sure the way is clear, I go up to the main entrance. The glass door closes behind me and I turn down the corridor, walk with rapid, silent steps.

I stop in front of her door.

I reciprocate the tiger's staring eyes.

Adrenaline and emotion rush around me as I think about the alarm cord and the night porter, and how I had to flee from here last time.

The longer the tiger's teeth, the more forbidden it is to enter.

I take out the scissors.

CHAPTER 32

I look over my shoulder before slamming the car door and running up the driveway into the house. As I raced past the church, I saw them getting ready for the midnight service. The dancing lights of the torches outside should have calmed me. Instead, they only added to my goose bumps.

Despite me turning up the heat in the car completely, the cold hours on the farm still sit in my body. The police kept asking questions and my hands shake as I rummage in my bag. The smell of dead animals is still stuck in my nose, and I drop the keys on the doorstep. Pick them up and turn the lock. Slam that door behind me, too.

The house is pitch-black, except for the flickering glare of the television penetrating from the living room, and I walk quickly through the rooms. Check that all the doors are locked. That all the windows are closed, and it seems like they are peeking in every glossy surface. The three carved eyes on the workshop table.

Do you need someone to drive you home?

You're not allowed to be here while we conduct the search.

Unfortunately, no. We're still looking for him.

The white of Steen's eyes stands out clearly in the dark bedroom. His eyes look frightened when they meet mine.

"Eva? Is that you?"

I throw my coat and boots on the floor and sit down next to him. Put my hands on his cheeks.

"Of course, it's me."

"It just didn't sound like you. Before."

"Before? When?"

"Before I fell asleep."

I look out the window. Behind the rolled-down blinds, I can hear the wind whistling.

"I wondered why you didn't come in and say hello," he says. "I heard you walking around the house. You were whistling that song." He tries to whistle, but ends up coughing instead.

A chill runs down my spine.

"Which song?" I whisper.

"When the night has come, and the land is dark ..."

His humming intensifies the icy feeling.

Outside, the wind howls louder. I go to the window and stick two fingers in between the blinds. Look out into the evening darkness that's as compacted as fabric. Bushes and trees rattle and I think of the hook without the rifle. Imagine the twin brother as a black shadow in the night. That he's standing out there, keeping an eye on the house.

When I turn around again, the bedroom looks even darker. Why didn't Klara burn a candle? I turn on Steen's bedside lamp and sit back on the edge of the bed. His cheeks are warm when I lay my hands around them.

"Don't be afraid," I say. "I won't leave you again."

I take his hand even though he can't feel it. Caress it with small, quick movements.

142 missed calls.

We're still looking for him.

You were whistling that song.

My teeth chatter and I can't figure out if the cold is coming from the house or myself.

I lie down in bed and pull the duvet over us. Hold on to it with both hands.

"Eva?" he whispers. "What's going on?"

"You were right," I say. "Your brother is mentally ill. More than you know."

"What happened?"

Steen lies completely silent while I tell him about the carved-out eyes. The blood on the floor, the clothes in the bin and the rifle.

"The police are there now," I say. "They promised they'd call us."

I take out my phone. Turn up the volume.

"They offered to send someone here," I say. "To keep an eye on us. Police supervision. So we're not alone."

Steen looks horrified and I take his hand again.

"Don't worry," I say. "We won't leave the house until we've heard from them. I've locked up everywhere."

As soon as I say it, I think of the spare key. It's been out there the entire time. Wu-Chao could easily have managed to get a copy made. He seems calculating enough for that. Maybe it makes no difference at all that I've removed it?

A gust of wind hits the house, causing the woodwork to give. I imagine the brother letting himself in while I was away. How he sneaked around the dark room and tampered with our stuff. Looked through the bedroom door at Steen and whistled. I try not to imagine the melody, but I can hear it anyway.

Whenever you're in trouble won't you stand by me
oh, stand by me

"It must have been your brother who was whistling," I say.

"Why would he do that?"

"Because he was hoping you'd hear it?"

The clock on the wall ticks and I look up at the daddy longlegs on the ceiling. Try to think clearly. What am I missing? What?

Steen's hamster lying dead in the cage. Steen's broken arm.

And when you got pregnant …

I think of the blood dripping down from the workbench. Postpartum pads and the threads of blood swirling around the toilet bowl. As black as ebony, as red as blood.

And when you got pregnant …

Oh, God.

"What if …" I can hardly bring myself to say it. "What if the placental abruption wasn't an accident at all? What if it was …?"

I swallow.

"The doctors couldn't explain it. They said that my pregnancy had been completely normal otherwise, and then suddenly ..."

I press my lips together and look out the window.

"What if what?" says Steen.

"If it was your brother who killed her."

"How would that even be possible?"

"I don't know, but if he stole medicine from your mother ... He could have put something in our food? I did actually think some of the meat tasted a bit weird."

The more I think about it, the more it makes sense. The strong taste of tablets that I couldn't get rid of no matter how many Ga-Jol liquorices I ate. Was the taste there, too, even before I started taking sleeping pills?

It's like I can feel it in my stomach. The medicine penetrating my bloodstream. Tiny hands that can't defend themselves.

But there was something in his eyes. Something scary. It was lying completely stiff in the cage and I tried to wake it up.

"Eva?" Steen's voice tears me from my thoughts.

"Breathe," he says.

"I am."

"Remember," he says. "We still have control over our own thoughts."

"What does that mean?"

"That we have to keep a cool head. Not let our imaginations run away with us."

"How can you say that, after all that has happened?"

"Because that's exactly what he's waiting for. That we go right to the edge so he can push us down the stairs."

A new gust of wind makes the house creak and I look at my phone.

"Your stomach keeps rumbling," Steen says. "Weren't you supposed to eat at church?"

I shake my head. Continue looking at the phone even though the screen is black.

"They'll find him," says Steen.

"They haven't found Lotus."

"The best thing we can do is get something to eat and go to sleep. Do as we usually do. Stay together."

"What if it takes days?"

"Then it's good Klara filled the freezer."

We lie in silence for a while. Listen to the whistling of the wind and the clock ticking on the wall.

"What about your mother?" I say. "Was it when your sister died that she broke down?"

"She loved Father very much."

"So, she did everything he said? She even dressed her dead daughter in a wedding dress?"

He closes his eyes tightly.

"She was so small," he says. "She was so small and lovely."

I stroke his hair.

"How did you cope?" I say.

"I thought about how one day I'd have my own family. A beautiful and happy family. That was what kept me going."

I caress him again. My body keeps shaking. It feels like we're in a bathtub and the water has gently run down the drain.

"Sometimes I wish I was dead, too," I say. "So I was still with her."

Steen meets my eyes. I expect him to scold me. Tell me that I shouldn't say things like that.

But he just looks at me with his black eyes and I put my arms around him and hold him close to me. His cheek is warm against mine, and our breathing is fast and shallow, just like the day we went cycling together during the summer, my pregnant body, and Steen's breathless in sympathy. The smell of heather and triangular-cut sandwiches, with the egg salad squeezed out. The baby's little body that jerked every time she hiccupped. Ants crawling over my skin, drifting clouds.

Fatigue overwhelms me. A longing for sleep. To pull the night over me, like the duvet, to disappear.

But I keep picturing it. The eyes on the workbench. The rifle on the wall. The empty hook where the gun no longer hung.

I take the phone out again. Press the side to increase the volume, despite it already being at max.

"Why don't they call?" I say. *"Why?"*

The wind whistles and shakes outside. I feel ice-cold even though I'm lying under the duvet and I jump when there's a knock on the windowpane. A hard, determined knock I can feel all over my body.

Blood rushes in my ears and I scout around the bedroom for something hard.

"Stay here," I say, laying a hand on Steen.

"I'll try to," he mutters.

I pull the duvet aside and open the wardrobe. Rummage on the shelves and find Steen's football boots. The ones with iron studs. I take one and look towards the window. It's quiet again. Only the wind is blowing out there. Still, it's as if I can sense eyes. Something living.

With the football boot in my hand, I go to the window, take the blind cord, and pull. The garden is dark and deserted. In the middle of the glass is a round spot. Below it is a little red.

Blood?

My heart pounds faster. Carefully I open the child lock and push open the window. There's something in the grass. I turn on the light on my phone. Shine it down.

On the lawn, just under the window, is a dead blue tit. Its head is at a weird angle to its little body.

I sweep the torch through the garden. Light in the direction of the cherry tree, the pile of planks, and the hedge facing the black fields.

With a hard tug, I get the window closed again. I push in the child lock and pull down the blinds.

"What was it?" says Steen.

"Just a bird."

I put down the football boot. Rub my face.

"I'd better go out and make some food for us."

I put the duvet closer around him. "I'm going to close the door into you. Just in case …"

I don't quite know what I want to say. Rationally, it makes no sense, yet it feels safest not to leave the door into him open.

When I've closed the bedroom door, I go out into the kitchen. Despite there being several kilometres between us, I have a feeling that the eyes on the workbench keep looking at me.

I pull up my sleeve and look at my arm. Given how painful it was when I cut myself on the broken window, I was expecting a huge wound. But there's only a superficial scratch. Like nothing had happened.

I press around the cut with two fingers, but I can't get any blood out. There's only a thin streak of pink skin. A fly lands in it. The proboscis moves in and out and I slap it away. Brush all over my body with hectic movements before pulling my sleeve down again.

The insect flies through the kitchen and lands on the edge of a red bowl. I feel the tenderloin. It's not cold anymore, but it seems okay.

I take out a frying pan and put it on the stove. Blue gas flames rise, hissing, and I melt butter. Push the moist tenderloin out of the bowl and into the pan. It sizzles loudly and I inhale the aroma. Lift my arm and sniff my armpit. It's there again. The strange smell of something earthy. Smoked bacon and dust.

I bend over and sniff the tenderloin. Wrinkle my nose and look around the kitchen.

The day before yesterday, it was so bad that I thought I'd left some food somewhere. That in my distraction, I'd put some of Dad's bloody pieces of meat in a cupboard or a drawer. I asked Steen if he could smell it, too. He said, of course the house stank when there was an adult man shitting in a nappy. I said sorry. I opened all the windows and aired the place out. It helped. The smell had already subsided the next day. But now it's back. Not as strong, but enough to make me think the whole house must be about to decay.

I hold a hand up in front of my mouth and breathe into it. Sniff it. Open the cupboard under the sink and smell the rubbish bin. The smell is like a spirit or ghost appearing and disappearing, and suddenly it dawns on me what it reminds me of.

The farm in Hvide Sande. The west wing with the dead animals.

The smell was different there. More animalistic and dusty. But there's a connection, I'm sure.

A panicked tingle spreads through my body. The sound of footsteps and *Stand by me.*

He walked around our house while I was away. Dragged the smell of death after him as he rummaged in our drawers and stuffed poison into our food in the same way he stuffed wood fibre and glass eyes into dead animals.

I turn off the gas burner and throw the tenderloin in the bin. Take out my phone and check the time. It's been an hour since I left the farm.

A bluebottle lands on the back of my hand. I shake it off and put the phone in my pocket. Every time I breathe in, my body becomes stiffer and tenser. The air feels like wood fibre and I feel like opening a window but I dare not. Instead, I turn on the cooker hood and open the cupboard with the pots.

The best thing we can do is get something to eat and go to sleep. Do as we usually do. Stay together.

Even though I have no appetite, I open the freezer. There's a bag of frozen beetroot soup that Klara made. I cut it open, dump the contents into a pot, and turn on the ring.

The soup melts slowly and I push it with a spoon.

My phone rings.

I fumble it out of my pocket and look at the screen.

Torben. Finally.

I take a breath and put the phone to my ear.

"Hi," he says. "How are things going at home?"

"You know yourself."

"I thought I clearly told you to let us do our job and not to do anything stupid."

"And I said you should go out to the farm. Did you find him?"

"Unfortunately, not. He seems to have gone underground."

There is something macabre about the expression that makes me think of the sound of the graveyard's gravel when I walk around between the graves.

"And the eyes?" I say. "Do you know if …?"

"Not yet."

In the background, I can hear a police siren and the sound of crunching gravel.

"We'll send someone over to you," he says. "But unfortunately, I can't promise when. It might not be until tomorrow."

"Tomorrow?"

"If you feel unsafe, you're welcome to come down to the station and spend the night here. Maybe you can get someone to help you move Steen?"

"Why can't you get anyone here until tomorrow?"

"Sorry. I thought we had some officers to spare. But something else came in."

"What?"

"I'm really sorry to have to be the bearer of more bad news."

He clears his throat, and there's a scratching sound as if he's rubbing his beard.

"It's about Steen's mother."

"Okay?"

"She's disappeared from the nursing home."

"Disappeared how?"

"Earlier this evening. We're not sure when. The staff noticed there was something wrong with the drawing hanging on her door. When they went in to see her, she was gone."

A chill runs through my body.

He said he would come back and that next time he would make sure the porter couldn't stop him.

"The alarm cord was cut," says Torben. "No one heard anything. Whoever it is, he was thoroughly prepared."

"What do you mean, there was something wrong with the drawing?"

"I don't know if you've seen it. It was quite nice. A large tiger with orange and white fur. Very lifelike."

In the background, I can hear running steps. A voice shouting "Over here."

"Someone," Torben says, "had cut off the tiger's teeth and painted a red smile instead."

The words send another chill through me.

I look down into the pot. The hard lump of soup that is slowly getting smaller.

"We have called in backup for the search," he says. "We're doing everything we can."

I nod, even though he can't see it.

"There's a good reason why I can't call Steen and tell him," he says. "But as I said, someone will come out to you tomorrow when more of us are on duty. Hopefully, she'll be found safe and sound."

I think of her frail body in the big coat. The narrow, white bed with the blue metal legs. The pillow.

"You'd better stay inside," says Torben. "Not to worry you, but we have to face the fact that there's a pattern. Steen's daughter and father. And now his mother, too."

"I'm not leaving him."

"Whoever it is, he's persistent. But also impatient, I sense. Three people have disappeared in three days. If it's the same culprit."

"Four," I say.

"What?"

"It may be four. Lotus hasn't been found yet, has she?"

Torben falls silent. There's a clicking sound like from a pen being clicked in and out.

"We don't know whether there's a connection between Lotus's disappearance and the others yet. We're keeping all lines of enquiry open."

Someone calls him.

"I have to go," he says. "Promise me you'll be careful."

"We promise. Thanks for ringing."

After I hang up, I stand for a long time staring down at the soup. It's completely melted now. Thin, white steam rises. I stir one last time and turn off the gas burner.

My hands shake as I lift the pot and pour it into two bowls. I breathe on Steen's portion. Check the temperature with my little finger.

As I walk towards the bedroom with the two soup bowls, I think of the photo of the two children getting married. A dead little sister and a living brother. His tense smile. The frightened, black eyes and the far-too-long tie.

I put my elbow against the handle and press down. The door opens and I stop. Stand in the doorway with the two bowls of soup as I feel an eerie sensation spread through my body.

It looks like Steen is lying in a completely different position in the bed than he was before.

CHAPTER 33

The sofa creaks as I turn around onto my other side. It's far too short and groans every time I change position. For the first time since giving birth, I haven't taken any sleeping pills.

Not being drugged by the medication is strange. There's something frightening about it, but also something strangely uplifting.

The door to the bedroom is closed. I couldn't stand lying in there. Couldn't let go of the thought that Steen was suddenly lying in a different position. When I asked him if there was any improvement, he blinked twice. I pinched his toes, lifted his arms, and let go. They fell back heavily on the mattress.

"What are you doing?" he said, and I pulled the duvet off him. Lifted his legs and let go. They fell in the same way as the pig carcasses at the slaughterhouse when they were cut from the iron chains in the ceiling.

"Do you need to be stressing me out like that?" he said. There was something new in his voice. The sound of tears or anger and I couldn't stand it. The restlessness in my body, the sudden urge to push him out of bed and see what would happen. His confused, helpless eyes, and how we stared at each other. I seized my duvet and strode out of the bedroom.

So now I'm lying on the couch, not knowing what to believe. I think of the candles in the writing bureau, which may or may not be gone. The man in the graveyard. Klara, who shook her head and said I didn't see anyone.

Maybe Steen wasn't lying differently at all. Maybe I wasn't looking properly.

I think of the blue bucket in the kindergarten sandbox. The claustrophobic feeling of having loved a child who didn't exist. Still loving this child who doesn't exist. It's an insane, inhuman love that burns inside, like forest fires that leave vast areas of land desolate.

I pick up my phone and go into history. Scroll through the many articles I've read aloud to Steen.

Living death rituals around the world: In Indonesia, they dig up mum to be photographed with her every year

Grave robber steals 29 child corpses

Pictures from Anatoly Moskvin's apartment: Made corpses of girls into dolls and held a birthday party for them

The sound on the television gets louder when the commercials are on. My heart beats faster and I put the phone down.

The last few nights, we've slept with the television on to drown out the silence in the house. The flickering light of the screen makes the shiny surfaces of the living room a bluish tinge, and I look at the shadows being cast. Look at them until they appear more real than the people on the screen. More real than myself, and it all blurs into hazy images that make sense without making sense.

I wake up on the sofa, confused, with a sore back and my head full of incoherent dreams. It's dark in the living room, except for the flickering light from the television.

I rub my face. Hadn't expected to actually fall asleep, but I must have been more exhausted than I thought. I lean off the couch and pick up my phone from the floor. The time is 03:49 and there are two missed calls from Klara.

Only when I have pressed call do I think they're probably sleeping and I picture them in my mind's eye. Alfred and Klara in the double bed. The kids in their rooms, little soft faces and colourful bedclothes.

It rings five times before there's a rattling on the line. A short cough, then the sound of Klara's sleepy voice.

"Eva?"

"Hello, sorry if I woke you. I saw you rang."

"Yeah. One moment."

There is a creak, footsteps across the floor, and the sound of a door being opened and closed.

A bluebottle flies around the living room, glowing in the same colours as the pictures on the television before landing on the screen. It's a beauty spot on a chin, a spot on the full moon, a hole in the map of Denmark.

"I'm here again," Klara says. She already sounds more awake. "It's not like me to ring so late, either, but I just wanted to talk to you. How did it go at the midnight service?"

"Why do you ask?"

She sighs.

"I had to put down twenty-two pigs. Really ugly fire. I only got home a couple of hours ago."

"Okay."

There's a short pause, as if she's taking a run-up to the next one.

"I know our relationship has been a bit up and down lately," she says. "And I know I've probably pushed you too hard and not always listened to you."

"Yeah …?"

"But you know I'm always here for you, don't you?"

"I do. Thanks. Is that why you called?"

"I just wanted to say it. Before I tell you about the dog."

"What dog?"

"It was yesterday afternoon. Before I went out to you. I had an urgent call out to a Labrador with a spinal cord injury."

"Right?"

"It'd been hit by a car that morning. Not so hard, thankfully, and the owners actually thought it had walked away from it. But it started to walk funny and fell over several times during the day. It stopped jumping and refused to go up the stairs. Eventually, it lay down in its basket and stayed there. So they called me."

"And I need to know this because …?"

"It turned out that the dog was completely paralysed. I recommended it have a CT scan and told them about decompression surgery and that rest was important. I said they should replace the dog basket with an air mattress. That an air mattress was very important."

"Right?"

"An air mattress, Eva!"

There's something in her voice that makes my muscles tense, like I'm about to jump into very cold water.

"I don't know why I didn't think of it before," she says, "but it's like I've been saying all along—I'm not a doctor."

"Think about what?"

"Bedsores."

My pulse increases. With the phone to my ear, I look over at the bedroom door.

"We should have turned him," she says. "You can't stay in the same position. What might we have done to him? His body? His skin?"

She's speaking in the same way as when she receives an emergency call on her work phone. As if there's a bleeding animal somewhere and we need to think fast.

"Fourteen days in bed without being turned," she says. "Steen should have terrible bedsores by now."

The sofa gives way beneath me as I sit up and push off the duvet.

"A grown man," she says. "On a crumpled sheet. And in the stuffy heat and urine and sweat and moisture. His skin should be completely destroyed. I don't understand how we've been so lucky."

Goose bumps spread on my arms as I look at the handle into the bedroom.

"Eva? Are you there?"

"I have to go. Thanks for telling me about the dog." I hang up, sit with a pounding heart in the dark.

Slowly, I get up from the couch, pick up my dressing gown from the floor, and pull it on. I tighten the belt.

With the phone clasped in my hand, I move across the living room floor, through the restless shadows of the television. Gently, I push the bedroom door open and peek inside. Steen's body is a silhouette in the bed. There are no snoring sounds and I can sense his insomnia in the room, like electricity. I take a deep breath. Try to get my feet to go to him, but they stay put in the doorway.

He should have terrible bedsores by now.

The clock on the wall is ticking and I keep a hold on the door handle as I look at my husband's body in bed. I imagine him suddenly getting up. Like Frankenstein. Moving about the room with his arms outstretched towards me.

I jump as the ads come on TV. The sound is loud, as if someone has turned up the volume, and behind me the darkness is filled with rapidly flickering light.

I look back at Steen. He's in the same position. Doesn't say anything. There's something ominous about his silence.

"Are you asleep?" I ask, despite me knowing he's awake.

He doesn't respond.

I remain standing in the doorway. Can't get myself to go inside.

Specks of dust hang in the air between us, spinning slowly around as if they can't find rest.

My little son. He was so scared to go to sleep.

The phrase echoes in my head as I look at my motionless husband.

He fell asleep and woke up with the sensation of the emperor's cold hands around his neck. The emperor was strong, and the worst thing was that my son could not move.

I picture Steen's mother in front of me. The dead butterflies and her eyes gleaming as she spoke of her frightened, sleepless boy.

He wanted to push the emperor away, but his arms did not work. He was wide awake while his body was still asleep.

Only now does it dawn on me. Maybe she wasn't talking about the twin brother? Maybe she was talking about Steen?

I stare at the silhouette in the double bed. Now that I think about it, she didn't once mention them by name. She said: The one who has sunk into darkness. The one who lives in pomp and splendour.

Maybe Steen was the one who woke up with the feeling of not being able to move. Maybe it's all repeating itself?

"Tell me about the old emperor," I say. "The one who tried to strangle you at night."

Still no answer.

I try to picture the emperor in my mind's eye. The long black beard, the long braid and silk kimono with embroidered gold dragon, and I don't understand why I'm only thinking of it now.

Sleep paralysis, Wu-Pei called it, and my fingers type it quickly into the phone. That would explain why Steen was suddenly lying differently. That would rule out all the gruesome diseases Klara listed, brain damage and meningitis …

"Listen," I say. *"During REM sleep, the brain 'turns off' the body so we don't carry out the movements we dream of. Normally, muscle paralysis is relieved before we wake up, but if you suffer from sleep paralysis, the body remains paralysed. The condition is typically associated with anxiety and panic. Many people experience suffocation and perhaps also a feeling that there's someone in the bedroom while lying paralysed and helpless. For some people, the condition becomes recurrent. Most often caused by high emotional stress."*

I inhale, breathless from reading so fast.

"Do you know what I think?" I say. "I think the old emperor has returned."

I take a short break, try to get control of my thoughts.

"And not just that," I say. "He's stronger now than when you were a child. So strong that he has kept you paralysed for days."

High emotional stress. It all makes sense now and a wave of hope flows over me.

"The good thing is," I say, "that he may finally be getting tired."

I put the phone back in my pocket.

"Do you understand?" I say. "You can get well again. We can be us again."

Not so much as a sound escapes him.

"Steen?"

Hesitantly, I release the door handle and move towards the bed. It's so dark in here that he's only an outline, and only now do I notice that his feet aren't protruding from under the duvet like they usually do.

And his head?

In one movement, I jerk the duvet off him, and a chill runs through me.

The bed is empty.

CHAPTER 34

Steen's duvet falls out of my hand and I look around the empty bedroom as a tingling anxiety consumes me.

"Hello?" I turn on the ceiling light. "Steen?"

My voice is woolly and doesn't come out of my throat properly.

In the living room, the commercials have been replaced by a debate programme. Excited voices keep interrupting each other.

I walk through the house and look out into the driveway. Our two cars are still parked there. The front door is locked and Steen's jacket is hanging on the coat rack beside mine. I go out into the kitchen and turn on the lights. The fridge hums faintly. Otherwise, it's quiet. I go to the bathroom and push the door open. Expect to see him lying on the floor. Imagine him staggering through the house, euphoric about being able to move, but his legs suddenly failing again. Imagine him falling face forward and banging his head on a hard edge.

The ceiling light turns on with a click, and three bluebottles take off from the floor buzzing. I look at the toilet and the shower curtain, the shelf with the nappies and the blinds that don't close properly. One fly follows me as I walk out of the bathroom again.

I've heard that when a traumatised person suddenly livens up, it can be a sign that … well. Klara's flickering eyes and the way she ran the zip of the raincoat up and down.

With a jarring sound, I push the back door open and squint out into the darkness.

The bare crown of the cherry tree sways in the wind, and he stood just over there waving at me. He was wearing sandals, sunglasses on his forehead, and had a mosquito net in his hands. He laid it carefully over the stroller.

Nothing was allowed to crawl in while she took a nap, he said. No one was allowed to do anything to her. He was careful to pull the mosquito net down on all sides. Smiled and waved at me through the window. Looked happy and devastated at the same time.

I close the back door again. Tighten the belt of the dressing gown and shoo the fly away. The thought of the empty double bed gives me the shivers. I go back to the bedroom. Open and close the tall wardrobes and look under the bed.

"Hello?" I say again.

Only the silence answers and I put my hands against my temples. Press on my skull to collect my thoughts.

My two sons are my yin and yang.

The light and the darkness? What else? I press harder on my head. *Think now, think!*

One son lives in pomp and splendour in his imperial residence. The other has sunk into darkness. I don't hear anything from him anymore.

Then it dawns on me: *If I've always had them confused, then the brother must be the one who has sunk into darkness.*

His phone in the bin. All the missed calls.

Of course!

But … My hands fall down along my sides again. If it's Wu-Chao who *sunk into darkness.* Then Steen *lives in pomp and splendour in his imperial residence.*

What does that mean?

I think of when Steen told me about his dead little sister. About his parents who put her in a wedding dress and I asked: *How did you cope?*

I thought about how one day I'd have my own family. A beautiful and happy family. That was what kept me going.

Something about the words makes me uneasy, but I can't figure out what. The thoughts are narrow passages that end blindly. As if I'm trapped in a maze of dark glass.

The time is now 04:00. Time for the news and weather forecast.

The sound from the television pulls me out of my reverie and I go to the doorway and look at the screen.

Police are still looking for the five-year-old girl who disappeared from a kindergarten in Hemmet almost two days ago. They would like to hear from anyone who may have seen or heard anything suspicious in the area.

The photograph of Lotus gives me chills and I take the remote control. Press hard. The living room is swathed in darkness.

I can hear the clock ticking from inside the bedroom. I look around at the shadows of the furniture. Where is he? Where?

He lives with his family in a magnificent palace. He often calls and tells me about it. The flower garden. The tea parties and the children.

I rub my temples.

Then I hear a sound. It's coming from the basement.

A bright voice.

Is that someone singing?

CHAPTER 35

"Up in the sky, everything will return to its proper form. Paper houses become real houses. Feathers turn into birds. The dead come alive again. Isn't that beautiful?"

No answer.

"Don't you want to hear a fairy tale?"

Still no answer.

"In the beginning, everything was chaos. Every day, Death came flying down from the mountain on the back of a dragon. The dragon was green and scaly, built of cans and tin plates. It knelt and lay down in the grass, like a great dog, and Death dismounted. With long strides and his silk kimono fluttering around his back, Death walked through the imperial garden and looked at everything with his large, empty eye sockets. Every so often, he would bend down to smell a paper flower.

"'For you see,' said Death. 'One never knows what will come of real flowers. They can wither and die and be lost. But paper flowers are faithful. You can open them up and see how the folds are, how they are put together and you can own them forever.'"

The butterflies stop in the air. They are made of paper. White, pink, and red.

"So what do you think happens?"

Still no answer.

I dip the brush into the red paint and let it slide over the duct tape covering her lips.

She's smiling now.

"Family is the most important thing," I whisper.

Her smile is big and red and I smile back at her.

It's a good day. We will soon be complete in number.

CHAPTER 36

My breathing sounds loud and I hold it inside. Listen. A cold sensation spreads within me as I grow more and more sure: There's someone down in the basement.

I get down on my knees and put my ear to the floor. Stick a finger in my other ear and the song becomes clearer.

no I will not be afraid
just as long as you stand
stand by me

It's a child singing. A little girl.

She doesn't sound very old. Some of the words are pronounced incorrectly, and she hesitates occasionally, as if she's nervous or in doubt about the lyrics.

My heart pounds hard in my chest as I walk out of the bedroom and towards the closed-off basement stairs that I've been avoiding for so long. The thought of going down there gives me the feeling that a thousand spiders are running over my skin.

I take out my phone and look at the time. It's the middle of the night. Should I call the police? But what am I supposed to say? There's a girl singing in my basement?

I put my phone back in the pocket of the dressing gown and open the child lock on the safety gate we mounted at the top of the stairs. The basement door at the bottom is closed and everything looks like it normally does. But the song is still there, very faint, like a radio turned down to the lowest volume.

The steps groan beneath me and I hold on to the bannisters as I move downwards. The deeper I get, the worse the smell gets. I have to hold my sleeve in front of my nose and mouth when I reach the basement door. I hesitate for a moment before pushing the handle down.

The door creaks and the cold inside me swells. There's something very wrong. As if I've opened the door to a strange, distorted nightmare or an eerie part of my own subconscious.

White sheets hang from ceiling to floor, hiding the rest of the basement, like a curtain on a theatre stage. I touch them with my fingertips and squirm as the light suddenly turns on.

"Hello?" I whisper.

My voice is so low that I can barely hear it myself.

Narrow strips of paper are attached all over the sheets with pins. As I look closer, I can see Chinese characters written on them. I don't understand what they mean, but one sign I do know. It's written in many places. *Family.*

The blood rushes in my ears. What's going on here?

The sheets meet in a narrow crack that leads into the rest of the basement. A reddish light penetrates from within. Most of all, I want to turn around and go up the stairs again. But the girl's thin voice makes me press my sleeve harder against my face and step in between the sheets.

Two green eyes meet mine and it takes me a few seconds to understand what I'm looking at. The old metal dragon that stood in the garden when we took over the house from Steen's parents. I refused to have it on display. Called it a deadly pile of junk with its rusty car parts and razor-sharp lids sticking out of the empty cans.

Hesitantly, I walk around and it's as though I've stepped into a feverish dream. I don't recognise the basement at all. There are things folded in paper everywhere. Houses, birds, fans.

The boxes of baby things have been pushed in front of the windows. All the lights are on. They're wrapped in red tissue paper that illuminates everything in a murky semidarkness, which amplifies the feeling of walking around in a delirium.

The basement air is cold and stagnant. The smell makes me think of meat that's been in the fridge for several weeks past the expiration date.

I can hear the girl's bright voice singing "Stand by Me" the entire time. Each time the song ends, it starts over. The repetition gives me the creeps. The increasing sense that something is so very, very wrong, and then I see it.

The teddy bear with the pink satin heart. *Love you to the moon and back.*

It's on top of our chest freezer.

The hairs on my neck stand up as I walk closer.

Something is sticking out, clamped under the freezer door. A snippet of white fabric. It's crumbling. But I recognise it.

It's the dress the baby was buried in.

My whole body contracts and I press my sleeve harder against my face to hold back the nausea.

"No," I whisper.

I want to scream, but can't. Just stand there, inhaling the stinking air down into my lungs while everything spins around me.

Torben. I have to get hold of Torben. I fumble to find my phone, scroll down to his number, and press call.

The phone is silent.

Shit, I forgot. The basement doesn't have any signal.

My neck tingles as if someone is looking at me and I look over my shoulder. There's no one there. Still, I can't let go of the feeling that someone is sitting in the dark watching my every movement.

"Steen?" I whisper. "Steen, is that you?"

There's a faint rustling and I turn around abruptly. Look at the metal dragon. The paper houses.

"Steen?"

My heart is pounding and my mouth is so dry I can't swallow. I can't bear to look at the freezer.

Darkness crawls up and down my neck and I walk hesitantly in the direction the sound came from. The whole the time I have the feeling I'm being watched and I stiffen. Don't understand what I'm looking at. It looks like large dolls sitting down. Life-size dolls wearing suits and ties.

They are positioned in our garden furniture. One in the lounge chair. Sitting up straight, with round eyes and a big smile. One in the hammock with stiff arms and a newspaper attached to his hands so it looks like he's reading.

The round glass table between is set with teacups and a vase of paper flowers. They have steel wire stems and petals and are similar to the one I found at the grave.

I look at the big dolls again. Something about them makes me uncomfortable and I give a start when a bluebottle lands on my neck.

I flick it away. Approach slowly. There's a buzzing sound from several flies taking off and I shiver as I realise what I'm looking at. The doll in the lounge chair ...

It's a skeleton.

A skeleton, wearing shiny shoes, a suit, and a black wig with a side parting. There are still tendons and remnants of skin. Small, greyish flakes. Two glass eyes are pressed into the eye sockets. A large, red smile is painted on the skull.

Acid reflux fills my throat and I press my lips together. Stare at the nostrils and the thin finger bones that have the same colour as tanned leather. A sick, uneven colour that penetrates me and makes me gnash my teeth. I freeze, like when you have a fever or go out in a snowstorm with too few clothes on, and I feel like fleeing up the basement stairs again.

Instead, I turn towards the hammock. Look at the newspaper and the two stiff hands.

Before I can regret it, I grab the newspaper and pull it away.

Gasp loudly.

Steen!

He has wide-open eyes. His lips are painted red. A thick line that goes beyond the corners of his mouth and up into two arches so that it looks like he's smiling.

I throw away the newspaper and grab him by the shoulders.

"Steen? Sweetheart?" I shake him.

His head falls forward with an eerie sound. As if something is broken. The arms are still stretched straight in the air. He's wearing a tie like the skeleton, and I feel dizzy when I discover the thread in his neck.

With a pounding heart, I pull out the shirt collar. The thread is thick and skin-coloured and runs all the way down his spine. The stitches are coarse. His back must have been cut up and then sewn back together.

The floor sways underneath me and I have to blink hard to focus. It seems to have been done in a hurry. I panic. The skin around the glass eyes is frayed. They look surprisingly lifelike except for the staring expression. And except that they never blink, and I put my hands around his face. Despite it being made up, I can see the fear chiselled into every single feature. As if it's penetrating through the shiny glass eyes.

I want to say something to him, but can't. His skin is so cold and I let go of him again. Step away.

Then the sound is there again. A rustling, as though from a mouse. It's coming from inside the pantry, and this time it keeps going. A persistent, scraping rustle. Something that looks like old cream has run out under the door.

Hesitantly I go over and push the door open.

The first thing I notice is the rocking horse. The one we bought online and never managed to pick up. Now it's on the basement floor with reins and a braided tail.

The smell in here is different. Urine and faeces, and I jump when the rocking horse sets in motion. The pointed horse's head moves forward. Then back. The stirrups clink against the wood, and my heart beats like crazy.

No one is sitting on the horse. *The rider is a ghost*, I think. I am frightened by my own thoughts.

Only after a few seconds do I notice the feet sticking out from behind a bookcase. Two little feet belonging to a child. They are the ones pushing the rocking horse.

I squeeze down along the rows of tins of chopped tomatoes and white asparagus. I can see the legs now, too. Thin legs in nylon tights and I hold my breath as I lean forward.

It's a little girl. Squeezed inside between the wall and the shelf of tinned food. Her ankles are tied together and she has duct tape over her mouth. A red mouth is painted on the duct tape so it looks like she's smiling. Her eyelids are clumsily made up and she's wearing a wedding dress. There's a large yellow spot on her crotch. Her eyes are wide open and frightened, and her hands are tied together in front of her. They're holding something. A white lily?

With an eerie delay, it dawns on me who it is.

Lotus.

Little Lotus from kindergarten.

Oh, God. My head starts swimming. She's lying completely still. Only her eyes blink as she stares up at me and I edge over the clutter and boxes to get over to her. Her hair is gathered in two pigtails just like the day in kindergarten when she jumped on the couch. The day she disappeared.

Something crunches under me, and a sharp pain shoots up through my foot.

The floor is full of shards of glass. A bottle of olive oil has broken all over the place. She must have tried to get out, but the splinters of glass forced her to stay in that awkward position.

The rustling sound gives me a shock. This time, it's coming from behind me. From the cupboard of jam jars.

I pick up a shard of glass. Hold it in front of me as I walk over there.

Oh stand by me

stand by me

The song forms a grotesque sound curtain, fills the basement with the light, nervous childish voice, and with a jerk, I step forward.

Wu-Pei is tied to a water pipe. Like Lotus, she has duct tape over her mouth with a big, red-painted smile.

In the middle of the tape is a small hole. I only discover that now. It's neatly made, as if cut with a tiny knife, and I look towards the creamlike liquid on the floor. Notice the range of protein drinks with straws. One of them is knocked over.

I squat down to free her, but stiffen as I hear footsteps. She throws her head as a sign that I should run.

Dazed, I get to my feet and hurry out. Only make it to the garden furniture with the dead before a door slams, very close by. I crawl into hiding behind the box of garden cushions. Hold my breath. The sound of footsteps gets louder. Then a jingle, as if something is being put on the glass table.

As quietly as I can, I change position. Find a peephole between the box of cushions and some cardboard boxes.

A man in a suit walks around with a teapot. Wu-Chao! A shudder goes through me. It's him. Less than three metres from me. Steen's twin brother.

He's wearing a black tie. His hair is combed in a sharp side parting.

My heart is beating so hard I fear he may hear it. I can see one of Steen's arms sticking out of the hammock. The last time I saw him, he was lying in his bed, and my stomach turns when I think about how he must have been dragged down here without me hearing anything. Without him being able to resist. And now he's sitting there. With grotesquely erect arms and glass eyes.

I don't understand how Wu-Chao has managed to achieve this. Cut him up, sewed him together. I can't wrap my head around it. The black crow on his workbench. The wing filled with animals and the hundreds of times he's practised.

He must have stuffed the body to prevent it from rotting before he was done with whatever he's doing down here. Still, there's this heavy smell in the basement. An odour reminiscent of smoked serrano ham.

I try to breathe through my mouth to avoid the smell, but that's even worse. It's like I can taste death.

Wu-Chao picks up the newspaper from the floor. Smooths it and puts it back between Steen's lifeless hands.

Then looks directly at me.

Everything in me freezes when we make eye contact.

"Would you look at that," he says. "Now we have Mum. I wasn't actually going to get you until everything was ready."

He extends his arms out towards me.

I duck my head. In a fog of panic.

"Don't be afraid," he says.

My thoughts whirl trying to grasp it. The twin brother I've been looking for is right here. In our basement. Has he been here all along? While I was driving to Hvide Sande and ringing his doorbell in vain? While Steen and I were right upstairs? Gooseflesh forms on my arms and I crawl farther behind the box of cushions.

What does he want? What?

My brother became so jealous. Everything I had, he wanted, too.

I look at Steen. Feel like calling him. Shouting for help. His head hangs on his neck just like on the blue tit that flew into our bedroom window.

"I made room for you here." Wu-Chao pats the hammock so the hinges creak. Steen's arm moves in time to the rocking.

"You killed him." My voice doesn't come out of my throat properly.

Wu-Chao comes closer. His movements are strangely stiff. He lifts his legs high with each step and stops right in front of me. His body odour makes me hold my breath. A mixture of aftershave, sweat, and putrefaction.

I can't stand to look at him. The slender, boyish body, the dark eyebrows, and the slanted eyes. He looks so much like Steen. Steen, back when everything was still good.

Only the tie and the side parting are different. His caricatured facial expressions and the strangely stiff body language.

"Come, sit down." He smiles, but there's something threatening in his expression.

I look towards the door. It has swung shut, allowing only a narrow sliver of light into the murky basement.

Wu-Chao squats down, forcing me to make eye contact. Something in his eyes terrifies me. A desperation.

I get up slowly. We are far too close.

"What is this?" I whisper. "What do you want?"

"I want you to sit down."

The part of my brain that's still working yells at me to obey. But I can't bring myself to sit next to Steen's corpse.

Wu-Chao pulls up his shirtsleeve and looks at his wristwatch. "There's an hour and twenty-one minutes left."

"Until what?"

He pulls the shirtsleeve back down and gestures with his arm.

"I think you should let us go." I try to sound composed, but the words tremble as they come out of my mouth.

"It's too late."

"Lotus is just a child. Let her go, at least."

He shakes his head. His body is uneasy. He straightens his tie and smooths his hair. As if he's trying to hold something inside, and his upper body jerks nervously all over. His head turns backwards and his shoulder pulls forwards and I don't understand how the twins can look so much alike. Right down to the weird tic I've seen so many times and that I'd swear could only belong to one person … An icy chill floods my body as it dawns on me.

"Steen?" I whisper.

He blinks once.

I feel faint as my brain struggles to comprehend.

The body in the hammock isn't Steen.

Steen is standing in front of me right now.

He's alive.

He can walk.

He …

In an eerie slow motion, it dawns on me what that means.

"What have you done?" I whisper. "What have you done?"

He puts a forefinger on his lips.

"Don't panic."

He extends his arms and I recoil.

"Don't touch me!"

"I'm sorry I lied to you," he says. "But I couldn't tell you until I was finished."

The words don't penetrate properly. My brain is struggling with the shock. Steen can walk. Steen has murdered. He's kept people locked up while I was just upstairs.

The more it dawns on me, the more my legs start to give way under me.

"You kidnapped a young child," I say. "You dug up corpses in the graveyard!"

"I got them. For us."

CHAPTER 37

The chest freezer has wheels underneath, and Steen pushes it over to the glass table. Places it as if it were another piece of furniture.

Seeing him move again is surreal. The big body movements make him look like a mechanical doll that's been pulled up a little too hard. All the hours in bed must have made his body stiff.

"Stop," I whisper. "I can't …" I press my hands against the temples. "We have to call the police."

"We are who we need to be."

I don't understand how my husband is standing in front of me. I don't understand how all this happened without me noticing anything. The madness must have lain hidden beneath the surface, just as this whole gruesome array has been hidden under the floor of the house. Despite all of Klara's examinations, we never realised he was being eaten up from within.

"Let's go upstairs again," I say. "Calmly. Then we'll figure all this out."

"I've already figured it all out."

"Think of Lotus's parents. Think of them, Steen!"

"My name is Wu-Kang. I am her father, and you are her mother."

There are two blue flies sitting on his cheek, but he doesn't wave them away. Doesn't seem to notice them.

"I'm looking forward to showing you all of it." He gestures with his arms again. It's as if the madness has set itself in his movements. As if his body has to exaggerate to feel itself.

The chest freezer. The smell. My head is reeling, making it hard for me to breathe.

"I'd really like if you would sit down," he says.

When I don't respond, he steps up on a stool and retrieves something from a high shelf. My blood freezes when I see what it is.

The rifle. The one that was missing from the hook out at the brother's yard.

He aims at me.

"I'm sorry. But we have to do it right."

"Do what?"

"I'll tell you when you're all sitting down."

With horror, it dawns on me that it doesn't matter what I say. The way he says *you're all*. It's a stranger standing in front of me. A stranger with a rifle.

On shaky legs, I walk over and sit on the hammock next to Wu-Chao's corpse. The stench is even stronger here. A smell of rot and old jam jars. The thought that I touched the corpse makes me sick. I had stood and held my hands around its face.

I move as far to the opposite side of the hammock as I can.

The wheels of the chest freezer rattle against the floor as Steen pushes it even closer. He wipes his forehead and sits on the teak bench next to me. Right at the corner, so we're sitting only a few centimetres apart.

He sets down his rifle on the glass table. Takes a deep breath and exhales.

"Finally," he says. *"Finally."*

The chest freezer is right behind us. So close that I could touch it if I reach out.

I try to breathe through my mouth. To sit as still as possible so as not to set the garden hammock in motion.

There's a buzz at my ear and I glance at the corpse. Some of the skin on the cheek looks like it's about to loosen and I press my lips together to keep the nausea inside.

"Would you like a cup of tea?" Steen asks.

"No." I have a hard time recognising my own voice. Feel like I'm being strangled from within.

He leans forward and lifts the teapot. Pours into a cup and pushes it towards me.

The tea is red and I recognise the smell. Panyang Golden Needle.

"Isn't it nice for once?" he says. "That I'm serving you?"

He's gone crazy. Does he even know that they're dead and I'm alive? Can he see the difference?

Sweat trickles down my upper lip. I look at the rifle lying on the glass table. I don't know whether it's a coincidence or whether his head is clearer than he seems, but the gun is lying so I can't reach it. Not without getting up. Not without him reaching it first.

I take a breath. Have to make an effort to get the words out.

"So ... you can walk again? That's nice to know."

"I'm sorry I didn't tell you. I could suddenly move my fingers one day and I was so happy, but also so scared."

"Scared of what?"

"Life."

I can't believe we're having this conversation. That this is happening. The dead around us. Lotus and Wu-Pei in the pantry.

The chest freezer. The stench tears my nose every time I breathe in.

"So what?" I say. "You've just been pretending all this time?"

"You can't pretend that kind of thing."

The flies are still crawling on his face.

"The day we left her in the hospital," he says. "It was as if all the life disappeared from my body. I felt so weak that I had to go and lie down. When I wanted to get up again, I couldn't. My body was completely dead. It was so scary, Eva. But in a way ... it was also a relief."

One fly crawls up his forehead. Sits polishing its wings while he speaks.

"It was as if my body thought: There's nothing left to get up for. So I might as well stay put. For ten days I lay like that. Do you know what day was the worst?"

I shake my head. Try desperately to collect myself, but I continue to have a foggy, nightmare-like sense of unreality.

"The worst day was when you put on your black dress and drove to her funeral. Without me. All day I lay thinking about what it must feel like to lie in a coffin underground. It was the scariest thought in the world. I waited for it to go away, but the next day it was even stronger. Her sweet little face in the dark earth. I kept picturing it."

The fly takes off from his forehead, flies away buzzing.

"It was as if the thought shocked me," he says. "Like a defibrillator, just from the inside." He slaps both palms against his chest. "Bang, bang, BANG!"

He says it so loud that I jump. Still with his palms raised, he leans closer to me. There's madness in his eyes.

"It went on for days," he says. "And then suddenly one morning, Eva, it was magical. Suddenly, I could lift my hand. I was just about to call you. But I didn't. Because I knew it wasn't for fun that my body had woken up. I knew I had an important task ahead of me."

He looks at me expectantly. As if he wants me to show him that I understand. I try not to look at the dead, but end up doing it all the time. The artificial red smiles. The glass eyes.

"What was the only thing we thought about?" he says. "What was the only thing we wanted to get back?"

I can't get a word out, but it's not necessary—my eyes flicker to the chest freezer of their own accord, and Steen nods.

"Exactly," he says.

He reaches out and strokes the lid of the freezer. His caresses are gentle and careful just like the day we brought her home from the hospital. The day she lay with her little white hat and we put a blanket over her so she wouldn't freeze.

Lullaby and good night with roses bedight, we sang as we peered down into the cradle.

"Lay thee down now and rest," Steen sings now, again, as he caresses the freezer.

When he reaches the chorus, he looks at me. Makes signs I should sing along. My throat is so dry that it feels like I've eaten raw flour. Steen mimes the first words of the chorus and I shake my head.

"Lay thee down now and rest …" Steen takes the chorus himself. Looks at the freezer all the while he sings and there's something both eerie and sad about him. A father who wasn't allowed to be a dad.

I pull my eyes away. Blow away a fly and try not to listen.

On the table are candlesticks with burnt-down white candles. Wax has flowed out onto the tabletop and I feel like my brain is doing the same. Flowing out.

Everything appears in a mist, as if it's something I'm dreaming. I have no sense of time. I have no idea how long I've been in the basement.

When Steen has finished singing, his eyes have changed. There's a seriousness there that's almost more sinister than the madness. As if he's fully aware of what he's doing.

"I was lucky that your sleeping tablets were so strong," he says. "You didn't notice anything when I got out of bed and went out and started the car. Later, I thought you might just be pretending to sleep. Because you wanted this, too."

I shake my head. My whole body trembles.

"You dug her up!"

"I just wanted to keep her. Not to lose her, too."

"Too?"

He looks towards the pantry.

"Family is the most important thing," he says.

"You taxidermied your brother," I say. "Taxidermied!"

"I didn't know what to do. You were already complaining about the smell up there and there was no room in the freezer. And then I saw the crow he'd stuffed."

"You've been out at his farm?"

"The plan wasn't to get him so early."

He changes position. Tells me incoherently that he went out to the farm to practise on a hamster. That his brother was suddenly in the doorway and that he panicked. Grabbed a crowbar and one blow led to another.

I think of the bloody crowbar that lay on the workbench the night I found the carved-out eyes.

Think about how he stood and painted the headstones in the graveyard. How he must have lifted the dead up into his twin brother's blue pickup truck.

It was huge work. He had plenty of time to think in the meantime, plenty of chances to realise what he was up to and stop himself.

But he didn't.

"You're sick," I say.

"What's sick about wanting a family?"

The words scare me. The morbidity in them. That he has gone to such great effort.

"We are good parents," he says. "Father and mother. We are a good family."

It feels like my guts are twisting inside.

"They're dead, Steen. Dead!"

"What difference does that make? What is the difference between life and death? When I lay up there in bed, I felt dead. Every time I thought of our daughter, she felt alive. As if she was everywhere. As if she was more alive than I was. Than we both were."

He looks at me as he says the last thing, and the cold from the basement floor penetrates all the way into my bones.

Sometimes I wish I was dead, too. So I was still with her.

"We have to ring Torben," I say. "He'll understand. He'll make sure you get help."

"We don't have to ring anyone. We're the only ones who need to be here."

"Steen … Listen to me."

"My name is Wu-Kang."

He takes the rifle from the glass table and points it at me. Panic rushes through my veins. I'm trapped in my own basement. I'm trapped by a man I no longer know.

"Was that what you were called as a child?" I try to sound calm, hoping he will lower the rifle again.

He nods.

"At the time, I thought my father's ideas were scary. I found my Danish name in my mother's books of fairy tales. As revenge."

I think of the pen lines in the book upstairs.

"Before, it was Death who decided. Now it's me." He smiles, but there's fear in his eyes.

With a sudden movement he gets up and kneels in front of me. Still has the gun in his hands, and in a dizzying moment, I don't know whether he's going to free me or kill me.

"Reach out your arms," he says, and I don't dare do anything but obey.

The blue plastic clothesline bores into my skin as he ties my wrists together. Then my ankles.

He rummages in the pockets of my dressing gown. Takes something out from there and there's a crunch when he steps on my phone.

"Sorry."

Without waiting for an answer, he takes a red silk ribbon and fastens it around one of my ankles. There's a little bell hanging from it.

"So we can hear each other. So no one goes missing. No one is allowed to go missing."

I follow his gaze. Notice that his father and brother also have a silk ribbon with a bell around their ankles.

The rifle points at me as he walks towards the pantry. Clinking comes from in there and I glance at the freezer. Try not to imagine what's down there.

Then he's standing in the doorway with Lotus in his arms. He carries her to the teak bench and sets her down.

Her eyes find mine. They are full of horror.

There is a rattle, and Steen comes out of the pantry with his mother. He pushes her in front of him and down into the empty chair next to his father. Her nostrils flare as if trying to say something. But no sound comes out from under the duct tape with the red smiling mouth.

Steen sits down next to Lotus.

"Listen," he says, and for a long time only the light, delicate girl's voice sings. There is a slight crunch as if from a poor recording.

I can't get my eyes off Lotus. The wedding dress and nylon stockings. The duct tape with the red smiling mouth. The terrified expression in her eyes.

I should have called the hospital. I should have listened to Klara and called the hospital.

"Wu-Lin always sang like an angel," Steen says. "After our wedding, I made her a vow. I promised you that you wouldn't be alone. *Not alone.* Do you remember?"

He looks at Lotus, and only after a few seconds do I understand what he means. The ghost wedding. The boy with the tie and the big, scared eyes.

It was him. The eight-year-old groom.

He smiles just as stiffly as back then. The child's confusion and panic are trapped in an adult man's body while he holds a new, silent girl.

The realisations come in claustrophobic slow motion, as if my brain is resisting.

Lotus is to play the role of the sister he lost over thirty years ago.

I feel like I'm going to throw up.

"So everything you said about your brother being jealous and wanting to ruin everything …" I say. "The only thing you were afraid of was that he was going to destroy this?"

He holds out his right hand in the same way as in our wedding photo upstairs. Above his wedding ring is a thin gold-coloured ring that looks as if it's going rusty.

"In fairy tales, you can live happily ever after," he says. "Unless you wake up."

He sits in silence for a moment. Looks like his mind is far away.

I get the feeling that my own body is dead. That even if he loosened the clothesline around my ankles, it would be impossible for me to run.

I have no idea what to do.

"The emperor's dragon has five claws," he says. "There are five senses, five elements, and five tastes."

He points to his fingers as he reels off. "Sour, sweet, salty, bitter, and umami. And look! Five fingers, too."

He holds out his hand and gets up so abruptly that the teacups clatter on the table.

"It's a magic number," he says. "So, we leave at five o'clock."

"Leave?"

"To Holy Mount Taishan."

My heart beats faster as I look at the petrol can he sets out. His words make no sense, yet I feel a wave of horror.

He fetches two paper lanterns hanging on a pole painted red. It dawns on me that these are our broom handles.

"When the flames get going, you swing the lantern and say our names. It's important you remember all of us. That no one is forgotten."

I don't want to accept the broom handle. But my hands do it of their own accord. The movement causes the clothesline to gnaw deeper into my wrists.

Steen unscrews the lid off the petrol can. Concentrating, he begins to pour. The father's wig gets wet and my heart beats so fast it feels like it's making a hole in my chest.

I sit in the same petrified way as the dead. Listening to the eerie, scratchy song from the tape recorder.

No, I will not be afraid

No, I will not be afraid

"The life you don't want, anyway, will be over soon," he says. "Isn't that a relief?"

It feels like I have the flu. My body is shaking and I am sweating.

In eerie flashbacks, I see myself lying next to Steen and reading aloud from the internet. Stories of corpses in silk and families dancing around them.

It was so far-fetched that I didn't even consider how he could grasp it.

Maybe he'd searched through my history, too? All my searches for death and suicidal thoughts. Maybe he couldn't find a single sign that I *didn't* want this.

The thought makes me sick. Is all this my fault?

"Forty minutes to go." He empties the last of the petrol over Wu-Chao.

"Stop." My voice shakes. "You need help, Steen. You are …"

"I'm happy." Unlike me, he sounds completely calm. "For the first time since our daughter died, I'm happy."

He finds a new petrol can and unscrews the lid.

"You don't understand how I felt. There was no meaning to anything anymore. No reason to get out of bed. There was only pain."

"That's how I felt, too! Of course, I did. I wish you'd talked to me about it."

"There are no words for that kind of pain."

His eyes are darker than ever. He's trapped in there, in grief. It swaddles him in the same way that the ivy swathes the house.

"You don't ever become human again, Eva. A parent who loses a child. You never become yourself again. Isn't that right, Mum?"

He looks at Wu-Pei. The duct tape moves over her mouth. It looks like she's crying.

I think of the photos on the USB stick. The dead little sister in the wedding dress. Everything that his mother had prepared. Spring rolls, paper flowers, wedding gifts.

It startles me when the petrol hits my lap. I try to kick out at him, but he has bound me too tightly.

He pours petrol over everything. He moves quickly and restlessly between furniture and bodies, and I can already see the flames in his eyes. The fire in there, in his body. It crackles and blusters like his movements, all the energy that accumulated in all the hours he was lying in bed upstairs.

I hold on tight to the broom handles. My thoughts won't gather, they flutter around like fragments of ash; I think of her grave, of taxidermied birds, of strong red tea.

There's a ringing sound. Steen is standing with two silver bells. Swinging them back and forth.

"We are gathered today because family is the most important thing. Always." His black eyes shine.

He sticks his hand into his inside pocket and takes out a box of matches.

"Fire is a sacred force. What we burn rises to heaven as smoke. In heaven, everything returns to its natural, proper form. Paper houses become real houses. Feathers become birds. The dead come alive."

He looks around as if waiting for someone to answer.

"But before we leave, we're going to hear a story. Just like back then with the butterflies. Like when I read aloud to your tummy."

He smiles at me and for a dizzying moment there is a glimpse of the old Steen. A minute glimpse, but enough to give me hope. If my husband is still in there, behind the madness, there's a chance I can reach him.

He opens a box and takes out some papers. They're frayed on one side, as if torn from a book. He clears his throat.

"It was the middle of winter, and the snowflakes were falling like feathers from the sky, and a queen sat at her window working, and her embroidery-frame was of ebony. And as she worked, gazing at times out on the snow, she pricked her finger, and there fell from it three drops of blood on the snow. And when she saw how bright and red it looked, she said to herself, 'Oh that I had a child.'"

He emphasises the last sentence and looks up from the book. Looks at the chest freezer.

The papers rustle as he flips on to the next page. Reads aloud with thought. Even doing voices, like I always do in kindergarten.

He looks like an unhappy dad. For long painful moments, that's all I can see. The unhappy father surrounded by all those he loves.

I see myself in the same way. Sitting on the couch next to a chest freezer. The unhappy mother.

My whole body shakes, and as Steen reads on, my thoughts fall apart more and more.

I close my eyes and try to concentrate on my pulse. The faint rush of blood running through my veins. My heart and muscles.

"The dwarves would have buried Snow White, but that she looked still as if she were living, with her beautiful blooming cheeks. So, they said, 'We cannot hide her away in the black ground.'"

"Wait!" My voice comes out like a gasp.

He looks at me questioningly and there's a new clarity in my head.

"Do you know what would make this perfect?" I say. "If I put on my wedding dress."

"Now?"

"Like Snow White. Like Wu-Lin."

"Where is it?"

"In my wardrobe. At the top."

I'm surprised by how composed I sound. Steen looks down at me. My bare toes and the dressing gown's tatty terrycloth.

Then he shakes his head.

"Maybe you could get it?" I say. "So I can be as nicely dressed as the rest of you?"

"You must not ruin this, Eva. We've had so much destroyed already."

There's a pain in his voice that makes my stomach clench.

"Do you remember the day we were out cycling when you were pregnant?" he says. "We brought a picnic blanket and ate triangular sandwiches."

"With egg salad," I say in a weak voice.

He nods.

"We talked about how soon the baby wouldn't be in your womb, but on the back of the bike in a little child seat. Do you remember?"

I nod.

He turns and takes something from a shelf. It's a little paper bicycle. It's folded so neatly that it must have taken hours. At the back of the bike is a child seat in miniature.

All those hours. Alone in a basement.

"It's lovely," I whisper.

"Isn't it? She can sit there."

He points to the child seat, which is as small as a thumbnail. He looks up and his black eyes are so full of pain that my insides rush. I tear my eyes away and look at the white candles that have flowed out over the table.

"You were beautiful with your pregnant belly," he says. "You were so beautiful."

I press my lips together. The tears sting behind my eyes.

When the night has come
and the land is dark

"Maybe you're right," I say. "Maybe I did really want this all along, too."

As soon as I've said it, I feel the dizzying sense of it all blurring together again. The baby's lifeless body. Steen's lifeless body. Melting plastic beads and snails that can't escape their shells.

"I can't imagine a life without you. So better …" My voice breaks and Steen lays his hands on my cheeks. Holds them, just like I used to, and the tears come violently and loudly, like water that's been held back by a dam.

"Sweetheart," he whispers. "Sweetheart, it's okay. I'm here."

I can't stop. I cry over everything that has happened. Over little Lotus in the wedding dress, over the baby's heart stopping, over Steen marrying his dead sister. It all blends together and I cry and cry.

Steen holds my face all the while. There's panic and confusion in his eyes. Again, he looks like the eight-year-old boy I saw photos of on the computer. The way he stood in his slightly oversized wedding suit, trying to understand what was going on.

Most of all, I cry over not calling the hospital. Over how I might have prevented everything from getting this far. Over the nauseating thought that I might have, somewhere, deep in my subconscious, known what was going on, but failed to intervene.

The doubt makes me sob even louder and Steen lets me go. He's starting to get tics. They come again and again. As if his head is trying to wrestle free of his body.

"Dearest," he says. "Won't you stop?"

It only makes me cry even louder. He shushes me, but it doesn't help. It's like something's been broken or released inside me. I have thought so much about death. Have felt like it was already sitting in my body. But now that I'm facing it, I feel a new and stronger longing.

"Please," he says. "Please stop."

I can sense that something is happening inside me. That the crying isn't just powerlessness.

"Eva, for God's sake. Stop."

That the crying is also power.

"Okay! Okay. Fine. I'll get it."

My tears stop just as abruptly as they began. I watch him as he opens the basement door and disappears up the stairs. For several seconds I sit dazed in the garden hammock.

It must be a kind of survival mechanism, like when an octopus sprays ink or a lizard sheds its tail.

Lotus and Wu-Pei look at me as I struggle to get up. The movement causes the clothesline to cut into my ankles. I bite back the pain and jump, legs together, over to the metal dragon. Upstairs I can hear Steen moving quickly across the floor and my arms shake as I run the clothesline between my wrists back and forth over one of the dragon's sharp tin can lids. I sweat all the while. Above me, I hear something heavy fall on the floor.

Pain shoots up my arm when I hit my skin. I file faster, ignoring the pain. Sweat runs down my back. My wrists are pounding—maybe the lids are too old. Maybe they can't ...

There's a crack and I jerk my hands. I pull. Unravel myself free of the cut clothesline. Loosen it around my ankles.

The next moment goes so fast that it all glides into one motion. Footsteps on the stairs, on the floor, and Steen knocking the sheets aside and coming to a standstill. Standing in the middle of the paper houses, staring at the gun in my hands.

"Now we're going to ring Torben," I say. "We're going to calmly go upstairs and call Torben."

"We are a family."

"Now, Steen."

"Mum and Dad are not allowed to leave."

I grab the rifle's safety and hold his gaze while I pull it back and turn it to the right.

As a child, I hated it when Dad took us hunting, but now I'm grateful for the sure movements of my fingers. The little click that tells you the gun is cocked.

"Go up the stairs," I say.

He shakes his head.

"It'll probably all work out," I say. "Torben will understand. And I am here for you."

"But they are not." He looks towards the garden furniture.

My husband. In a flash, he's standing clearly in front of me, and I don't understand how it's happened, but amid all the horror and disgust, I can still feel the love I have for him.

There is a hesitation in his eyes, which strengthens my hope.

"We'll figure it out," I say. "Maybe you'll be locked up for the rest of your life, but you'll still exist. You'll still be able to keep alive the memory of our daughter. If we die, no one will remember her."

He looks at the chest freezer.

"We are the only ones who loved her," I say. "If the basement burns down and we both die, there'll be nothing left of her. No one would be able to tell that she existed. Only an empty grave and a headstone without a name."

He's quiet for a moment. Shakes his head very slowly.

"I can't."

"Steen, sweetheart." My voice trembles. "We can't give up."

He hesitates. I can see how the emotions are fighting inside him. His body twists, making me think of the scene in *Poltergeist* where the demon finally lets go of its victim.

"We survive for her sake," I say. "We can. We still have each other and she can go back to …"

"No!" He raises his voice. Comes towards me.

"I won't lose any more. I can't take losing more. Give me that."

He grabs the barrel of the gun. I feel dizzy inside as he pulls and it slides out between my sweaty hands.

I grab hold of it again, tug the rifle to me, and step backwards.

Steen follows me.

"Stop!" I take aim at his chest. The gun shakes in my hands.

"You would never shoot me," he says. "We are the only ones for each other. We both know that."

"Stop!" I repeat, louder this time.

There's panic in his eyes. He extends his arms out towards me.

"I love you," he says. "The only thing I want is to be together forever."

I take a step backwards and he keeps his arms outstretched as he comes towards me. Closer and closer, until I'm standing with my back against the cold basement wall.

Without breaking eye contact, he opens the matchbox. Fumbles to get a match out.

"That's why I'm doing this," he says. "Because I love you."

I sob. Clench the rifle harder and aim it at him.

"I love you, too," I whisper.

And then I shoot.

CHAPTER 38

The rifle slips out of my hands and hits the glass table with a clonk. I shake all over and the knots slip between my fingers as I untie Lotus and Wu-Pei. I push them in front of me and fall. A red-hot pain darts up through my foot where I stepped on the dragon's metal claws.

Steen is lying on the floor. His face is turned away so I can't see it. Wu-Pei helps me to my feet. Pulls me until I stop looking at Steen. The sheets hit us like giant cobwebs, and then we're out.

Then we're out.

Relief rushes through me and I lean against the wall of the house. My foot throbs and burns.

"Run away," I say. "All that petrol. I don't know if it'll suddenly explode."

They look towards the house. Their faces are pale and the wide red smiles stand out clearly in the moonlight.

I help them to get the duct tape off.

"Go!" I push them.

"What about you?" asks Wu-Pei.

"I can't. My foot."

"But ..."

"Find a phone and call 112. Now! Go!"

They set off running. Lotus in front, Wu-Pei behind, unsure and stiff-legged. They disappear out onto the road and I sink into the grass. Only now do I realise how exhausted I am. Above me, the early morning sky is grey with a clear, circular moon. It casts silver light over the quiet landscape around me, and I stare at the basement windows. Imagine Steen's body in there, among the dead.

My throat tightens and it's all there again. The hair-raising seconds when he still stood up, in shock. The pain in my shoulder because I forgot about the rifle's recoil. The sound as his body hit the floor.

I hope he didn't feel anything. I hope it went quick.

The thought makes me dizzy.

My husband. My child.

I start rocking back and forth. The movement makes me feel the bulge on my stomach. I stick my hand up into the dressing gown and pull out the teddy bear with the satin heart. It all happened so fast. I didn't have time to think about it until I'd taken it.

The strangled feeling increases and I rub my eyes. Try to breathe all the way down into my stomach as I listen for sirens.

But the only sound is the bell around my ankle. I rip it off and throw it in the grass.

The silence is unbearable. Maybe the nearest neighbours won't open the door. Lotus and Wu-Pei might need to run several kilometres. An old lady and a child.

I try to get up and pain shoots up through my leg. I pull my sock off and tie it tightly around my foot. Hobble to the house and try to look inside.

Steen's phone. It has to be in there somewhere.

The basement windows are blocked with cardboard boxes. I look for a crack and wince when the boxes fall down.

The expression in his eyes when I fired.

He was standing right in front of me.

He is standing right in front of me.

Suddenly, he's standing right in front of me, on the other side of the basement window. There's a big red stain in the middle of his white shirt.

For several seconds, we look at each other through the windowpane.

He's still alive. *He's alive.*

I move closer. Want to say something.

He immediately retreats. My heart beats faster and I look towards the door. Expect him to come out and point the gun at me.

But the door is still closed. The leaves of the ivy rustle. Otherwise, there's no sound.

I go all the way to the pane and put my hands against it. It takes a few seconds before I can focus.

Then I spot him. He's sitting in the garden hammock. Next to his dead twin brother. With the silver bells in one hand. In the other hand he has ... A creeping horror runs through me. Go. Go. My brain screams the word while I stand paralysed. Steen strikes a match and then my body finally reacts. I run with everything I can. There is a deafening roar that pushes me forward. There is wave of heat and I just manage to see flames shoot out of the basement windows before I fall.

CHAPTER 39

I'm standing now. I close the garden gate behind me. My palm is sweaty from having held on to the metal for so long.

The gauze around my right foot is making my shoe too tight in places and I shift my weight on the crutch. Hobble up the driveway.

The sky is heavy and lead-coloured. It hangs like a shadow over the treetops and windmills.

The cardboard boxes in the front garden are no longer there. Klara and Alfred dealt with them. Now there are only some square patches of flat grass.

It's hard to walk. My foot. The crutches. My thoughts.

My steps grow slower and I stand for a moment and look down. Build myself up to raising my gaze.

Our home. It looks like the ribs of a large animal. The rafters protrude like arms reaching for someone in vain.

Through the broken windows I can see in to what was once our living room. In a flash, I see how the flames twisted in there, furious, red and white.

It's quiet here now. Black flakes of ash swirl up every time there's a gust of wind. The rest is a smattering of sticky firefighting foam. It smells sour.

I bend down and lay a white rose in the ashes. Now there are six. Lying in a row next to each other. One for every day that has passed since the fire. The petals of the first one have browned and dried. The new one is chalk white.

I wish it would start to rain. A great downpour that would wash away all the black.

But there's only the heavy sky above me.

I can't. My foot.

I don't know if it was just my foot.

I don't know.

I think of Steen's words. *You never become yourself again.*

I start when a hand is placed on my shoulder.

Klara's windbreaker is open over a black dress.

"We thought we'd better come by. So we knew we'd catch you."

I turn around and look at the road. There are two cars in addition to mine. Alfred and the children are in one. In the other, my mum and dad. They're wearing black clothes. Their finest. Dad's had a haircut, too.

"Are you ready?" asks Klara.

I shrug.

"It'll all be fine," she says.

Ash flakes sail through the air like blackbirds, and over the burnt-down house, the clouds are full of water that doesn't fall.

"You were right," I say. "We should have asked for help."

"Yes, well. We're looking to the future now."

I look at the six white roses and imagine I hadn't pulled the trigger.

Klara pats me on the shoulder. "We're looking to the future now, Eva. Aren't we?"

That I hadn't pulled the trigger.

There's a wrinkle between Klara's eyebrows. I don't know if I've said it out loud.

She looks at her watch. "I'll just tell the others that they can drive on ahead."

Her windbreaker says *scritch, scritch* as she walks through the front garden. I look at my palm. Discover that I'm bleeding. I must have held on to the rose too tightly again.

I can hear their low-pitched voices out on the road. A little after, the engines start. The cars drive away. Now there's only mine out there and Klara is back in the garden.

"I see the estate agent already has the sign up. I did ask him to be quick about it."

I nod. Want to say thank you for her help but just stand there.

"It's a good site," she says. "With the fields and the view and what have you. And it's probably not that expensive to build yourself anymore."

Somewhere a tractor is driving. A faint hum in the distance. Everything continues.

"The woman from the chemist did it," says Klara. "The one with the birthmark, you know. Built a new house with her husband. It turned out really well."

"The birthmark," I mumble.

I can feel Klara's eyes, but pretend I don't.

She opens her bag and takes something out. "You forgot this at home."

I look at the teddy bear's black glass eyes. The satin heart.

"Shall I keep it until we get there?"

I nod. She puts it back in her bag and I look at the bare rafters protruding towards the sky. The remains of walls.

I open and close my hand. The blood has settled in the lines of the palm. Looks like a pattern that has some sort of meaning.

"Did you cut yourself?" asks Klara.

I shake my head.

"I have a plaster, if you need it?"

I shake my head.

Klara finds a wet wipe, opens my palm, and pats it gently.

"Everything will be all right again, Eva. It's just going to be different to how you imagined."

The words are so heavy. Like my thoughts. Like the crutch and the idea that I didn't pull the trigger. That I had let him have his way.

Scritch.

Klara opens her windbreaker. Takes something out of the inside pocket.

A packet of Viking cigarettes.

She holds it up to me.

"What's that?" I say.

"Cigarettes."

"We don't smoke."

"Nooo."

She continues to stand with it and I take out a cigarette.

"Why are you carrying them around with you?" I ask.

"It's good to have something a little healthy when the vet's been over."

She takes a cigarette for herself, too. Puts it between her lips and finds a lighter in the inside pocket.

I've never seen Klara smoke before. The sight is so surprising that I put my cigarette between my lips, too. I haven't smoked since I was quite young, but I can still remember the feeling of the soft filter. The smell of tobacco. The crackling sound as Klara holds the lighter under the cigarette and I inhale.

It burns all the way down my windpipe. Warm and nice. I take another inhalation.

Klara lights her own cigarette. Coughs.

I thump her back and we smile.

Then we grow serious again. Stand next to each other in silence as we look at the burnt-down house and smoke our cigarettes.

Above us, the clouds are the same colour as iron. A heavy water-filled membrane that looks like it's about to burst, but doesn't.

While we're in the church, the sky gets even darker. Heavy, heavy rain that doesn't come. I stop in the doorway and look towards the spire. The bells are ringing up there.

Someone pushes me forward.

Now I'm standing by the grave. The metal windmill spins around.

Klara opens her bag and hands me the teddy bear. I put it on the grave. Now it's on the gravesite again.

There are many flowers.

Hands press mine.

The clouds hang so low that it looks as if they're hitting the church tower. There's a cross at the top. It's pointed and metallic and I think of needles.

Now the vicar is there again. Pressing my hand.

"Thank you," I say.

She nods. Holds my hand in hers for a long time before letting it go.

This is the first time a reburial has taken place here. I had no idea such a thing existed. I had no idea people would show up.

Loads of people have come. Torben and Dagmar. Helen and Tanja and Bjarke. Dr. Møller. Some of Steen's old colleagues. A couple of parents from kindergarten. Some people from the supermarket. People I only know peripherally. Black clothes and muted voices.

Condolences.

I still don't know how to answer.

Just nod. Try to read their facial expressions when they think I'm not looking.

I can't remember when I was last with so many people.

Klara's children jump into a puddle.

"Stop," says Alfred.

They keep jumping. Laugh all the while.

The sound of laughing children.

I look back at the spire. Wish I had chosen some other hymns than the last one. Other kinds of flowers. At least a different colour of ribbon. But I couldn't think clearly. Her body was largely untouched by the fire. The chest freezer had protected her. Torben told me as if it should come as a relief.

It should come as a relief.

The kids laugh again and people glance at me. I'm sure they are, despite them always managing to look away.

The repetition. The little coffin. The repetition.

Like a creepy loop. A nightmare I can't wake up from.

"Stop," says Alfred.

To be here without Steen, just like last time.

And yet not at all like last time.

I move the crutch over to the opposite hand. Can feel the weight of the sky up there. The tears sit in my throat. A constricted feeling that makes it hard to respond when people say things to me.

The wind has loosened a tuft of hair from my bun. It flutters on the edge of my field of vision, and in the tree above me some magpies cackle.

It's nice to be outside again. To stand up and not hold a hymnbook. Still, I can't really move naturally.

I jump when I feel a little warm hand in mine.

"Come here. Leave Auntie be."

The hand slides out of mine again.

"Thank you for coming," says my mother. "There's coffee and cake at home on the farm for those who'd like to come back."

People crowd out into the car park. Seem relieved to have something concrete to do and I go to follow them but then suddenly she's there. Standing in the car park next to a black car. Henriette. She's changing her high heels to flat shoes. Has she been here all along? I don't remember shaking her hand.

I lost a child. I saved a child. That's what I say to myself. Still, I dare not go over to her.

Maybe she can feel me looking, because she looks over here. For nerve-racking seconds, we hold eye contact. Then she draws her eyes away. Knocks on the car window. I try to see who's sitting in there, but Mum gets in the way.

"It went well," she says. "Do you not think so?"

I shrug.

"Should we warm the pastries, do you think? Before we put them out?"

I shrug.

"I asked the neighbour to let in whoever arrives first. So they don't have to stand waiting for us. I could ask her to put the pastries in the oven, too?"

My shoulders can't move up anymore.

Mum wrings her hands.

I think of all the days they could have rung.

All the days.

"Okay. See you at home then." She stands for a moment. When I still don't say anything, she turns around and walks over to Dad.

Henriette has bent down. She's talking to someone through the wind-screen of the black car.

An empty plastic bag rolls across the car park. Looks like it's searching for a place to do away with itself.

"Do you want to come with us?" Mum's voice.

She looks old. Dad does, too. Old with a fresh haircut.

"No thanks. I'll drive myself. In a moment."

They get in their car and I think about all the things they arranged for today. Pastries and extra chairs. Hours of preparation.

Spring rolls, paper flowers, wedding gifts.

The thought makes me dizzy. All the things that repeat themselves.

Again, I wish it would start raining. A huge downpour.

A man approaches slowly. He walks bent over, as if carrying something heavy on his back.

Only when he's close can I see who it is.

Lotus's father.

He shakes my hand. "My condolences."

I nod.

He puts his hands in his pockets. Looks towards the church.

"It was a nice ceremony," he says.

"Yes."

I want to say something else. But what are you supposed to say?

"And your husband?" he asks.

We both wince. Or maybe I just imagine it.

"He'll be buried in a week," I say. "In an unmarked grave."

"I see."

"Yes, it's a bit much. Two weekends in a row. But I didn't think … to hold them together. I don't know."

"Of course."

We stand for a moment in silence.

"Well," he says. "I also just wanted to apologise for not saying hi to you that day. In the graveyard. I was beside myself."

"What?"

"I'd just been told. About Lotus. And I didn't know what to do with myself. I raced over here all the way from Herning, but what could I do? I ended up trudging around in the rain."

Slowly, it dawns on me.

The man in the cemetery. The man standing in a black raincoat with his hood pulled up. His sloping figure and his hands tucked in his pocket, just like now.

"So yeah, I'd like to apologise for not saying hello," he says. "I just couldn't do it. You know. Someone from kindergarten."

"I understand."

We fall silent again.

"How is she doing?" I ask.

"She's doing better. Thanks for helping."

His jaw is tense. As if it's taking all his strength to take things so nicely.

"I'm really sorry …" I stop.

Some awkward seconds pass where we can't look at each other.

"Where is she anyway?" I ask.

"With her grandmother. We didn't think she should be here today."

"Say hi."

"Will do. Will you be going back to the kindergarten?"

There's something tense in the tone of his voice and I shake my head.

"I'm on sick leave now. And I don't really know about afterwards. I might move to Herning and look for something there."

He nods. Looks relieved?

"Well," he says. "Isn't there coffee somewhere? I could do with that."

"Yeah."

He nods at me before walking across the car park. To the black car where Henriette is waiting. They say something to each other and Henriette squints at me. It's like I can hear the whole city whispering. A shaking and rustling in the treetops.

Shortly afterwards, they are all gone.

A butterfly flutters by me and into the graveyard. I put my hands on my knees and take a deep breath.

Everything will be all right again, Eva. It's just going to be different to how you imagined.

The butterfly flies farther into the graveyard and I follow it with my eyes. The fluttering, uneven path, and at first I think I'm seeing visions. The figure on the bench sitting all alone, in the shade of some tall, steel-blue cypresses. Her eyes are closed. The coat is adorned with glass stones, and the more I look, the surer I am.

The sound of my steps in the gravel makes Wu-Pei look up.

"We're done," I say.

"I know."

"Were you in the church?"

She shakes her head. "I couldn't figure out how to go in."

I sit down next to her. Follow her gaze towards the graves with the low, sharply cut boxwood hedges and conifers. I still remember many of the names from the nights I spent googling.

Bird's nest spruce. Thuja 'Tiny Tim.' Sander's Blue.

A gust of wind swirls through the graveyard. It makes the branches and leaves rustle, and I don't know whether it's my imagination, but for a brief moment, it's as if I can make out the sound of silver bells.

CHAPTER 40

I'm lying in bed with all my clothes on. Jacket and shoes and trousers. It's dark in my childhood bedroom. We still call it that, even though the only thing left from that time is the blind and some holes in the wall where my mirror hung.

A moth sits on the ceiling. I don't know whether it's alive. It's not moving. I look at the wings. Wait for it to do something.

Mum has laid out a pair of pyjamas on a chair. I consider putting them on. Brushing my teeth. I've been thinking about that for a long time. Now the house is quiet.

Outside there's a peal of thunder.

The moth crawls across the ceiling. I point the phone's torch up there and am amazed by its patterns and colours. I always thought of moths as grey shadows in the dark. But now I can see that it's at least as detailed as the butterflies you see during the day. On all four wings, it has large, peacocklike eyes in shades of blue. It reinforces the feeling that it's keeping an eye on me.

I turn off the torch and pull myself up to sit. The bed creaks and I get up. Walk across the wooden floor. Through the quiet house and out.

The garden stinks of the pigsty and wet moss. Rain whips against my face and my shoes sink into the lawn. I can hear the pigs. Their scratching and unease behind the barn door. A new crash of thunder vibrates in the pit of my stomach. I stand still in the storm. Think of Steen's lifeless body. All the weeks he lay in bed and I had to get up to take care of him. When I think back, it feels like I was the machine he spoke through. As if Steen was the living one, and I just a machine.

I open my palm. The blood keeps dripping out. I clench and stretch my fingers. A red tree. The tree of life. Placenta.

The life you don't want anyway will be over soon. Isn't that a relief?

The sky lights up as if a large match is being struck. Shortly afterwards, the bang comes, and more heavy, blue-black rain pours down on me.

I lean my head back. Look up at the falling drops.

Isn't that a relief?

An arm is placed around my shoulders.

Klara's hair is wet. She's wearing pyjama pants under her rain jacket.

"What are you doing out here?" she asks.

"Couldn't sleep."

"I couldn't, either."

The next clap of thunder comes right after the lightning, and Klara gives my shoulders a squeeze.

"Come on. Standing out here is dangerous."

The thunder lasts a long time. It rumbles under my skin, deep and threatening.

"Let's go inside," Klara says. "I'll make some hot coffee for us."

I remain standing. Rain pounds down on us like a thousand glass balls.

"Eva?"

"You're right," I say. "It'll all be all right again. It's just going to be different to how I thought."

She sends me a small smile.

We stand together, looking up at the black clouds. The sky being ripped apart by lightning and patched together by darkness.

I think of the butterfly that fluttered into the graveyard. Only after several steps did it dawn on me that I was following it.

I put my hands on my stomach and let them slide over the bulge.

I couldn't help myself. The glass eyes looked at me that way.

Love you to the moon and back.

ABOUT THE AUTHOR

Sarah Engell is the author of books for both teenagers and adults. She has received the Carlsen, Blixen, and Claus Deleuran prizes, as well as a grant from the Danish Arts Foundation. *Dig Two Graves* is Engell's first adult novel.